Alia Henry and the Ghost Writer

Christine Betts

ISBN: 978-0-6486880-6-8 Large Print
ISBN: 978-0-6486880-5-1 Paperback
ISBN: 978-0-6486880-4-4 eBook
Copyright © 2018 Christine Betts
All rights reserved. Time Step Press

If a man can bridge the gap between life and death, if he can live on after he is dead, then maybe he was a great man. ~ **James Dean**

Busted

Except for a scratchy grey blanket, Alia Henry was naked in the most famous food hall in London and it wasn't a nightmare. A young police officer led her towards the lifts, the throng parting like a Red Sea of camera-phones. Someone called her name and Alia looked up to see the crowd filled the floor above and the one above that. She smiled and lifted one blanket-covered hand to wave. Somewhere in the crowd a woman called out, 'I love you, Alia,' and a cheer went up. Alia grinned at the frowning officer, who only nodded at a hidden walkway behind a raised display of mannequins showing off the latest summer fashions. Alia turned to smile at her audience, clutched her blanket, and walked to the locked security door behind the display. The cop covered her hand as she punched a code into a keypad. The door swung wide on an automatic hinge and they started down a linoleum corridor with cage covered bulbs on the ceiling. The door swung shut with a metallic thud, leaving behind the vocal and disappointed crowd.

The bare floor was cold underfoot. In all the years Alia had been shopping in Knightsbridge she had never suspected anything so utilitarian was hidden behind the elegant facade. She smiled up at a winking security camera at the end of the corridor. What a lark. She was about to be let off with a warning. Again. That would make it seven for the year.

'We have permission to film here,' she said as they arrived at a service lift.

'Not in the buff, you haven't, have you?' the officer said. It was a rhetorical question, but Alia felt she had a right of reply.

'It didn't specify…'

'Of course, it didn't, it should have gone without saying.' The officer spoke softly and shook her head sadly as she pushed the down button and looked at Alia. 'I'm worried they're going to throw the book at you this time. I think you should have given it a rest after the show at the Fringe. It was hilarious. That thing with the shopping trolleys.' She stopped and looked up at Alia. 'I follow all your stuff. You're an icon for a lot of young women and girls, so this looks really bad.'

Alia wanted to say something, but the lift doors opened. The call button didn't make a fun dinging sound and there was no cheeky, uniformed attendant in this lift. Just two huge cops who made even Alia look petite.

'Mind your step, Lady Thalia,' the young officer said. She was smiling slightly, her eyes kind, but as she turned to greet her colleagues, the sweet face became a mask. As Alia stepped carefully over the gap in the floor of the old service lift, she suspected she might have taken things a little too far this time.

How to deal with a Narcissist

Hours later, Alia was still wearing the blanket, still naked, and busting for the loo. She was being held in a kind of glassed-in no-go zone with administration staff on one side and detectives on the other. She was desperate to get someone's attention. Star had finally arrived but hadn't looked at Alia. Her agent was only metres away but hadn't acknowledged her favourite client in any way. Alia moved from side to side as much as she could in a bulky blanket, trying to catch Star's eye, but she was focused on the police officers, her back to the room where Alia was being held.

Alia watched, fascinated. She had never seen her agent so serious. Normally, she would be holding court, wildly gesticulating, making everyone laugh, but today she was sitting at a desk, soberly reading paperwork, and signing things.

'Hey!' Alia looked up at the blinking light on the security camera. 'I need to use the bathroom.'

She looked around for a response. Surely, somebody had to be monitoring the cameras. She gripped the blanket, shuffled over to the door, and tried the handle. Still locked. She looked up again at the security camera trapped in its little metal cage, and smiling, let the blanket drop. She turned towards the little knot of officers now standing around Star, but still nobody looked in her direction.

'It's as though they've all studied up on how to deal with a narcissist,' she said to herself, making a mental note to add the line to her next show.

She looked around the cell. She was cold and really needed to pee. She draped the scratchy blanket over the bench and sat, not even thrilled she was naked in a holding cell.

This isn't fun anymore.

Her shoulders slumped and she looked up at the camera again. 'Who am I without my audience?' she asked the blinking light.

Her partners in crime had been released. Gaynor, super-model, and best friend, had left with her lawyer, giving a wink and a nod to Alia.

No hard feelings. Hopefully, we are finally even for that little incident in Ibiza.

As usual, Gaynor's father would pretend to be mad for a few days then buy her a new car or something. The photographers had been freed by their agent, too. They had left without their camera gear, but the cops had obviously overlooked the iGlasses that were still on their faces when they left, no doubt still filming. With a cheeky grin, they had dipped the sleek glasses at Alia as they followed their agent from the station.

Alia sighed and shivered. She looked over at Star again, who was now sitting with the young policewoman from the food hall. They seemed to be signing wads of papers. At least Star was doing her job; signing wads of paper for her client was the least she could do for her 10%. All she usually did was go to festivals and get fucked up. Alia scowled at the thought. What good is an agent if they take this long to get you out of jail?

She gave up on glaring at the back of Star's head and knocked on the window separating her from the busy administration staff. The young officer at the closest desk looked over, a pen dangling from her lips. Her brows shot up at the sight of a naked minor member of the royal family. She frowned, pointed at the ceiling, and hurried from the room.

'She's either telling me to wait a minute longer, or suggesting I pray for help,' Alia quipped to herself. She sighed and sat back down. Life was no fun without an audience.

'What the actual fuck?' Star bellowed as she walked into the room. 'Have you finally flipped?'

'Star, you scared the living daylights out of me. I let a little bit of pee out. I'm going to have to keep this blanket now.' Alia screwed her nose up and stood.

'Sit. Down,' Star said.

Alia did not like her tone of voice but decided to keep that particular bit of feedback to herself. She had never seen Star in any mode other than what she referred to as 'pumped mode.' Arriving at the airport at three in the morning Star was pumped. On the last night of Glastonbury Star was pumped. In the lock up of the Knightsbridge Police Station, Star was most definitely not pumped. Her eyes were red as though she had been crying and she was wearing the most hideous coat. It may even have been a raincoat and it smelled like it belonged to an elderly man. She stood with her back to the door and said nothing. As annoying as Star in pumped mode could get it was preferable to Star in whatever mode this was.

Alia smiled. 'Star, thank the hairy goddess you are here, I have to pee. Not joking.' Alia ended up shouting this as Star raised her voice to tell Alia to shut up. 'Star, I'm in pain,' Alia whined.

The agent's shoulders dropped as the young officer from the food hall bustled in and pulled the blanket over Alia's shoulders.

'Lady Thalia, Katie Jenkins, remember?' The officer handed Alia a bottle of water.

'Oh Katie, thank the goddess you're here,' Alia said and was rewarded with a small smile.

Star rolled her eyes. 'She needs to use the bathroom,' she said, sighing heavily, she held out a shopping bag. Katie took it and led Alia to the bathroom.

When they returned the officer hugged a now-clothed Alia. 'Good luck with the books,' she said, gently squeezing Alia's arm.

'Thanks, Katie, and you tell your little sister to have more respect for herself,' Alia said.

Star let out a barking laugh. 'If that's not the pot calling the kettle a little twit, I don't know what is.'

Katie looked back at Alia, frowned, and looked sadly at Star.

'See,' Alia said, and Katie nodded. She patted Alia on the arm and gave Star a sad look as she left.

Wearing the outfit Star had brought, Alia felt as though she was late for her shift at the bank. Black trousers, black shoes, white top, accessorised with an acrylic wrap striped in multiple shades of pink. She handed Star the plastic shopping bag.

'Is it support a sweat-shop day? And what's with the fake wool serape?' The weather was unseasonably warm. Alia held up the wrap, her nose scrunched.

'That is for putting over your stupid face while we make a run for the bloody car.'

Alia held it up with both hands, nodding her head.

'Aah, good thinking. You are such a good agent.' She draped the wrap over her shoulders. 'Yes, it works doesn't it,' she said and turned back and forth for Star to see both angles. Star rolled her eyes again. 'Did you get my kimono? The one I took off in the video.' Alia grinned.

Star didn't respond.

'Star, that was my favourite. Oh, goddess help me, my navy silk.' Alia's hand went to her forehead, her eyes closed. She opened one eye to see if Star was watching but her agent only stared at the paperwork in her hands. 'Star?'

'Look, just don't.' She held up a finger but didn't look at Alia. 'Just. Stop. For one moment, stop being so…you.'

Alia looked out the window at the London traffic. The dash to the car had been a hoot. Strutting might not have been her thing but running the paparazzi gauntlet was right in her wheelhouse. She'd had her game face on, which no one could see because it was swaddled in the bright pink scarf. Alia Henry was a distinctive-looking woman, apart from the fact that she was in *Hello* magazine every second week. She stood out even with a scarf wrapped around her face, but Star always said photographers couldn't sell a photo of what could be just about anyone. That is anyone over six-feet-tall, and in this case, they would have to be wearing a too small top with no bra. Star had seemed legitimately sorry about forgetting to buy a bra; even the world's best agent got it wrong sometimes, Alia had assured her.

In the safety of the car, its heavily tinted windows coming in handy, Alia watched her agent from the corner of her eye. They had never had so much as an angry word.

'Can I have my phone?'

'No, you bloody can't.'

Alia slumped in her seat. Once they were alone, she assumed Star would return to her default setting, her usual, enabling self. Alia was confused by the change of attitude.

'I've done some pretty ballsy stunts and you've always been up for anything.'

'Thalia, you were naked. In Knightsbridge. What the fuck? What was with all the shortbread and stuff?' She sounded tired.

'You never call me Thalia. I hate it. Why do you have to suddenly call me Thalia because you're mad at me? You're not my real mum.'

Star rolled her eyes again. 'Of course, I'm mad at you, you twit.'

'We were…shoplifting…naked, it was to make a point.'

'Oh really? What point? That you can't shoplift when you're naked?'

Alia hesitated and looked out at the traffic. 'Uuummmm. Climate change?'

'Don't be a bloody idiot.'

Silence settled over the car. The heavy afternoon traffic crowded in from every side. They stopped at a red light. Star sighed. 'Alia…' she smiled a tight-lipped grimace.

Alia nodded. 'That's more like it.'

'I was visiting my parents. My dad's poorly. I told you that, but you don't listen. Can't stop mucking about for one day.' She took another deep breath. Star shifted in her seat to look at her client. 'Honey, we've talked about this. They want to get a ghost writer and if you keep this up, I just don't know what will happen. We fought to get you to write those books yourself. Well, I fought.' She swiveled back around in the seat and bowed her head. The light changed to green, but Star didn't move, her fingers pinching the skin between her eyes. The car behind sounded its horn and Star sat upright, middle finger raised facing the driver behind and slammed her foot on the accelerator. Tyres squealing, she sped into the intersection.

'They've given you a month. They are being very generous.'

'A month in jail?' Alia's hands went to her throat. 'I'll die!'

'No.'

'A month wearing this outfit?'

Star snorted. 'Why do you have to be so funny all the time, even when you're not trying. I bet your mum had trouble scolding you when you were little.'

Alia put her finger up at Star. 'For starters, I am always trying to be funny and… thirdly, my mum was never not high. Half the time she didn't even remember she had a daughter, so no it wasn't an issue.'

Star rubbed her forehead. 'Ali, you've got a month to finish your manuscript which is great because you're under house-detention for a month.'

Alia nodded. A month at home, sleeping, watching Gaynor on Top Model. It wasn't the worst outcome. 'Okay. As soon as I get home, I will get down to it. I'll have a shower and eat something, and then I'll start.' She reached for her phone but remembered she still didn't have it. 'I can start now if you give me my phone.'

'I'm not giving you your bloody phone. You've already missed the deadline and after what you did today, well, drastic times call for drastic measures.'

Alia had no idea what Star was talking about. 'I know I should ask what you mean, but I've lost interest in this conversation.' She was sifting through the contents of the glove compartment and let out a low whistle when she found a small bag with one white pill in it.

'Don't,' Star said. She sounded tired.

Alia looked down at the pill on her finger and back at Star. 'Stop me,' she said and flipped her agent the bird as she put the pill in her mouth and swallowed it with the last of her prison water.

'Star, can we stop at that offy? Oh, and a kebab? Can we get a kebab?' Her finger jabbed at the window.

Star didn't respond. She didn't stop at the off-license and Alia nearly cried as her agent drove straight past the best Kebab shop in London. Alia stared out the window as Star drove in silence, her eyes glued on the road. Alia sat back in her seat, pulled the pink, striped wrap over her head, closed her eyes and waited for the tablet to kick in.

The Driver

A bump in the road smacked the side of Alia's head into the window. 'Owww,' she said and rubbed her eyes. About to complain about Star's driving she pulled herself free of the wrap and shrieked. She shifted her body away from the man at the steering wheel and put both palms up to face him. Her eyes darted around the vehicle. She was still in Star's car, but this was most definitely not her agent driving. The beginnings of a smile twitched on the corner of his mouth, but he didn't take his eyes from the road.

'Good afternoon, I'm Phillip. I'm your driver.'

'Where's Star? Am I being kidnapped? Where are we?' Alia swiveled in her seat as green countryside sped past. She turned back quickly to the driver, scrunching her palms into fists like she was about to spar. Phillip put his hand to his lips.

'Are you laughing at me?' She tried to put her hands on her hips, but the car seat made it difficult.

He cleared his throat. 'No, no, I'm not. Sorry, Star did say you'd be quite disoriented when you woke up.'

'Yes, because I am supposed to be at home writing my book!' She kept her eyes on the driver but unlocked the car door.

'You can't open the door; we're doing seventy on the motorway,' he said, not taking his eyes off the road.

She slumped in the seat. 'So, this is how I die.'

Phillip snorted softly. 'She also said you were quite the drama queen.'

Alia put her head back and laughed. 'Who am I kidding? I'm a ride-or-die chick and you're a hottie, I'm not going to lie. Can we have a rest stop though? I need the loo.'

Phillip stared at the road ahead, but again a smile played around his lips.

'Oh and P.S. I am a professional working comedian not a bloody garden variety drama queen so you and Star can both pull your heads in. Who exactly are you anyway? Uber Luxe?'

'I'm the driver for Whitehall. It's my job to deliver packages and clients.' He nodded at her to indicate that she was his delivery for the day.

'Okay,' Alia said, looking around the car. There was a document box on the back seat. Satisfied with the answer, she reached into her back pocket. 'Phone,' she said and held out her hand.

Phillip stole a look at her and then looked back at the road. 'I don't have your phone. Star has it. She warned me it would be the first thing you'd ask for.'

'Damn straight it is. It's my livelihood. Gotta keep being funny slash deep and meaningful for my peeps.' Her open palm was still sitting expectantly between them.

Phillip shrugged. 'Sorry, I don't have your phone…'

'Do you know who I am? I could have you arrested,' she said and jabbed her finger in his direction. 'Whatever they're paying you, I'll double it.'

'I'm sorry Thalia, I don't have your phone.'

She sat upright and placed her folded hands in her lap. 'That is Lady Thalia to you, and I really have to pee, so we'd better stop soon. And don't call me Thalia.'

'My apologies, my Lady.' Phillip leaned forward and punched a command into the dashboard. A voice told them there was a convenience stop in less than ten miles.

Alia swiveled around to look in the back seat. 'What's in the document box? Is that your delivery? Oh no, that's me isn't it? Your delivery. Is there a human head in there? Is my phone in there?' A soft dinging sound came from the dashboard as she unbuckled her seatbelt.

'Just boring paperwork, really boring. Badly written.' The smirk still played at the corner of his lips. 'Seatbelt.' He reached over and pushed the buckle back in its cradle.

Alia wasn't listening. 'You're really good looking. Are you one of Star's clients?'

He snorted softly and his cheeks flushed pink. 'Like I said, I'm the driver.'

Alia sat back in her seat and drummed her fingers on the leather. 'You could give me your phone.' She turned to face him again, a playful smile on her lips.

'I can't. Look, Star said to tell you, you've been cut off.'

She glared at Phillip. 'What do you mean cut off? I am a grown-ass woman. You can't just take away my phone! You've carjacked Star, for all I know. I'm too trusting.'

She stopped talking and ran her hands through her hair. She was thirsty.

Perhaps I shouldn't have taken whatever that was in Star's glove compartment.

Alia's thoughts were interrupted by Phillip's phone ringing. The dashboard display announced the caller was 'Star – Whitehall.' Alia was about to ask who that was when the car answered the call automatically. She thought Star's surname was Christodoulou. Phillip and Alia began talking over each other and Star responded by screaming at them to shut up.

'…just a quick check in, I've only got a minute.'

'Fuck you,' Alia said.

'Charming. That's the thanks I get for keeping your stupid arse out of jail?'

'I got off with a bloody warning so don't exaggerate your usefulness. I am supposed to be at home writing. Remember?'

The car was silent. 'Okay, so Phillip hasn't explained the situation yet, I see.'

'She's just woken up. I was still dealing with the phone situation.'

Both Alia and Star made a noise that sounded like 'harrumph.'

'Phil, I'll let you explain everything, and I'll check in when you're further away.'

Star didn't sign off; the line just went dead. Alia turned to Phillip, but his eyes were glued to the road. 'So, explain.'

'Do you want me to tell you now or after you've, aah…' He pointed to the convenience stop. The car had barely come to a complete stop when Alia tumbled from the car and ran into the building leaving Phillip to run after her, the pink scarf trailing from his hand.

Ten minutes later Alia pulled open the door of the ladies' bathroom to find Phillip stationed outside like a bodyguard. It was at this point she realised he probably was a bodyguard. Driver was obviously a euphemism. She was about to jump into his arms and get him to carry her to the car when she noticed a queue of women standing to one side, behind him. Alia had been asked for a selfie in the bathroom before but usually at a nightclub or festival. She looked down at her clothes. Her fans were important to her, but she really wasn't dressed for the occasion.

She rolled her eyes at Phillip and turned to speak to the gathered women but before she could say anything the first woman bustled past her followed by the rest of the group.

'About time,' the last member of the queue muttered as she let the bathroom door slam behind her.

Alia turned back to Phillip; his mouth was a line. There was a strange sensation in the pit of her stomach. It felt a little bit like sadness and a little bit like anger.

Oh, maybe this is embarrassment.

She'd never been embarrassed before. Phillip held the pink scarf up to her. 'I have food and water in the car. We should get moving if we are going to make the ferry.' He moved towards Alia and she held up both hands.

'Before we go anywhere, you're going to tell me what's happening.'

'I'll talk if you walk but please let's walk because those women will be much less annoyed at you when they've used the bathroom and will actually want a selfie. And then we'll have a new problem.'

'Okay, what is this about a ferry? I've had enough of whatever joke this is that you and Star have cooked up to teach me a lesson. I want to go home.'

'Please, I'll explain everything in the car. Thalia, aah, Lady…' He shook his head and looked at her. 'Alia, please don't try to run off because if you go to the police, they will lock you up.'

'Spoken like a true Gaslighter.'

Phillip frowned. 'We can talk in the car. It will all make sense, I promise. Then we can phone Star and you can yell at her for a full minute.'

Alia was about to protest further but the idea of yelling at Star sounded great. She turned to lead the way, but Phillip quickly fell into step with her. They exited the tiled bathroom area and headed through the service centre shop as the double front doors slid back to welcome a group of schoolgirls into the air-conditioned space. Phillip took Alia's arm and steered her towards the section that sold roadmaps and scented car fresheners in the shape of lemons and portraits of David Hasselhoff. 'Let's just take a look at these oil filters.' He pulled Alia down into a crouch next to him.

'Oh, look, these are on sale,' Alia said. She took two off the shelf and put them next to her ears. 'I'm Princess Leia.'

He rolled his eyes at her, but he had a small smile on his lips. He took the oil filters and put them back on the shelf. 'Can you be serious for one second? This is no time to practice new material.'

'I detect a hint of condescension in your tone and I don't like it,' she said, but stayed in her uncomfortable crouch position, the too-small trousers Star had bought cutting in. 'You might as well start talking now, I can't see us getting out of here until those girls are back on their coach.'

Phillip shifted his weight and turned towards her. 'Okay, your little stunt at Knightsbridge did not go down well with Whitehall or Mrs Grant, and now Graeme is on the warpath. I am in the middle of the most important semester of my life but of course it's my job to deliver packages for Whitehall. So, I have to get you out of here before you get into more trouble and Whitehall decides to terminate you.'

Alia was stunned. 'Terminate me?'

Phillip shook his head. 'It's just a contractual term. There are costs involved and of course if you break the terms of the contract, you'll have to go to court.'

She blew out a puff of air. 'Thank goodness for that, I thought you meant I was like Sarah Connor and you were Arnie. I mean you are kind of built like him. May I?' she said and reached out to squeeze a bicep. 'Wait, court? But I got off with a warning.'

Phillip shook his head. 'No, you didn't. Whitehall called in a few favours.'

Her hand was still on his bicep. He looked down at it and she pulled it away as though she'd been bitten. Phillip shook his head. Alia had a knack of bewildering even the most level-headed of people. 'Do you understand?'

'Yes, but can you just clarify a few things?' The group of schoolgirls had spotted the MacDonald's and had thankfully left the shop in a hurry.

Phillip nodded. 'Like what?'

Alia took a deep breath. 'Like, who is Graeme, and what exactly are these used for?' She pulled a pair of bright yellow wheel chocs off the shelf, sending another dozen clattering to the floor.

'You have an amazing knack for attracting attention,' Phillip said. Alia was smiling, Phillip not so much.

'And what does Whitehall want with me? Isn't that the government? What's in the package you're delivering? Is it drugs? Are you a sex trafficker? Am I about to be Taken?' She made air quotes when she said taken.

Phillip looked down and sighed heavily. He shifted his weight and stood up then held his hand out for her to stand.

'Okay, listen carefully. Whitehall International is the parent company of your publisher of which Mrs Grant is the CEO. I work for Whitehall as does Star. Graeme Jones is the in-house legal, and you are, as I said, the package I am tasked with delivering to the house in Paris. So, if it please my Lady, can you put that big pink scarf over your head and get to the car before I throw you over my shoulder and deposit you in the boot?'

Alia threw her head back and laughed but clamped her hand over her mouth. 'Naughty,' she said through her fingers, then held out her arms to him. 'Let's go, big guy.'

He looked stunned for a moment but then reached out and dragged the scarf over her head. She waved her arms in protest. 'I'll do it,' she said. 'Savage.' She draped the wrap over her head and shoulders, then went to the spinner holding dozens of cheap sunglasses for sale and checked her reflection. She took a large black pair from its little plastic peg and tore the tag off. Phillip sighed but held out his hand for the price tag.

'I guess you'll be paying for these because I don't seem to have my purse.'

He was still standing next to the oil filters when she turned. 'What are you waiting for?' she said and stood near the front door, tapping her foot.

Phillip paid and held out his arm for her to take. She lifted the oversized sunglasses and winked at him eliciting another eye-roll. 'You know, if you keep rolling your eyes, you'll eventually see your brain, and no one can handle that. Incidentally, what would you have done if I'd tried to steal these?'

What Would Dame Judy Do?

The sun was setting behind them as the ferry left Dover. Alia was relieved to find numerous pieces of her luggage stacked in the boot of the car, pulled an outfit together and was about to strip off in the vehicle hold.

'Hey, no. You're lying low, remember? Trying to behave? There are tons of cameras here.' He pointed to the roof of the enormous vehicle bay.

'Sorry, I'm unfamiliar with this term; Behave?'

Phillip pressed his lips into a line, an expression he probably called smiling. 'Well, you think before you act. That's the first step.'

'Right… Sorry still don't get it.'

He laughed softly. 'Okay, before you do anything, ask yourself WWDJD.'

Alia's eyes rolled and travelled from left to right as she tried to work out the acronym.

'What would Dame Judy do,' he said looking proud of himself.

Alia snorted with laughter. 'You don't know Dame Judy! She'd give me a run for my money, and she'd run rings around you. I tell you what, I'll use WWDHMD.'

It was Phillip's turn to try to work it out.

'What would Dame Helen Mirren do?' she said, as she started to peel off her top. She stopped and looked at the shirt Star had bought for her. 'This is cute enough… but the trousers are off to Oxfam in the morning…although they might need a wash….' She looked up at Phillip. He had turned his back, but she could see his ears were bright pink. 'Are you shy?'

'Yes,' he said.

Alia was surprised by his response. She tried to remember if she'd ever heard a man admit he was shy. She shrugged and pulled her favourite Tommy Hilfiger shift dress over her head and shimmied out of the black trousers. She screwed up her nose and rolled them in a ball and tossed them in the boot. 'Okay let's go get a drink,' Alia said slamming the boot shut.

'No, no, no, we can't,' he said, still facing away from her.

'What about the Club Lounge?'

Phillip groaned when he turned around and looked at her. 'Can you wear something a little less conspicuous.'

Alia looked down at her bright red dress. 'I don't own anything inconspicuous.'

Phillip shook his head. 'No, we need to stay in the car. I just thought you would like to get changed.'

'Star didn't mention anything about staying in the car,' Alia said, shrugging her shoulder.

'No, and she didn't mention anything about swimming to France, either.'

They stood and stared at each other. Alia wrinkled her nose. 'I could do this all day. I win every staring competition I get into.' She squealed.

Phillip spun on his heel and spread his arms wide. Alia hunched over and laughed. 'Hey, you are a bodyguard! I'm not sure what this was going to achieve.' She spread her arms to mimic his move.

'What the hell were you screaming about?' He looked annoyed.

'There's a huge RV.' Alia skipped towards an enormous RV parked to one side. 'Hey Phil, I'll pretend it's mine, take a photo.' Alia reached around her back as though there were pockets there and when she found none, patted herself down frantically as though she was on fire. 'Oh, that's right. No fucking phone.'

Phillip stood and watched her.

'What?' she said. 'Never seen a woman completely and utterly confused about what's happening to her life?' Her shoulders slumped. It had been a very long day.

'Oh, come on, it's not that bad,'he said. The phone trilled again. He snatched it out of his pocket and stared at the screen for a second before answering it.

'Hello?' he said and then nothing more for whole minutes. Alia wandered around the RV and Phillip followed her. Finally, he spoke. 'Okay, thanks. Yes, she's here. Where else would she be?' He mouthed the word 'Star' at Alia. Alia held her hand out for the phone.

'Hi Star. Fuck you,' she said and jabbed the red 'hang up' button. She handed the phone back to Phillip and turned towards the stairs up to the decks.

'Alia, wait,' Phillip said.

She had only walked five feet before the phone rang again. Star would not be happy about her hanging up like that, but she hadn't really given Alia much choice. Star should understand from experience that she would be dying for a drink or something harder by this stage of proceedings. She turned back to Phillip. After his initial greeting he hadn't said much since; Star must be in one of her 'monologue moods.'

Two young girls appeared next to Alia, broad grins on their faces, offering up their phones for a selfie. 'Hi girls, do you have any money? How about I do a selfie with you if you go and get twenty pounds from your dad? Euros will do too…'

The grins began to disappear, but suddenly Phillip was at her side prattling about how funny Alia is, how she's working on new material. Phillip pulled a white bundle from his jacket and handed it to the girls. They unrolled the little fabric packages to find a limited-edition t-shirt and two pins for them. 'Head back to your folks, girls. Right now,' he said.

He turned his back to them and asked Alia to go back to the car.

'We saw you on YouTube, Alia. It was hilarious when that short security guard tried to cover you with the blanket and his eyes were the same height as your boobs,' they called as they ran back up the stairs.

Alia stopped walking. She tried to stifle a grin, but it was brilliant to get even that little bit of feedback about the video.

'We'd better get back to the car before they go and tell their friends,' Phillip said.

'What's the big deal? Tomorrow one of the Kardashians will do something and no one will care about my boobs.'

'Walk,' he said. He wasn't aggressive but he left Alia no room to refuse.

'Phillip?'

'Yes?'

'Just so you know, before all this is over, I will get you to carry me like in the Bodyguard movie.'

'I'm sure you are very used to getting your own way.'

She climbed into the backseat of the car and pushed the box on to the floor. 'Oops, I hope that wasn't fragile…' She saw Phillip flick a switch on the inside of the car door before shutting it. When he was settled in the front seat, she leaned forward and slapped her hand on the leather. He let out a yelp.

'I'm sorry, did I scare you?' she said. 'I am scared right now because I saw you put the child lock on my door. Do you understand how this feels for me right now? I am a lone woman, locked in a car. I'm vulnerable…'

Phillip turned to look at her. He smiled and spoke softly. 'You're safe, I promise you. I'm sorry, I really am, but I work for Whitehall and they asked me to take you to Paris. I have my orders.'

He held up the phone for her, but she waved it away.

'Wake me up when we get to France,' she said as she threw the sunglasses on the seat and pulled the scarf over her head.

The car slowed, telling Alia they had probably arrived at their destination. She had slept all through the journey and didn't remember leaving the ferry. She wondered what kind of papers Phillip was carrying that allowed him to take a sleeping woman to France in the back of a black Audi. Alia imagined a scene reminiscent of the movie,

Transporter. Phil did look a little bit like Jason Statham in his diving years only with a little more hair.

He had said the house was in Paris, so she figured if the 7pm ferry docked around 8:30 and the drive to Paris was around three hours, it had to be around midnight. The car swung to the left and the crunch of gravel told her that they had either arrived at the house Phil kept talking about, or he was really a kidnapper. Was she about to be shoved in a buried shipping container with a reverse osmosis machine to make drinking water from her own urine?

Speaking of which, she could do with another convenience stop. Shifting her weight carefully so he wouldn't notice the movement, she watched Phillip through the weave of the pink scarf. She had stopped referring to it as a serape. It was a horrible scarf and it had been thrown over her head a lot in the past twenty-four hours. The crush of photographers outside the police station had given her plenty of ideas for new videos. She wondered how long it would take to get permission to film at the *Old Bailey*. She and Gaynor could dress up as Defendant Barbie and Barrister Barbie.

She heard a click as Phillip used the automatic window opener and the cool night air rushed into the car. They seemed to travel for minutes along a gravel road and after driving in a wide arc, came to a stop. Over the smell of dust and her own sweat, Alia could smell something else. Trees, grass… earth? Star had said the house was on the outskirts of Paris, but this place smelled like the countryside. Phillip killed the engine, and she watched his silhouette in the glow from the interior light through the scarf. He took his cap off and ran his fingers through his hair. His eyes flicked towards the rear-view mirror and she squeezed her own shut. He said her name quietly, but she didn't move. He got out of the car and she could just hear his footsteps on the gravel. For a big man, he walked the earth lightly. He soundlessly opened the door on the other side of the car and said her name again, a little louder this time. She breathed deeply and sighed, pretending to be slightly roused from her peaceful slumber.

'I'm not going to carry you like Kevin Costner,' he said, directly into her ear, making her jump.

She sat up and threw the scarf at him as he ducked out of the way, a grin on his face. How did she not hear him walk around to her side of the car? 'But you're my bodyguard,' she whined theatrically.

This guy has an excellent stealth mode.

She crawled out of the car and stretched her long legs. The house was in darkness except for a single light above a huge ornate front door. It had obviously been beautiful once, long ago. Paint peeled from the window ledges and the tiles on the terrace were chipped and faded. She opened her mouth and yawned then stretched her arms over her head, waved them around and turned in a slow circle to see the rest of the property.

Phillip stopped piling her luggage on the terrace and stood watching her.

'What?' she said.

He raised his eyebrows and smiled. 'You can't do anything the normal way can you?' He held out a pack of cigarettes to her.

'Nope.' She took a cigarette and put it in her mouth the wrong way. 'I'm hilarious.' She turned to look at the house and took a drag on the cigarette. 'How big is this place? It's a mansion not a house.'

'We're in France so technically it's a château. It used to be known as Château de Bellevue, but Whitehall plan to call it Château de Rêves, castle of dreams. It is about half the size of Sandringham Palace, so not huge by English standards but still a decent sized project. The land was bigger too. It's only about sixteen acres now. Not what it used to be. See those lights? Houses.' He sounded sad. They both stood looking up at the house.

'How far are we from Paris and can I get an Uber without access to a cell phone? I'm asking for a friend.' She looked him straight in the eye.

Phillip smiled at her. 'You're funny. I mean what you say isn't that funny it's…'

'…all in the delivery?' she said arching an eyebrow at him.

'Yeah, I suppose it's timing isn't it?'

'Stop changing the subject. Oh, Alia you're so funny. Ha, ha. How far is the city?'

'We're in the Loire Valley, so about three hours.'

Alia's mouth hung open. 'You said the house was in Paris.'

'It's close enough…'

'That's like saying Norwich is in London!'

He shrugged. 'Would you have stayed in the car if I said I was taking you to a run-down château on the edge of a light industrial estate?'

She lifted her cigarette in the air. 'Touché.'

They stood in silence for a few moments. Phillip cleared his throat. 'Is her real name Star?'

'Who?'

Phillip hunched his shoulders and laughed quietly, scuffing his shoes in the gravel. Alia watched him as she took a deep drag on her cigarette. He wasn't a laugh-out-loud kind of guy. 'Nah, it's Stella but she thought it wasn't cool enough. Besides it kind of rhymes with Alia, her most famous client,' she said, and gave a little bow.

'Right…I don't want to say that makes sense to me but hey, who am I to judge?'

Alia nodded in agreement.

Phillip shuffled the gravel with his foot. 'Star gave me… umm… instructions, detailed instructions about you, and one of those was that you were not to be woken if I wanted to keep both eyes in working order.'

It was Alia's turn to snort with laughter.

'I really wanted to stay awake, to see where you were taking me, but I got bored and after my very eventful day, I couldn't keep my eyes open. Who knew all it took was getting arrested, then kidnapped and driven to France?' She didn't mention the tab she'd found in Star's glove compartment.

Alia was wide awake, but Phillip was yawning after the long drive. He took a small black cylinder from his jacket, opened it, and jammed his cigarette butt into it. He held it out to Alia, but she shook her head and took another drag.

'I'm trying to give up, but that's difficult in times of stress,' he said. He replaced the lid and put the cylinder back into his coat.

'I should quit too, but hey, who can be bothered?' Alia said, looking at her cigarette. She took another drag, pinching the butt between her fingers. She blew the smoke up into the air and laughed softly, threw the butt into the garden, and turned toward the house. She reached the terrace and picked up her makeup case from the pile of luggage, before turning to see Phillip, bent over in the garden. 'What have you lost?'

'You tossed your butt in here. I can't…' he said, his voice lost as he turned away to keep looking.

She watched him for a moment, shook her head, and marched across the gravel and into the garden bed. She found the discarded butt and held it out for him.

'Stick that in your little black pipe and smoke it,' she said and walked back towards the house.

Exiled to the Château

Next morning, if you could call quarter to midday morning, Alia woke with a pounding head and a mouth dryer than her father's wit. She was disoriented and sweaty. The sheet over her head felt warm to the touch and for a moment she thought the room was on fire. Pulling the sheet back just far enough to see, she was temporarily blinded by the sunlight pouring through the floor-to-ceiling windows. She groaned and buried her face in the covers. The bare windows needed curtains, block-out curtains, maybe curtains made from steel. She'd be giving the room a 1-star review on TripAdvisor.

'The light, it burns,' she wailed, channelling her inner Dracula. She crawled from the bed and staggered to the bathroom.

Although there was no door, the light in the bathroom was more subdued. The deep blue tiles seemed to absorb the bright sunshine coming in from the other room. Once her eyes had grown accustomed to the dimmer light, she could see the bathroom was smaller than she was used to, but it was perfectly designed, with a clawfoot bath and the glassed-in shower had jets facing in different directions. It was modern but had that charm the French do so well.

'Dick and Angel would be proud of this room,' she said to the mirror as she checked out the brass tapware. 'At least I feel like I've been exiled to a château.' She reached down to where her phone usually stuck out of her back pocket, despite the fact she was wearing just a t-shirt and hadn't seen her phone for nearly 24 hours. 'Fuck,' she said, slapping her own left butt cheek. She groaned as much from the missing phone as from the self-administered slap.

Not having her phone was killing her. If anyone else had been there, she would have launched into a description of how it was probably literally killing her. It was killing her not knowing what was going on in the world generally and specifically, she had no idea what had happened to Gaynor and the boys after they'd left the station. She wasn't worried about Gaynor; she was famous, and her dad was stinking rich, but the boys might have found themselves in a spot of bother because their parents were just regular rich. It was killing her too, that everyone was right about her being addicted to her phone.

Back in the bedroom, her eyes shielded from the sun, she hauled her large vanity case into the bathroom, propping it on a thoughtfully placed wooden shelf. On another shelf below the basin, a very considerate person had placed three large fluffy towels, a carafe of water and a glass, and a selection of essentials including a toothbrush and one of those useless combs they give you in 4-star hotels. She poured herself a glass of water and sat on the tiled floor, flipping open the clasps on her vanity case. She admired the beautifully packed case, each product in its own compartment and a slim drawer stocked with a small selection of over-the-counter pain relief, and her jewellery roll. Sighing with relief, she popped a couple of headache pills into her hand and downed them with the rest of the water. She flicked the shower mixer on, letting the warm water run over her hand, then stood for a long time in the shower.

The last 24 hours had been eventful to say the least. She was supposed to be sorry for what she had done, but she laughed out loud at the fact that she had shoplifted naked and sat wrapped in a prison-issue blanket for six hours in a police station. She didn't care what Star thought; she was doing her bit for personal freedom. She wrapped her wet hair in a towel and looked in the mirror again. The words 'personal freedom' ran around in her head.

'Really?' she whispered to herself. Did she really believe what she had done was anything more than a laugh for her mates and her followers? Her stomach lurched. What would her followers be thinking about her radio silence? She reached for her phone.

'Arggh,' she said at her reflection. Along with the extreme withdrawals from social media accounts she felt bad about letting her followers down.

They rely on me to cheer them up on their way to their crappy job or school.

She went back out into her bright bedroom, head pounding. Coffee! She desperately required coffee and a cigarette before she could do another thing, although clothes were probably a good idea before she could go in search of coffee or she'd end up in even more trouble.

She and Phillip had stacked the luggage in the corner of the room next to an ancient looking armoire. She spread the cases around the room on all available horizontal surfaces and stood back to see exactly what she had to work with. Not that it really mattered because no one was going to see her. It was obvious that Mrs Plant had packed the bags. They were military neat. If Star had packed for her yesterday, based on the mood she was in, there would have been nothing but old sweatshirts and holey yoga pants. Alia smiled at the thought of her housekeeper. Calling her Mrs Plant made her sound like an old-fashioned nanny, but Mrs Regina Plant, or Mrs P as everyone called her, was amazing. She stood nose to nose with Alia matching her height of 6'1"and before coming to work at the house, she had been in the forces for twelve years. She was more like an older sister than an employee, although Alia often complained dramatically that she insisted on being paid like an employee, a running joke between them. Mrs P was like a neat, kind flatmate who did all the shopping, cooking and housework. Mrs Plant was no plant; she was Alia's rock.

Alia felt a tear pop into each eye and fiercely pushed them away.

'Obviously I am desperately hungry. No point getting sentimental over a stupid suitcase,' she said to the room.

The closest bag contained part of her collection of vintage Kimonos. She pulled out a jacket made from old silk and draped it over her shoulders. 'Might be a bit much for breakfast,' she mumbled. She folded the exquisite jacket but couldn't fit it back in the suitcase the way Mrs P had. She ran her hand over the neatly folded silk and satin jackets and dresses in ivory, jet black, the deepest blues to the palest of pinks. Her hand stopped lightly on a baby pink wedge of fabric. She pulled it out and a flowing silk dress unfurled like a particularly fast blooming flower. Laughing, Alia pulled the dress over her head and it fell to her feet. She'd had it made in Thailand for about five Pound and it was immediately her favourite dress even though she had completely forgotten she owned it.

Back in the bathroom, she brushed her long hair and piled it on her head. Holding it with one hand, she reached into her vanity case and pulled out a vintage comb decorated with Jet beads. She stuck the comb into her messy bun to keep it in place. She felt her right-hand twitch, the caption for the photo already typing itself out in her head.

'Argghhhh,' she yelled at the mirror. Her shoulders slumped and she stared at her reflection. Drawing a deep breath, she pulled herself up to her full height and smiled. 'You can do this,' she whispered at her reflection. 'It's a phone. Get over it.'

She opened her bedroom door and sniffed at the air. Something smelled like food but there was an overlay to the smell reminiscent of burnt hair. She scratched her nose. There was a glue smell also and she could hear the faint sound of a power saw. The entry had been very dark on their arrival and while her own bedroom was elegant and had obviously been re-modelled recently, the hall looked shabby. The worn carpet on the hall didn't continue down the stairs; they had been recently repaired judging by the amount of fresh new timber underfoot. She looked up at the high ceilings. The crown mouldings, scrubbed back ready for painting, were in place but she could make out faint traces of graffiti on the walls and even the ceiling.

She wandered down the stairs, enjoying the smooth feel of the balustrade that had been stripped back, ready to be stained. Alia had grown up in a stately home and inherited the estate on her 18th birthday, one of the perks of being an orphan she had once told her audience at Edinburgh. They had laughed but her therapist didn't think it was very funny.

'What have they done to you, old girl?' she mumbled as she took in the patched plaster and new treads. The house must have been magnificent in its day, but it had obviously been abandoned to its fate like so many other stately homes in Europe. They were notoriously expensive to maintain. Alia kept walking, following the smell of food, the scent of building work growing fainter. She came to the entry foyer and looked up at the stripped walls and the ornate ceiling more than thirty feet above her head. The place was enormous.

'Hello,' she called, and a voice echoed back to her. It took her a second to realise that it was a man's voice and not an actual echo.

'In here,' the voice said. It was Phillip. He was sitting at the far end of a long timber table, a laptop and neat piles of paper in front of him. At the other end of the twelve-seater table sat a woman and small dog, both on grand upholstered chairs. Phillip greeted her again but seemed distracted by his computer, while the woman stood to shake her hand.

'Hi. Camryn, artist in residence. I'm working on the stained glass in the château.' She was wearing coveralls in a bright turquoise. On the table, dozens of intricate drawings in jewel colours covered every available surface.

'It's lovely to meet you. These are stunning,' Alia said, peering at the artworks.

Camryn smiled. 'Working sketches for the glasswork.'

'I love Art Nouveau,' Alia said, leaning over the table to get a better look. The little dog jumped down from his chair, stood in front of Alia and cocked his head to one side as if trying to work out what she was.

'He probably thinks you're a tree,' Camryn said and chuckled.

'What's your name?' Alia said, scratching the Jack Russell behind the ear. 'You look like a Jack? Or a Russell?'

'Ha! His name is Watermelon.' Alia stood up and looked at Camryn as the dog ran in circles around his mistress, 'My nephew had a dream about a Jack Russell eating watermelon and went out the next day and found this little guy at the dog's home. He went travelling, so Watermelon here, moved in with Aunty.'

Alia smiled. She desperately wanted to make a smart-arse remark about the name but watching Camryn with the little dog made her stop.

'He keeps me company, I keep him in treaties, and funnily enough, he doesn't eat watermelon.' She sat back down, and the dog jumped up onto the other upholstered chair, turned around once, and sat down.

'There's bread and a toaster. Cold cuts and yoghurt in the little fridge, pastries and fruit,' Phillip said, pointing in the general direction of the sideboard. His eyes didn't leave his laptop.

Camryn patted the seat to her left. It was a hard timber chair, but it was obvious that the plush seats were taken. 'Sit down, love. We won't bite,' she said. She quickly stood up again and carefully gathered her drawings up in a stack. 'Sorry about that.'

Alia took her allotted seat. 'Coffee?'

Camryn pointed at the pot on the sideboard.

'Any chance there's Kombucha?' Alia asked.

Camryn scrunched up her face. 'Not bloody likely.'

'Write it on the list and I'll see if I can get some in the village, but don't hold your breath waiting.' Phillip pointed at a cork notice board on the wall. It was empty except for the sheet of paper entitled 'shopping list.'

'Can I come with you? Which village?'

'Star didn't say anything about excursions. You're here to write,' Phillip said, eyes glued to his screen.

Alia made a face at him and went to the cork board and picked up the pen. She jerked at the black cord attaching it to the notice board. 'Having problems with thieves? Particularly desperate thieves?'

Phillip looked up finally. 'Things go missing from time to time. Ghosts. It's annoying not having a pen when you need one.'

Alia nodded. 'I live in an old house. It's like Hogwarts sometimes, even got our own moaning Myrtle but that's just the housekeeper.'

Camryn laughed.

'Actually, my housekeeper is lovely. Don't pay any attention to me, I joke about everything.'

In large letters she read aloud as she wrote 'Kombucha, White Rum, cigarettes, chocolate. And freedom.' She stood with the pen, still attached to its long cord, in her mouth. 'My five favourite food groups.'

'I wouldn't put that in my mouth. You don't know where that pen's been,' Phillip said.

She dropped the pen. It swung back on its black cord and smacked on the cork. Alia went to the sideboard, chose the largest mug, and turned to Phillip. 'So just the filter coffee, then?'

He didn't look up, just made a grunt sound that Alia took for an affirmation. She filled the mug and grabbed the plate covered with pastries and took them back to the table.

'Don't you love France?' she said, taking a huge bite of a croissant.

Camryn packed up her notebooks, Watermelon watching her every move. She smiled at Alia. 'What are your plans today?'

Alia swallowed her bite of flaky pastry and opened her mouth to speak.

'Writing.' The response came from the other end of the table.

'Oh Alia, your ventriloquism is coming along nicely,' Camryn said.

Alia snorted. 'What he said. I'm on a deadline and you know what they say about deadlines?'

'If you don't meet them it costs you and the company around five hundred thousand quid in legal fees and costs?' Phillip was smiling but it wasn't a terribly kind looking smile.

Alia frowned at him. 'I'd better get on with it then,' she said and stood up.

Phillip closed his lap-top and stood.

'Oh, such a gentleman, standing when a lady leaves the room,' Alia said.

'Ah, no, actually, I have all your writing stuff.' He made speech marks in the air as he said, "writing stuff."

'What's with the speech marks?'

'Sorry, it's just that if you're writing six books, it's a little light on.'

'Don't actually need your professional opinion, thanks, *driver*.'

He took a deep breath and walked over to pick up the document box sitting next to the sideboard. He put it on the table next to her. Alia picked up another pastry.

'Isn't this the delivery you had in the backseat on the way here? "The boring paperwork" you called it. Like, "really boring, badly written" you said.'

'Sorry, yeah, that was a bit rude of me, but then I am only the driver.'

Alia stood and pulled the lid off the box. There were four of her journals and about a hundred sheets of loose-leaf paper printed on both sides.

'Six books…?' Phillip said as he peered into the box.

'Uh huh,' she said with her mouth full of pastry. 'And they gave me a whopping advance, too.' He didn't look at her. It was a waste of a smug grin.

Camryn cleared her throat. 'What are the books about?'

Alia finished her mouthful. 'My life, really, how I live, my view on things. My poetry, obviously, how to live free-range.'

'Free range?' Camryn said.

'You know, without restrictions.'

She heard Phillip snort softly at the other end of the table but ignored him.

'How old are you? 25? I couldn't have filled a page with my thoughts at 25,' Camryn said.

Alia felt that as an artist, Camryn seemed more understanding of the situation. It was good to have some moral support. 'I'm 26, I think. It's a matter of finding inspiration. I'm worried that being stuck here, away from the vibe in London, that I won't be able to write the way I normally do. I actually write a lot on my phone. It's an art in itself.'

Camryn smiled and put her hand on Alia's. 'I know what you mean but we professionals can't afford the luxury of inspiration; we just have to get in and do the work. Speaking of which, I have about forty square metres of glass to finish and a show to prepare. See you at dinner?'

Alia and Phillip both nodded and wished her a good day, and she and Watermelon left through a side door that Alia hadn't even noticed.

'What about my laptop?'

'Star didn't mention it, but I think its absence speaks for itself. Did you say you *think* you are 26?'

Alia ignored the last question. *This guy does not understand my humour.*

'No phone, no laptop. I really don't know what I am supposed to do.'

'You're creative; you'll think of something,' he said as he sorted through his own neat stacks of paper. A small smile tugged at the corners of his mouth.

'Why are you enjoying this so much? What did I ever do to you?' Alia didn't wait for a response. She jammed the lid back on the box, went to the sideboard and refilled her coffee and put a chocolate croissant in her mouth. She balanced the coffee on the top of the document box and left the room.

The Write Stuff

Alia pushed her door open with her backside and nearly made it to the bed before dropping the mug of coffee. She tripped on the mug, sending it hurtling across the bare timber floor where it smashed against the armoire.

'Are you fucking kidding me?' she said through gritted teeth.

She threw the box on the bed and went to the bathroom to get a towel to clean up. The cup had been lovely and now she was picking shards of porcelain off the beautiful hardwood floor. The morning had started with such promise and had gone downhill faster than a Tory politicians' credibility. She threw the coffee-stained towel into the shower and switched on the water. The brown towel slowly turned back to white as the coffee ran down the drain.

She returned to her writing stuff.

Bloody Phillip. Who is he to tell me my writing is boring?

She rifled through the printed sheets to see if Star had hidden any contraband but considering her agent was the one that banished her, it was a long shot. There was a sheet of palest pink paper at the bottom of the pile. It was a letter from Star. She obviously hadn't expected Alia to get down to work so soon because the opening line read "in the unlikely event of you getting to the bottom of the pile and finding this letter…"

Rude.

She sat on the sticky, coffee-scented floor to read.

Alia,

I'm writing this in the unlikely event of you getting to the bottom of the pile and finding this letter, (unless you were looking for hidden treats in the box.)

I hope I can impress upon you the importance of the coming weeks. I'm sorry if you think I am being unsupportive when I feel as though I am finally doing my job after these past three years of mayhem. Please – just get in and write! It will not be easy.

Let me repeat that – writing is not easy!

Yes… I think you have bitten off more than you can chew, but my girl, I hope you get in and chew like crazy because you are so very talented. Don't take the easy road like you always do! I want you to get these books written because I believe you can write them. But I want to warn you - I have just heard there is a ghost writer working on the project this minute, and if your work isn't acceptable the publisher will simply go with her stuff. (She's a lot cheaper than you, too! And it's all right there in the contract – remember?) I beg you, use your time well. You might never get this chance again!

Stella-Maria

p.s. You can ask Phillip (the driver) for help if you need it. He's studying literature or something, so he might know a thing or two about words.

She sat back against the bed frame. Things had to be serious for Star to sign off using her real name. 'And what about ol' Phil the dark horse, studying literature. No wonder he was so smug about my writing stuff,' she mumbled, re-reading the letter.

She stood up and looked around the room. Obviously the first thing to do was to make a writing space. There was no desk just the two huge armoires on the wall opposite the bed. She had seen her fair share of old handmade furniture, so she went to the first cabinet and opened the door. It was clean and smelled like camphor and old flowers, and as she suspected it wasn't an armoire at all, but a writing cabinet with a fold out desk. It was a beautiful piece of furniture. Her hand went to her back pocket in search of her phone. She gritted her teeth and gave a little grunt of laughter. She really was addicted.

She opened the other armoire and started to unpack her clothes into it. There were no hangers, so she folded everything neatly and stacked the suitcases in a pile on top, a benefit of being tall. No laptop in her luggage but she did find various little gifts left by Mrs P. Two family size bars of Cadbury's, a lighter but no cigarettes, a quarter of a bottle of rum, her old camera, and three rolls of film.

She picked up the rum, unscrewed the lid and necked what was left. 'Oh hello, darkness my old friend…' she murmured.

She replaced the lid and stood the bottle on the windowsill. With any luck there would be a wonderful cellar full of bottles of rocket fuel under the old house. Looking around the room she felt a flutter in her chest. It could have been her grandmother's house. The photogenic room made her phone hand twitch again. She was dying to post photos. She made a square with her fingers and held them up to her eyes. Remembering the camera, she snatched it up, flicking the power switch to 'on.' Mrs P must have put in a new battery. She was always trying to get Alia to go back to her photography.

She put the camera up to her eye. It had been her father's and she felt a pang of…something…when she looked through the viewfinder. It felt like sadness but was mostly resentment. The room looked even better through the little square. She snapped a few shots of the space.

She looked down at the camera. What was the point of taking photos that no one would ever see?

Conversation floated up from outside. She went to one of the four tall windows that flooded her room with light to see Phillip standing on the drive talking to an older man who was covered in splatters of paint. She lifted the camera again, fitting the two men in the little square. The paint splattered man was laughing.

Surely not at something Phillip said.

The men were holding large paint swatches, talking animatedly. They were also smoking. Alia almost threw the camera down and bolted down the stairs to bum a smoke, but for some reason the goddess had seen fit for Phillip to take his shirt off at that moment. She forgot for a second that he was pompous and mean and had a chip on his shoulder the size of an ancient pyramid; he was a fine-looking man with a broad back and slim waist. Without thinking, she lifted the camera to her eye and snapped a photo of the two men. Well, maybe just of one of them.

Phillip turned his shirt inside out and shook it violently. He must have had an insect crawling on him. He turned to face the house, and she took another couple of shots. The contractor nudged Phillip and pointed up at her. Phillip turned as he pulled his shirt over his head and Alia was startled by what she saw. He had angry red scars running across his torso and down his left arm. She dropped to the floor and lay still, her heart pounding in her chest. He already thought she was an idiot; what was he going to think now? That she was a pervert, a voyeur? He would think it was a digital camera.

She was still lying on the floor when the knock came. After the coffee spill she hadn't shut her bedroom door. To be honest, she wasn't one for privacy and was often told off by Mrs Plant for leaving her front door open, even when she stayed in the city house.

'You okay down there?' Phillip said.

'Yeah…I…fell…'

He stood in the doorway.

'I…I don't really mind people looking at my scars, but photos are a bridge too far.'

Before she could answer he had walked away. She was appalled at herself. If it had been a digital camera, she could have deleted them. Without giving it a second thought, she flipped open the film housing and pulled the roll free, exposing the photos and destroying the whole roll.

She pulled herself up off the floor and flopped on to her bed. It was covered in sheets of paper. She lay face down for a few minutes and rolled over, collecting the covers and papers as she went, making herself into a burrito.

Writing. It's harder than you think.

A knock at the door woke her. She was sweaty and disoriented, still rolled in her duvet.

'We didn't see you at lunch so when dinner time came, I thought I'd come and find you.' Camryn stood in the open doorway. Watermelon trotted into the room and sniffed at the armoire. 'We're just down the hall.'

Alia stared at her. 'I just wanted to check on you. I'll see you at dinner?'

Once again, the person at her door was gone before she could answer. Her head was pounding. She unfurled herself from the duvet and stumbled to the bathroom. She drank the water in the carafe and refilled it, draining it again. Sitting on the loo she took a couple of painkillers. She was having withdrawals and not just from TikTok. Her hands were shaking, and her mouth was dry. Star's note said, "use this time well." She would have known exactly what was going to happen because she was privy to all the excesses in Alia's life. Star was often the source of those excesses.

She cast her mind back to the yoga retreat she and Gaynor went to in Greece. After two days she thought she was going to die, but on the third she had woken with a clear head and felt better than she ever had.

Tomorrow, my second day...

The cool shower was wonderful on her feverish skin, but her scalp protested as she tried to pull a comb through her hair. She gave up and twisted a silk scarf over it instead. She pulled on a slip dress and belted a jacket over top.

Too much? She consulted the mirror. *I won't wear shoes...keep it real...*

The painkillers seemed to be helping so she went down to dinner. If she didn't face Phillip tonight, she would have no choice but to make a run for it.

Piles of painting equipment sat in the middle of the entry hall, along with buckets and mops. A shiny red machine stood at one end of the foyer, hoses coming from it. She smiled. It was a wall-paper remover. She had seen one of those when she was remodelling the country house. Okay, so it was a stretch to say *she* had done any remodelling, but she had paid the bills. She looked up at the towering walls covered in peeling wallpaper. The contractors certainly had a lot of work ahead of them.

Phillip and Camryn were in the dining room, with Watermelon sitting on what was clearly his chair. Alia sat to the left as she had that morning.

'Good evening,' Camryn said.

'Hello, hi…' Alia gave Phillip a wave too. He nodded in response but was once again glued to the screen.

'Dinner looks amazing,' she said, taking her plate to the sideboard. She loaded it with salad and leaned in to inhale the aroma of the pasta dish. Her stomach was doing flips, but she was starving.

'Wine?' Camryn was holding up a bottle. 'I brought it from home.'

Alia's mouth watered at the sight of the wine bottle. She sat next to Camryn, put her plate down and snatched up her glass.

'Lovely, thanks. And where is home?'

Camryn reached over and took the glass, smoothing Alia's shaking hand on to the tablecloth.

'California, but as you can hear from my accent, I'm Welsh.'

Alia's head was fuzzy, but she must have responded positively because Camryn went on to talk for the better part of dinner. It was pleasant listening to her accent and her amusing stories of art shows and the intricacies of travelling with a companion animal. Her words washed over Alia as the wine washed down the salad.

'This is lovely.' Alia held up the glass and admired the golden liquid.

'It is, and no nasty side-effects.'

Alia tilted her head at Camryn the way Watermelon did. 'Like, as in, organic?'

'Like, as in non-alcoholic. Because I am. An alcoholic,' Cam said, looking far too happy about it.

Alia had trouble disguising her disappointment. It tasted lovely but it had been the nasty side effect she was particularly looking forward to.

'How's the writing going?' Phillip piped up from the end of the table to spoil the evening.

Alia smiled. 'Welcome to the conversation. Umm… Writing. You know, it's harder than I thought it would be.'

Phillip and Camryn both burst into peals of laughter. Alia sat in mortified silence as they laughed, setting each other off again as they struggled to gain control. Watermelon stood on the chair and hopped up and down with excitement.

'You are wonderfully funny,' Camryn said.

Alia stood up and crumpled her napkin on the table and the other woman stopped laughing. 'Alia, please I'm sorry. I didn't mean to offend you. You're a comedian; I thought you were joking. It was funny. You have to admit that.'

Alia smiled and slid back into her chair. 'Yes. I guess so…' She smiled and held her glass up for Camryn to fill.

Normally, Alia wouldn't be upset by something like that, but she was feeling fragile and desperately needed a drink or three. Camryn reached across and scratched her dog's head and he settled down on the damask seat cushion. Alia knew all kinds of artists and performers, but she had never met anyone like Camryn. She had a quality Alia couldn't quite put her finger on; it was as though she actually liked other people. She smiled at Camryn and made a mental note to add the joke to her next show.

She raised her glass to her dinner companions. 'In the absence of all other people, you guys are a great audience.'

She relaxed a little and the conversation flowed then as they learned a little more about each other. Alia was surprised to find she had much in common with Camryn and even Phillip dragged himself away from his laptop long enough to join in the conversation a few times. When he did though, it was to talk about Alia, her deadline, and the various daft things she had done in her career. He seemed to enjoy watching her squirm and it was Camryn who was her saviour each time. She was kind and caring and had an almost motherly quality to her, even though she was probably only a few years older than Alia.

Phillip started to run through some of the crazier stunts Alia had pulled on her YouTube channel. She found her cheeks were burning.

'So, you're obviously a huge fan. You know all my greatest hits. For your information, I read English at Oxford.'

Phillip looked up at her. 'What? As in you went to a pub in Oxford and read the menu? In English.'

'Ha bloody ha, ha. As in I attended university at Oxford and actually graduated. I am *actually* quite smart, ask anyone who knows me, I just act like a mad woman; it's my stage persona.'

'So, you were on stage during the drive here? You certainly acted like a mad woman.'

Camryn sat watching them both. 'Oh, you kids are fun,' she said. She was smiling but Alia could see the conflict was making her uneasy.

Alia leaned back in her chair and looked at Phillip.

'Look I know I am a bit of a joke to you, but I write on my phone. I have nearly a million followers. I'm not a complete twit but I'm finding it hard without it… or my laptop. Writing by hand is different from typing, don't you think?' She looked from Phillip to Camryn. Camryn nodded her head.

'I know…I'm just teasing you,' Phillip said.

'Well, that's okay then. As long as you're doing it for comedy,' Alia said.

'There are a couple of old typewriters here if you want to use one. You want to come to the cave and take a look? Cam, you want to come?'

Camryn was already on her feet. 'Perfect timing; we need another bottle. C'mon Melon.' The little dog leapt down from his seat.

Phillip went to the sideboard and took out two torches, handing one to Alia. 'You'll need this at night. The power isn't connected to some rooms while the work is being done so don't leave home without it.'

He led the way through the concealed doorway that Camryn had used that morning. Alia could have sworn she was feeling the effects of the wine, but it was probably just the sugar or the fact that she was detoxing. Watermelon stayed close to his mistress as they took the long hallway lit only by Phillip's torch. Alia flicked hers on and for an instant Watermelon was distracted by the new pool of light in front of him.

'He's a great dog, does he ever bark?' Alia asked.

'Don't tell him he's a dog, he thinks he's people!' Camryn said in a stage whisper. 'He only barks at the ghosts, eh, Phil?'

Phillip put the torch to his face and did his best Vincent Price laugh, which really wasn't that great.

They stopped at a set of double wooden doors. Phillip handed the torch to Alia while he opened them, took it again, and told the women to wait. Alia watched as the little pool of light bobbed away down the stairs. There was a clicking sound and a bank of temporary lights on a stand lit up. The sight made Alia's head feel like it was about to take flight.

'It's a fresco. We were all surprised when the contractors found it,' Phillip said from the other side of the space.

Alia switched her torch off and stared up at the ceiling. Camryn stood looking up for a few moments then headed for the wine stored at the end of the cavernous room.

Alia watched her go, wondering if there was anything more potent than the Californian lolly water she was drinking. She was reluctant to ask, unsure of the protocol of drinking with someone in recovery. Phillip was standing under the painting, smiling. He seemed to love the old house. The ceiling was a shallow dome carved out of the limestone the château was built on.

'The figures look as though they are dancing when you have candle-light down here,' Phillip said. He was whispering. 'The former owner must have had it covered over before the war. An expert from the Louvre is coming out next month. It could be old. Apparently, the château belonged to a mistress of Good King Henri… Henri the fourth…she was a musician and wrote music for the court, a remarkable woman. The expert seemed really excited about the photos, said it might have been done by a Venetian master.'

'I've never seen anything like it…' Alia said in a whisper. The deep colours looked as though they had been rendered yesterday.

'It's the nine muses…' Phillip whispered.

They stood in silence for a few moments while Camryn cheerfully chatted to her little dog from the depths of the cellar. Alia gently cleared her throat.

'I'm sorry… I've deleted them…pulled the film out. I can give it to you if you want. The film, it's an old 35mm, not digital, so I can't share them…' Alia's voice trailed off.

It took a few seconds for Phillip to respond. 'Uh, oh? It's fine… thanks…yeah…let's get you that typewriter.' He walked away.

After looking up for so long Alia was swaying. She walked over to the stairs and sat down heavily.

'Okay, hen?' Camryn asked.

Alia nodded. 'Tired. I know that's fake wine, but I feel a bit drunk. I'm just a long way from home and…'

Phillip joined them holding a dusty black typewriter. 'There are two or three more down there, but I know this one works because someone's been using it.' The typewriter had a sheet of paper in it and a few words had been typed.

Summer in this valley is not kind. It's hot and bright and the storms can tear the roof from a structure. The lambs of spring no longer bound about but find shade with their mothers….

'That's lovely,' Camryn said. 'I wonder who wrote it.'

Phillip put the heavy typewriter down on the broad stone stairs and tapped out a few letters.

'It's perfect,' Alia said. Her head had started to tap out a few letters of its own. 'I think I need to go to bed…'

Phillip picked up the typewriter and placed it on her forearms. It was lucky she was sitting down because she almost dropped the heavy old thing.

'Torches,' he said. He walked back into the room to turn off the bank of lights, leaving the group in darkness until he could fumble around and switch his own on. Alia sucked in a breath and hauled herself and the typewriter upright in the darkness just as Watermelon began to bark.

Admonition

Alia woke with a start, the morning light was pouring in through the windows, she pulled the covers over her head. She was a little fuzzy from too much fake wine, but she felt better than she had in a long time. Watermelon's barking had freaked them out and she and Camryn had run the length of the corridor, laughing. They had stood in the dining room, clinging to each other but Camryn had had to go back and call the silly dog as he stood barking at the cave door. Phillip had followed at a more mature pace, carrying the typewriter Alia had left behind on the stairs.

In her bedroom, they'd set the typewriter up in the armoire and she and Camryn had talked for hours, only heading off to bed when the local roosters had started their crowing for the day.

She laughed as she thought about it, sitting up to look at the typewriter in her writing area. Phillip, who couldn't seem to work out if he was a hero or a villain in the story, said he would buy more paper in Tours when he was running his errands but then suggested she might only need a few sheets.

Rude.

Alia didn't ask to go with him. He was such a prickly character, and she didn't care to be stuck in a car with him again for any length of time and she had to admit, she was itching to get started on her writing. She jumped out of bed and pulled the chair up to the desk. The paper from the night before was still wound around the barrel of the old typewriter. She moved it down a little and sat, fingers poised above the keys.

'What is there to say about making life up as we go along?' She said the words slowly as she typed them. Working on a laptop was far easier but that was a decent enough sentence to start with, she thought. She stared at the paper. She loved the way the little black letters looked on the page; imperfect, slightly askew, already bleeding a little at the edges on the soft, old paper.

She clicked the barrel down another couple of lines.

'Dear Mrs P…. (Regina),

I hope you are well and not missing cleaning up after me too much. Thanks for packing all my fave things. Did you sing like Julie Andrews while you were doing it?

Things are going okay here. I am writing (obviously) but it's quite hard. The view is lovely. I don't have my phone and my hand twitches every time I see a nice view or something else that might look good on Instagram. I'd send you a pic if I could. There are a lot of trees, it's a lot like being out at the Hertfordshire house. An artist is staying here too, she is lovely and doesn't appear to be here under duress as some of us are, although it sure as fuck beats being in the lock up.'

Alia sat back and re-read what she had written. An f-bomb on the beautiful old paper in those sweet, quirky letters seemed wrong somehow. She looked in the document box although she knew there was no white-out. She had seen people use a row of exes over the offending word to blot it out, but Mrs P wouldn't care.

'I am sure you have heard all the juicy gossip (which is all true) so I hope you don't hate me too much. I am going to get down to my writing seriously today but wanted to shoot this quick message to you to let you know I'm alive and okay, but I miss you and I miss my bloody life…'

She would have to ask Phillip to pick up an envelope along with the rest of the things on her list. She wound the paper down and typed her London address on the bottom of the page. It wasn't much, as letters went, and it wouldn't be the end of the world if Phillip read it. She chewed on her fingernail. Mrs P might not even receive it if she had been moved out to Hertfordshire for her safety. Alia imagined the usual three or four photographers who took turns staking out her house had swelled to a few more and she hoped Regina was okay. Her housekeeper had been mistaken for her in the past.

She took a quick shower then ran down the stairs to grab some breakfast. Camryn laughed at her as she filled her plate with scrambled eggs, and grabbed a pile of pastries, an apple, and a large mug of coffee. She was more careful with her breakfast than she had been the previous morning. As she headed back up to her room, Phillip was coming down the stairs.

'Good morning,' Alia said

'Morning. You are feeling better?' He smiled at her, but it was one of his tight-lipped smiles.

'I am. Hey, I really wanted to ask…'

'Please don't,' he said. 'I'm going to Tours. I have your list, I'll add paper, pens, white out, and there's this old place that specialises in stationery. I called; they've got a spare ribbon for the typewriter.' He stopped and looked at her.

She frowned. 'If you had let me finish, I wanted to ask if you can phone Star and ask her if my housekeeper is safe. What did you think I was going to ask?'

'Regina is fine. She is in very capable hands.'

Alia was dumbstruck that Phillip even knew who Regina was.

'Anything else you need? Coke? Speed?'

Once again, she was lost for words, but she quickly recovered. 'Couple of lines of Coke would go down a treat,' she said and headed for the stairs. 'I have a letter for you to post if it's not too much trouble. I'll leave it on the sideboard. Please refrain from reading it. This isn't an actual prison.' She was seething by the time she reached her room although she was careful to put the coffee down first. She bit into a pastry, took a mouthful of eggs, and went to the typewriter. She nearly spat the eggs out as she read a single line typed across the top of the page.

'Profane swearing never did any man any good. No man is the richer or wiser or happier for it.
Robert Lowth'

'Oh, you arse,' she said and tore the page from the barrel.

Ghosts for Breakfast

'How fucking dare you!' Alia said as she burst into the dining room. Camryn and Watermelon looked up in unison. Phillip didn't look up at all, a sure sign of a guilty conscience.

'What's happened?' Camryn said.

Alia waved the sheet of paper in the air. 'This.' She slapped the page down on to the table in front of Phillip.

He stared at it. 'What?' he said and looked up at her.

'Who gave you permission to enter my room? You might be my warden but seriously stay the fuck out of my room.'

'I didn't go anywhere near your room.'

'Right, so who the fuck wrote this smarmy fucking quote on here about swearing?'

Phillip picked the page up. 'I didn't write that, seriously I haven't been in your room. I promise.'

'Sure, right.'

'Might have been one of the other residents,' Camryn chimed in. Phillip and Alia both looked at her.

'Ah, yeah,' Phillip said.

'Whoever it was will get a face full of pepper spray if they come near my room again,' Alia said, looking pointedly at Phillip.

She didn't have any pepper spray but that was beside the point. She was a tall, well-built woman; one of her stand-up bits ended with the line

"I'd give myself good odds against any regular sized intruder that isn't armed, high or hot."

'Pepper spray won't hurt that lot,' Camryn said and ruffled melon's head. 'You sort them out don't you, buddy?'

Alia stared at her. 'Are you suggesting a ghost took me to task about swearing?'

Camryn nodded and as if on cue, Melon ran from the room to bark at the stairs.

'Oh, fuck off, are you serious?'

'Afraid so,' Phillip said.

She spun around to look at him.

'You said you were quite comfortable with ghosts, said you lived in a genuine haunted house. No, you said Hogwarts.'

Watermelon trotted back into the room, did a lap around the dining table, and jumped back onto his chair.

For the third time that morning, she was speechless. She stared at the sheet of paper. 'You guys are nuts,' she said, and left them to their breakfast.

Back in her room, Alia paced the floor. She couldn't believe the lengths to which some people would go, to alienate and bully a newcomer. Jealousy. That's what she put it down to. They were jealous of her 'lot' in life, she supposed. It wasn't her first ride in that particular rodeo. Growing up the way she had, she had come across her fair share of bullies and others offended by her wealth and position. She looked again at the letter she had written to Regina, screwed it up and threw it on the floor. She was going to need a waste-paper basket but there was no way she was going to ask Phillip to take up his precious time getting one.

She slowly ate her breakfast, ideas for poems chasing each other around in her head. There was no time to let pettiness distract her, procrastination and nicotine cravings were enough to contend with. She filled a glass with water and stared at it.

'I never pray, Jesus, I know, but if I could just ask this once, for you to turn this water into wine…' she looked up. 'No? Okay fine.'

She put the glass on the desk and settled into the seat, fingers poised on the shiny old keys. Her leg was itchy, but she knew it was just her brain trying to distract her. The rum bottle on the windowsill caught her eye. The sunlight glinted prettily off its silver cap, but it was still annoyingly empty. Her fingers brushed the keyboard. How is it possible for the mind to be completely blank when normally its positively awash with nonsense?

Running her hands through her hair she sat back and looked up at the ceiling. It was ornate with crown mouldings and tiny rosebuds painted every few feet. How had she not noticed this before? The decoration was intriguing not because it was beautiful but because it seemed almost pointless. She stood up to get a closer look at the flowers. They all appeared to be slightly different and were probably painted by hand. Standing at the keyboard, she pecked out the word rosebuds with one finger.

Okay, that's a start.

Suddenly thirsty, she drained her glass and went to the bathroom for a refill, wondering if there was anything cold to drink in the kitchen.

'Focus!' she yelled at herself in the mirror. How had she ever achieved anything in life? She couldn't believe how easily distracted she was, and she didn't even need a phone for it. Annoyed at herself, she stomped back to her desk but changed direction to close the bedroom door. She didn't want any of the local 'ghosts' coming in to critique her work again.

'What work would that be,' she grumbled, glaring at the almost blank paper.

Pulling her chair in towards the desk, she started to type. Nonsense, but words were words, as her first year tutor was annoyingly fond of saying. Just as some lines of type began to stack themselves on the paper, yet another niggling thought ran through her mind. She needed to know the time even though time was all she had at that point.

She retrieved her jewellery roll from the bathroom and pulled out her watch. She rarely wore it, but it was a family heirloom. She turned it over gently in her hand. It was old and had a couple of diamonds missing on the band, but it was beautiful. It almost glowed in the bright room. It had been her grandmother's and her father had had it restored and engraved for her 16th birthday, her last birthday with him. She had been rude to him that morning. He'd bought her a car, thrown her a party, and given her a thoughtful present and she'd been mean. She couldn't even remember what she'd said, but she remembered the expression on his face afterwards.

She gritted her teeth. 'Save the guilt trip, man. You were the best father a girl could want on her birthday but absolutely appalling for the rest of the year.' Sitting back down, she laid the watch next to the typewriter and got to work.

Twenty minutes later she came up for air. She sat back in the chair and read through the three typed pages. It wasn't her best work, but it was more than she'd had that morning. Star had mentioned something about needing around 250,000 words in total, including the poems. Alia closed her eyes and sat back in the chair. Three pages, she counted the words. That was about twelve hundred words. She groaned and stood up to stretch.

'Only another, billion more words to write,' she said and looked at her glass to see if Jesus was getting anywhere with the water.

A knock on the door pulled Alia out of her daydream. She shook her head, stared blank-eyed at the typewriter, and groaned. She had been daydreaming she was typing. She flicked through the pile of typed sheets. Twelve. She had stopped keeping a running tally in her head but knew twelve was both a decent first day's effort and patently not good enough.

'Coming.' She opened the bedroom door. It was Camryn, with a tray of food.

'You've got to keep your strength up.' She handed the tray to Alia. 'How's it going?'

Alia took the tray and nodded her head sideways for Camryn to follow her.

'This is such a nice set up you have here,' she said. 'I see you're getting some work down.'

Alia sat on the windowsill and picked at the salad Camryn had brought. Watermelon trotted in. 'Where have you been, mister?' Camryn asked him. He wagged his tail in response. 'He loves this house, so many nooks and crannies to check out.'

'And ghosts…' Alia said, rolling her eyes.

'Yes,' Camryn laughed.

'I'm sorry about my little rant this morning. I just can't stand that guy, he's so smug and for him to think he can just waltz in here and fuck with my work and with my head…'

'Do you think he would do that?'

'Yes…he thinks I'm a joke. Just because I'm…'

Camryn looked at her. The dog trotted back out into the hall and sniffed around. 'Young? He's only a few years older than you.'

'No, because I'm.' She stopped and put her hands on her hips. She sighed. 'Because I inherited money.'

Camryn put her head down and laughed softly. 'No, that kind of stuff isn't important to Phil at all. He's lived too much life to worry about that. You know he was in the military? I don't want to tell tales out of school but there's more to him than meets the eye.'

Alia nodded and looked out the window. That explained the scars.

'So, who came in here and put that bloody quote on my paper? It can't have been you because we were together. One of the contractors…maybe?'

Camryn shook her head. 'The two guys who work here speak only French and Spanish… and they wouldn't dare set foot in your room.' Watermelon walked back into the room and gave a tiny bark. Camryn turned to him. 'Time to go, guy? Okay! Let's go…' She clapped her hands excitedly.

The tiny dog ran back out of the room and turned right. Alia could hear him barking down the hall. A shiver ran up her spine. 'More ghosts?'

Camryn nodded. 'See you at dinner?'

'I'll be there. I'm going to try to double my output by then. That will give me about 6000 words for the day.'

'Good for you, chicky. Keep going.' Camryn followed the dog and pulled the door shut behind her.

'Bloody ghosts,' Alia said and ate her lunch.

Alia counted her typed pages. Twenty pages of words sat in a little stack on her desk. She was on a roll and tomorrow she would fill at least another twenty. She sat on her bed and read over a couple of passages. They weren't perfect but Star had said an editor would whip them into shape. All she had to do was get the essence down. She stacked the pages again. It would be a struggle to get all the words needed by the end of the month, but she only needed material for two books. For a start? Surely that would be enough to convince the powers that be to let her write the books herself. That ghost writer would have to find someone else to ghost.

She shivered at the word "ghost."

She'd missed dinner but she wasn't hungry. She couldn't believe how good she felt. She vaguely recalled Star and Mrs P both telling her she would feel good if she got more sleep, stopped drinking and partying so much, but that had seemed a little extreme at the time. She was sure Mrs P would be proud of her progress. Star would be stunned, then disbelieving, but finally at least a little bit proud. It was frustrating that Star hadn't been in contact at all, but then she was probably getting constant updates from smug Phil.

She wished she had a book to read. Lying on the bed, looking at the ceiling, the tiny rosebuds just visible in the gloom, she was restless, her mind racing. One of her new poems ran through her head.

Am I kidding myself? Who in their right mind would think I am a poet?

'Woah,' she said out loud, sitting up. She'd never had an inner critic before and was certain she didn't need one. She'd never been sober long enough to listen to it anyway, that's what drugs were for. She sighed heavily and leaned on the windowsill. Through the trees, the headlights and taillights wound their way towards Paris. The old house would have stood for thousands of nights, silent, except for the calls of birds or the hum of insects but in 2019, there was an ever-present hum of traffic. A full moon peaked its glowing head over the tops of the trees. She reached over and turned off the nightlight. A couple of bugs flew in circles around the now-dark lamp and out through the window in search of something more interesting. If only she could follow.

Alia sighed again, annoying herself. She went to the bathroom for a glass of water and flipped open her vanity case with her toes, a skill she had practiced with a drink in both hands many times. It was one of her followers' favourite talents. One of her most popular style of videos was a makeup demonstration filmed when she was either very drunk or very high, which always started with that particular trick.

'Huh,' she said out loud and slumped her shoulders. Even she had to admit she wasn't a great role model for the thousands of young girls who followed her.

She opened each compartment and took the products out, piling them on the bathmat. She was looking for something, but she wasn't sure what. The case was soon empty, so she ran her hand around the lining. Boom. She took a nail file and pried the lining away from the silver outer case and found the little bag of Edibles she had hidden there the last time she was in Amsterdam. She tore open the packet and shoved one then another into her mouth. They were sweet, a little crystallised with age. She'd probably be asleep before they kicked in.

The pile of cosmetics would have to wait until morning. She walked slowly around the dark room, stopping at the typewriter to check in with herself to see if she felt like writing. She didn't. She lay on the bed and stared up at the sky, letting the night air kiss her skin, shivering, accompanied only by the dark trees, an array of stars, and the bright circle that was the moon.

The days were so warm and bright in her room, but it was a different place at night. She found the shadows more welcoming somehow. Before drifting off, she dreamily took her watch off and lay it on the bedside table and switched off the light. 'Goodnight, grandmother,' she said looking at the watch. She rolled over and lay her feet on the pillows and her head at the end of the bed. 'Goodnight, moon…'

The Stairs

Moonlight woke her. It was like a spotlight in the sky had been switched on. She sat up, confused a little by her different orientation. The room was still and cool. How long had she been asleep? She checked her watch. Once she had it facing the right way, she could see it was just a few minutes after midnight. She turned back to face the windows. The full moon looked too heavy to stay hanging in the sky. There wasn't a light to be seen anywhere on the estate or beyond. Perhaps it was a power outage. She went to the bathroom and tried the light. The bulb glowed warmly. *Not an outage, then.*

A bird called out its haunting song and somewhere in the night, its mate answered. Her skin rippled with tiny goose bumps. She couldn't remember the last time she had heard a bird at night in the city, but at the country house she assumed you could hear them. She had to assume because the house was never quiet. There was always music or voices. She even used a white noise machine to sleep. Alia didn't like quiet.

She walked back to the windows and leaned out breathing in the cool night air. The garden was flood-lit by the moon. No, she thought, there's too much light. The light was coming from somewhere in the house. She leaned out as far as she dared and peered down to the side of the house. There was music. Music and light and…and perhaps voices.

She went to the armoire and took out one of her vintage kimonos and draped it over her shoulders, securing it with a gold belt. Back in the bathroom she ran her fingers through her hair and tied it up. She went to the bedroom door and put her ear against it. Nothing. She would have to investigate. If someone was having a party in the house, she wanted to be there. No, she needed to be there.

She turned the key and pulled the door open as quietly as she could and closed and locked it behind her. She wasn't sure why she was trying to be so quiet; it's not as though she was a prisoner. She was a VIP guest. She lifted her chin and her chest smoothing the silk of her kimono. Hesitating at the top of the stairs she strained to hear the voices. Music played. Old time music, but it was real; she hadn't imagined it. She moved slowly down the stairs, as if any sudden movement might make the music stop at any second. The foyer looked different at night, more elegant. As feared, the music became fainter as she descended so she went back to the top of the stairs. She felt like a little girl again, playing hide and seek. Her grandmother's house had been a great place to grow up. It had all kinds of little nooks to hide in. Alia shuddered and laughed. One girl from school had refused to play with her again after being forgotten in an epic game of Hide and Seek. Who knew it was that difficult to get a nine-year-old girl out of a priest hole?

Peering along the corridor she could see the bright moonlight on the curving wall. That was the way Watermelon had run, investigating and barking. She passed the door she had seen Phillip use and Camryn's was further along where the passageway detoured slightly to the left. Just past Camryn's door, Alia stopped and looked backed. The paint was new and the carpet under her bare feet was plush. Perhaps the section was an extension built on the old house at some time. She turned back towards the sound of the music and kept walking. The passageway opened out onto a tiled gallery, and from the gallery, a spiral staircase cut through the building. The ceiling above it was a stunning Art Nouveau style dome of stained glass with butterflies, dragonflies and bees. The light of the full moon shone through it, but it would have been spectacular by day.

The remodelling was complete in that area and the contractors had done an exceptional job. The papered walls glowed in the moonlight from a bank of windows along the wall beside the stairs. The old-timey music was louder, floating up from downstairs. She heard the unmistakable sound of an ice-cube hitting the bottom of a glass and felt a Pavlovian release of saliva in her mouth. She really needed a drink! After the week she'd had, she needed to let off some steam.

She started downward but stopped. Perhaps the elderly owner was having people to tea. She looked at her watch. A quarter past midnight was a strange time for a bed-ridden pensioner to be having tea. Her hand went to her throat and she giggled. What if she walked in on him entertaining his nurses? She shrugged and started back down the stairs, the sound of more ice cubes hitting a glass made up her mind. She didn't mind a few cavorting nurses. She'd cavort along with them if they gave her something to drink.

Moonlight flooded the entire lower floor showing jewel coloured carpet and artworks lining the walls, reminding her again of her Grandmother's house. The rug underfoot was silky and soft and when she reached the end of the hall, a tall double door with etched glass panels stood slightly ajar. She put her hand on the door but hesitated at a scratching sound. The music started up again, and… footsteps. She peered through the glass panel in the door. There were sofas and occasional chairs, stunning tiffany-style lamps, the odd trinket, and piles of books. One wall was given over to dark timber bookshelves lined with leather-bound volumes. She looked up at the ceiling, trying to picture the floor above, to figure out where in the house she was. Perhaps it was somewhere behind the dining room. The decor was definitely nicer than the rest of the house which was decidedly 3-star in places. This room was plush but quirky. Boutique hotel, perhaps, but in the West End.

'Are you coming in, or are you just going to stand there all night?' said a man's voice.

Alia laughed and pushed the door open. Across the cosy room stood a tall, elegant man with an old-fashioned gramophone record in his hand.

'These old things are a lot of fun but the new records sound better,' he said. He turned to look at her and let out a rather inelegant yelp. 'Where did you come from?' he said. 'Am I dreaming this vision?'

'London. Arrived a couple of days ago. Got anything to drink?'

He pointed to the well-stocked drinks trolley. She crossed the room and took a glass from the sideboard.

'Thank the hairy goddess,' she said.

He was staring at her.

'Are you alright? You look like you've seen a ghost.'

He shook his head and smiled. Alia looked him up and down. He was a very good-looking man. She waved the opening of a decanter under her nose. Brandy. And another. Gin. He was suddenly beside her.

'Gin and tonic?' He took the decanter from her hand and began to pour.

'A bit presumptuous don't you think?' But she took the proffered glass while he added the tonic. 'How do you know I'm not a whiskey girl?'

He smiled at her again, but his brow was wrinkled. He looked like he was enjoying a joke but didn't really understand it.

Alia took a sip. The clear liquid felt warm and cool at the same time. 'Who am I kidding? I'll drink anything. I'm not really supposed to be drinking. Promised Star weeks ago but never really stuck to it. Plus, she drinks more than I do. Give or take.' She shrugged and swallowed deeply. 'Star, From Whitehall. My agent,' she said, when his eyebrows arched in question.

He seemed to shake his head and nod at the same time. He poured himself a drink. 'My agent has been trying to get me to stop drinking since '44.'

'Ha!' Alia downed her drink and held the glass out for a refill. He didn't look a day over thirty.

His eyebrows raised, he took her glass and dropped some more ice into it.

'Have you got any cigarettes?'

'Of course,' he said, taking out a sleek gold case. He opened it with a flourish, and she took two, pocketing one and putting the other in her mouth.

'Got anything harder?' she said with a wink. 'These edibles have kicked in nicely.'

A slow smile crept across his face. 'Depends on what you had in mind…' He handed her the drink. 'Drink it slowly, give me a chance to catch up.'

'Oh, you'll have to work hard to stay up with me. I'm a triple-threat; booze, drugs and men…the harder the better, I find.' She twiddled the cigarette like she was channelling Groucho Marx.

The stranger threw his head back and laughed.

'You've been sent by the gods, right?'

'Oh, you are a keeper,' she said, forcing herself to sip the drink.

He laughed again.

'And you? You've got the looks. I'm guessing you're an actor…an American?' She scrunched her nose up and peered at him.

'Ah, No. I am a writer. Welsh but I've lived in New York on and off. My mother was American.'

'My mother was Greek,' she said, raising her glass at him, and he lifted his.

'Alia,' she said, her hand resting on her chest. 'Not that you asked.'

'Of course, she was. My apologies. Braith Evans-L… Just Braith is fine. Alia?' He said her name like he was tasting it.

'Short for Thalia. Actually, Lady Thalia if you please, but it's so old fashioned.'

He went to take a sip but stopped. He was smiling into his drink.

'You are?' He put his drink down and laughed, clapping his hands like a toddler. 'Oh of course you are. I should have known you.'

'Yeah, I'm kind of a big deal. And no, I'm not a model even though I recently walked in Knightsbridge.' She laughed at her own joke. 'Comedian. I mean with a name like Lady Thalia Penelope Heathcote Henry, what else was I going to do with my life?' She gave a shallow curtsey.

Braith was staring again. 'You are not what I expected,' he said, and raised his glass. 'I can't believe you're here, I mean, Thalia, Goddess of Comedy.'

Alia threw back the last of her drink and laughed. 'You most definitely are a keeper. I think I am going to like it here in France after all.'

'I love France, they all call me Braze. Makes me sound dangerous, but my agent says I'll have to use a nom de plume.' They raised their glasses again and drank. Alia kept her eyes on his face, and he seemed to be studying her.

'So, your father is Welsh, and your mother is American. How did you end up here?' She waved her arm around to take in the sumptuous surroundings.

'They were both from fine families. My mother was an heiress, and my father is in business, importing, manufacturing. Together, they made a lot of money and were so happy when I came home in one piece from the war that they gave me my inheritance.' He waved his hand around at the beautiful room. 'Music?'

He walked back to the gramophone. Alia went to follow him but as she passed the open French doors she was drawn to the moon-lit garden. The night birds were calling. Like the rest of the house, it was magnificent in the moonlight. Braith put the needle down on the record and walked towards her.

'Shall we?' he said, leading the way out on to the terrace.

'Can I get another of those lovely G&Ts?' She wiggled her glass at him.

The tiles on this part of the terrace were a deeper blue than she had seen earlier and the intricate pattern more pronounced. The remodelling of the château would be magnificent if the contractors kept up this level of craftsmanship. They felt smooth and cool underfoot and Alia was suddenly aware that she was wearing just a silk Kimono, as expensive as it was, and had nothing on her feet. It wasn't the least she'd ever worn when first meeting a man. She giggled at the memory… Burning Man, 2016.

'This place is far more beautiful at night, positively *Rousseau*-like, *Henri*, not *Jean-Jacques*.' As if on cue, the cicadas started their choir.

'And magical…I mean look at that moon.' She pointed up at the sky. The huge white orb hanging over the house didn't look real.

He nodded in agreement, handing her another drink. 'The full moon is my favourite time. I feel potent when the moon is full. How long will you be here?'

Alia was a little taken aback by his use of the word *potent*. The word had an energy attached to it, like the words 'moist' or 'panties'. She smiled into her drink. *Ha… moist panties.*

'I'll be here about a month. Gotta get this book written.'

He nodded and pursed his lips. 'Yes, your presence will inspire me. I have two deadlines hanging over my head. It's more nerve wracking than anything I've ever done. I wasn't this jumpy the day I signed up.'

'Phillip was in the forces, too.'

Braith nodded and sipped his drink. 'Airforce. Most of the chaps don't like to talk about it, but I think it's important not to forget. If we forget history, we are damned to repeat it.'

It was her turn to nod. There was no way Phillip was going to forget with those scars.

'I feel invigorated, just meeting you like this. Each morning I take a walk in the grounds before settling down to write in my studio. I would be honoured if you would join me. I start out at seven sharp, from this terrace.'

Alia drained her drink. 'I'm not much a of a morning person…' She was suddenly feeling tired and just a little drunk. 'I think I might go up to bed. It's been a very long day and those drinks have just hit my blood stream and gone straight to my head.'

Braith laughed as though it was the funniest thing he'd ever heard. Alia watched him, a smile on her face. He took her hand. 'May I?'

Alia laughed again but stopped. He was serious. She shrugged her shoulders and lifted her hand towards his face. He bent over and kissed it. 'I am feeling inspired already. My juices are flowing. You can join me if you like…'

'Oh, you're naughty!'

Braith began to splutter and cough. 'Forgive me, I didn't mean to suggest…that you…ah… I merely wished to say that you might like to join me in my studio.'

Alia laughed. 'Oh, sure…right. You can keep your juices to yourself…for now.' She fluttered her eyelashes at him. Moist panties, indeed.

Too early

Somewhere a rooster crowed or perhaps it was a car sounding its horn. The room glowed like the morning sun was rising inside the room. Alia groaned and rammed the pillow over her head.

'Curtains,' she groaned. Now that's something to add to Phillip's list. She crawled out of bed, groping blindly for her watch. She staggered to the dark, cool bathroom, peering at the dial. 7am. No wonder her head was pounding. She'd probably only had three hours sleep. Her head thumped in time with her heartbeat and she was parched.

'Braith,' she said out loud. 'What an odd dude…'

As good as she'd felt the day before, she had no regrets about the drinks. Detoxing was never part of the deal as far as she knew. Phillip and Camryn seemed to have a problem with booze but at least she now had a partner in crime. She didn't have a problem… what was that old joke? I drink, I fall down… no problem. Her shoulders shook with laughter. She looked at her reflection in the bathroom mirror.

'Wow, you need some serious stimulation, girl, if you think that's quality humour.'

She crawled back into bed to close her eyes for a few moments. Star always said nothing good happened before 9am anyway, except sex, and that probably wasn't on the table unless Braith was lurking outside with his flowing juices.

'Oh, you are going to feature in my next show, you strange, gorgeous man.'

Her head was still pounding when she woke again. No, that was someone pounding on the door. Even through the sheet, the room was like a supernova, bright and hot. She stumbled to the door and pulled it open, to see who was trying to kill her.

It was Phillip.

'I'm sorry to bother you, but I'm going to town.'

'Great, can you pick up a gun so I can shoot the next person who bashes on my door in the morning.'

Phillip made a huffing sound he must have picked up from his time in France. 'It's after midday. And I knocked…'

'Right. Okay, then I had a couple last night, I was up late with, what's his name?' She rubbed her temples.

Phillip's forehead creased down towards his eyes. 'Benito?'

'B…is it Benito? That doesn't sound right but yes, it did start with a B…' She felt like she was about to choke. Her mouth was dry.

Phillip shuffled his feet and turned to go. 'So, just the stuff on the list, then?'

Alia had already shut the door and was heading for the bathroom.

'Curtains,' she yelled as she sat on the toilet and cradled her head.

The Room

By the time she made it to the dining room, even the lunch things had been packed away. Alia knocked on the kitchen door but there was no response. She was famished. Surely no one would mind if she helped herself to some food. She pushed the door open and stuck her head through the gap. She was surprised to see a shiny commercial grade kitchen, expecting something far more rustic, or at least historically accurate. The kitchen would have been right at home in a major restaurant. In remodelling her own house, the Grade 1 listing meant she had to follow strict rules but maybe the French were simply happy to see crumbling old castles getting the love they deserve.

'Anybody home?'

She went to the fridge, taking a yoghurt and a couple of apples. She opened the upright freezer, noting a couple of bottles of vodka tucked into the bottom shelf. 'They might come in handy…' she mumbled.

She slammed the door with her backside as she bit into one of the apples. 'Spoon…' she mumbled, checking the sleek stainless-steel cabinets for drawers. There was nothing that looked like a cutlery draw so she began pulling open cupboards, working her way around the room. A door slid open on the far side of the room and a voice wished her a good morning.

'Good morning, Hi. Umm, spoon?' she waggled the pot of yoghurt.

He turned and retreated but a moment later returned to the room holding up a spoon for her. 'This,' he pointed back at the door, 'is the special room for all plates and utensils. It keeps everything clean.' He beamed at her.

'This is your happy place, isn't it, dude?'

'Yes miss, it is. Ah, tell me, why did you tell Phil that I have a party with you last night?'

Alia frowned. 'Oh… I said the wrong name… I'm sorry, you are Benito?' She put the spoon in her mouth and held out her hand for him to shake. 'It's nice to meet you. Sorry. It was someone else. I hope I didn't cause any trouble for you.'

He laughed. 'Oh no, Phil was joking with me, calling me Don Juan.'

Alia could feel her face burning with embarrassment. She didn't like feeling embarrassed. She took pride in almost never feeling ashamed of anything she did, no matter how stupid it was.

'That Phil, huh… he's a joker…' She was having trouble swallowing the yoghurt over the knot in her throat.

'I had a couple of drinks with the tall, dark hair… The owner?'

Benito puffed out his lips. 'Mrs Grant is here? In France?' Benito checked his watch which Alia thought was an odd thing to do.

'No, she's in America… I wonder who was here. This is very unusual. Maybe it was the ghost?'

Alia rolled her eyes. 'No, it was a guy, a man. I didn't catch his surname.' She looked over at Benito who seemed to have lost patience for the conversation.

'Miss, I must… this… to take into the…' he nodded at the things he was carrying. 'I'll see you perhaps later?' He smiled but didn't wait for a response. Resting the boxes on the stainless-steel bench he pressed a green button on the wall making the glass doors slide back. Alia took a step forward, as the door slid shut behind him.

She put her food on the bench and went over to the glass door. There on the other side of a terra-cotta tiled passageway was a cosy room but it was nothing like the sumptuous room she'd found the night before. For starters, the elegant glass doors were missing, plate-glass sliders taking their place. It would be lovely to see that room again, she thought, with its Tiffany lamps and sumptuous sofas. Through the two pairs of glass doors, she saw Benito put the boxes on a desk in the corner of the room and turn to come back to the kitchen. He looked at her, eyebrows raised as he pressed the door opener.

'Are you okay, miss?' He stood in the terracotta-tiled hallway. She could just hear his muffled words through the thick glass. She reached over and pressed the green button as she had seen him do.

'Uh, yes… um… I am just a little confused… I thought that was the room with the Tiffany lamps but it's not, is it? Is there…' she stuck her head out and looked along the passageway. 'Is there a staircase along there?' Alia felt a little dizzy.

Benito gestured with his hands that she should return to the kitchen and he bustled through, letting the door slide shut behind them both. 'There are stairs, yes, but not in use,' he whispered.

He ushered her away from the door. 'Miss, can I make you an omelette. You look like you could do with a good meal.'

Alia sat at the dining table and waited for her eggs. Benito's words swam around in her head. What did he mean? Did he mean the stairs were there, but no one used them?

He came out with a fluffy golden omelette and set it in front of her along with a steaming mug of coffee.

'Bon Appetit,' he said and disappeared through the kitchen door.

She ate slowly, wondering where the others were. She had missed the early morning walk with what's his name. Seven in the morning she muttered. How could anyone be inspired that early in the morning.

After eating, she took her plate to the kitchen. Benito was preparing something on the centre island. She thanked him and offered to wash the dishes, but he chased her away.

'Go and write, that's why you are here! Not to wash dishes in my kitchen.'

She felt restless. There was no way she could settle to write. Perhaps a walk around the grounds would help after all. It wasn't seven in the morning, but she'd read somewhere that Stephen King always walked in the afternoon.

The huge ornate front door stood open and the warmth of the day was creeping into the entry hall, even though the terrace was now in shade. She walked slowly along the faded blue tiles. Tiles were missing or cracked in places. She walked out into the sunny afternoon and looked up at the building. Her room was just above where she was standing, its curtain-less windows stood open like missing teeth in a beautiful face. She looked along the terrace to where it turned a corner, obviously mirroring the curve in the hallway above. The Tiffany room as she had taken to calling it, must be further along and around the corner. She set off to find it.

She came to the corner of the terrace and stopped. The floor stepped down a couple of steps, the tiles there were fresh and new as she had seen the night before. Two contractors sat in the shade of a tree, eating their lunch. Phillip had said that they spoke only French and Spanish, so she just waved, smiled and gave them the thumbs up. They waved their hands at her and one called out 'No walking, please.' Alia looked over at the new tiles and could see the little pegs used to space them were still in place. She gave the workmen a double thumbs up, crossed her forearms and said, 'No walking.' They gave her a double thumbs up in return.

She had walked on those tiles the night before. Alia felt a shiver go up her spine. She turned slightly to see if someone was standing behind her, but she was alone. At the far end of the terrace the French doors opened, and a kind of hospital bed was wheeled out and manoeuvred around to face the trees. A nurse in a pale blue uniform disappeared briefly to return with a chair before disappearing again. When she came back, she was carrying a mug and a book and chattering away to the patient. Alia could see her mouth moving but from that distance couldn't hear what she was saying. The nurse walked around the bed and seemed to be checking it was secure but eventually settled into the chair, reading aloud and sipping on her drink.

The nurse looked up and waved. Alia jumped, surprised. She felt strange, as though she had been invisible to the nurse somehow. She smiled and waved, and the nurse went back to her book.

Alia gave the contractors a little wave and set off along a path in the gardens. The sound of traffic was louder there. She stood on her toes to see the ribbon of highway stretching off towards the north.

Paris, London, and freedom, that way.

The sun was beginning its descent towards the west, but it was still strong, and Alia was sweating by the time she reached the studio in the grounds. She covered her eyes and looked up at the beautiful little orangery. Its walls were a series of archways of red and white brick, its pitched roof, faded grey tiles. An ancient looking vine climbed above the firmly closed door. She walked around the perimeter of the building, enjoying the shade from the older trees. The studio was larger than it appeared from the path, looking as though it had been extended and remodelled several times over the years. All the doors were closed but she could see Camryn's sculptures and work area. Each glass piece seemed lit from within with the bright sunlight pouring into the space from huge skylights. A statue of a woman dominated the space. It was translucent green and looked like the sea glass she'd once found on Naxos.

She knocked on the window. 'Hello?'

The place was empty. Alia continued her walk around the building, stopping to peer into each window, willing Camryn to appear and let her in. Alia was the first to admit she didn't like isolation. It wasn't that she didn't like her own company now and again, but it wasn't something she wanted to make a habit of. She trudged back to the house, her sweaty hair sticking to her face. Standing in the foyer she looked around and a shiver went through her whole body. Without Camryn and Phillip, as annoying as he was, the house seemed even more like a derelict building full of ghosts.

'Hello?' she said, to no response.

She took the stairs slowly, trying to decide if she would take a shower or just slide back into bed. As she opened the door, a piece of paper fluttered across the floor.

'What's this? More advice for life from censorious Phil?'

She picked it up and flipped it open. Four words only were written on the page, inscribed in neat handwriting.

'Taking Cam to train.'

Alia laughed out loud. Phillip was so economical with his communication. Not really knowing why, she tacked the note to the wall above her typewriter and placed her fingers softly on the keys.

'Aah,' she said to the room, and ran to the bathroom.

Her kimono from the night before was lying in a heap. She snatched it up and put her hand in the pocket, drawing out the cigarette Braith had given her. She stared at it. It was smaller and the paper creamier than usual. The night before had taken on a dream-like quality over the course of the strange day she'd had but the cigarette made it all very real again. Transfixed by the elegance of it, she walked to the desk where her lighter stood to attention, waiting for some action, lit the cigarette and went to sit on the windowsill. She sat forward and pushed the window further open. Smoke plumed above her. The air was so still the smoke seemed to sit in the air like a speech bubble. She watched the patterns as she waved her arm through the smoke in slow arcs.

Three in the Moonlight

The room glowed with moonlight as Alia dressed. It was midnight again and her new friend was raising the roof downstairs with his old-timey songs. She pulled her door shut and virtually ran down the stairs, listening to the music she wasn't sure her grandmother had even been around for. How the rest of the house was sleeping through the noise was a mystery to her, but then, as she hurried down the spiral stairs, she had a sneaking suspicion it was all a dream.

The parlour doors stood open, but the room was empty, the music coming from the gramophone on the far wall. She looked further down the hallway but there were no glass sliders in sight. The gorgeous Tiffany lamps were lit. Alia walked slowly through the room past each lamp, marvelling at their colours.

'Hello?' she called to the empty space. The terrace doors were open, and the lace curtains stirred with a soft breeze. She called again but there was no answer. The song blared on. The mysterious writer who made the excellent cocktails was around somewhere, but he probably couldn't hear her over his terrible music. She shrugged and went to the bar. She hadn't put her glad-rags on to miss the party completely, but she made two drinks in case what's-his-name should pop through the door doing the Charleston. She was halfway through her second drink when the record finished but the needle stayed down with that soft, repetitious grind and hum she had only ever heard in movies. A man's voice called from the terrace and she stood to greet him, slipping one of the glasses under the sofa as she did.

'Oh,' he said as his eyes fell on her. 'You're here.' He was whispering.

'Yes, I'm just as surprised as you are.' Alia felt a warmth flushing her cheeks that had nothing to do with two glasses of whiskey. 'Sorry, I heard the music.' She drained her glass and handed it to him. 'I see you have company. I'll come back.'

He stood awkwardly at the door holding her empty glass.

She didn't wait for his reply.

Alia hurried back up the stairs, fuming. She couldn't remember anyone ever treating her with less regard. She had to stop herself from slamming the door, settling for passive-aggressive mumbling. She crawled into the bed and pulled the covers up. There was a party going on in the house and somehow, she wasn't invited. She tried to get a grip on her frustration. She'd always had a pathological case of FOMO and it wasn't a millennial affliction, she'd inherited her fear of missing out from her parents, the original Henry party animals.

She curled herself into a ball to stop herself from stamping back down the spiral stairs and joining the fun by force. The taste of whiskey still on her lips, she stared into the sheet over her head. He hadn't actually asked her to leave but she could tell he was uncomfortable with her presence. He had the same vibe as a guy whose wife had come home early. She sat up and laughed.

'Maybe he has a wife or girlfriend. So what?'

She lay back down and took a deep breath, content that she hadn't done anything wrong. He just didn't want a third wheel on his hands. She sighed. He was so old-fashioned. Most guys she knew would say 'threesome', pour another drink, and put some decent music on.

Between the Sun and the Moon

Alia woke with a start; the room was pulsating with sunlight.

Between the sun and the moon, this house is trying to drive me mad.

She tunnelled back down under the covers and groaned but came up laughing as she pictured Braith's face. She felt a little ill from hunger, but grinned as she thought of his startled, guilty expression.

She dressed for breakfast, but there was a tray waiting for her when she opened the door. She lifted the silver cloche. She almost devoured the omelette where she stood but managed to carry it to the windowsill for a slightly more dignified meal. The omelette was cold but delicious. There was a note from Benito. He'd gone to town with Phillip.

She sipped the warmish orange juice and picked up her Grannie's watch. It was after eleven. She was certainly catching up on her sleep. Looking over at the small pile of pages next to the typewriter she hoped she might catch up on her writing in the same way.

Once again, as much as she wanted to write that afternoon, Alia couldn't settle. She was beginning to wear a path in the polished timber floor as she paced around the room. Her head felt light, as though it would float away if it wasn't attached to her neck.

She sat in front of the typewriter and forced herself to write. It was torture. Testing her ability to carry the heavy typewriter, she considered moving her writing stuff down to the dining room but that was Phillip's domain. She checked her watch so often she wanted to toss it out the window but got up and put it on the bedside table instead. Apparently, the cell phone wasn't the problem; her attention span was.

She poured a glass of water and settled on the windowsill. Swirling the water, she watched the sunlight glisten on the glass and send flashes of light onto her hand. A knock on her door startled her, making her spill the water all over herself. She got up, mumbling and cursing. At least she was a little cooler.

She pulled the door open, a smile already on her face. She was hoping to see Camryn and Watermelon standing there. Even Phillip would have been a welcome distraction, but she was facing a corridor empty except for a couple of boxes.

'Thanks Phil,' she called to the empty space.

Shaking her head, she dragged the box of paper into the room, shoving it under the desk. The second box was a little more fun, filled with all the things she had asked for, except the one thing she had actually been looking forward to. She wasn't fussy and would have accepted any alcohol, but it was a booze-free box. She muttered under her breath. At least the cigarettes she'd asked for were there. Phil would have had a riot on his hands if he'd forgotten those. A riot of one. He could hardly judge her for smoking; it seemed to be his only vice, even if he was pedantic about the butts. There was a handwritten note reminding the 'dear residents' there was no smoking in the rooms.

'Bite me,' she said aloud and balled up the note. How did they expect to run a writers' retreat if you couldn't smoke in the house? And where did Phillip get off being so sanctimonious?

She unravelled the note and spread it out. The writing was familiar. She jumped up and grabbed the note that had come with her breakfast and compared the two, then held them up to the note tacked above her desk. Phil might be smug and sanctimonious, but these notes were probably both from Benito. Somehow a no-smoking reminder from the head of housekeeping was okay but from Phillip it was unforgivable. She folded both notes, put them on the breakfast tray, and slid it into the corridor shutting the door behind her.

She threw the long, thin carton of cigarettes on the bed and shuffled the rest of the items around in the box. Pens, pencils, a couple of lined notepads and extra things that she hadn't asked for. There were a couple of disposable lighters, a few bags of pretzels, nuts and other snacks, tampons. Star must have told him to get them. Surely?

Shoving the box on the floor, she snatched up the cigarettes and flopped across the bed. A shaft of bright sunlight fell across her face as she ripped open the brown-paper wrapper and took a packet of the cigarettes out of the carton. Savouring the moment, she took great delight in peeling back the plastic wrapping and flipped open the little box. She put the neat row of cigarettes to her nose and inhaled.

Sitting up too quickly, she grabbed the lighter and lay back down, head swimming. The day, she'd decided, was a write-off, though there had been no writing to speak of. The room was stifling, and she had to get out. She went out into the corridor, pulled her door shut and locked it. It offended her deeply that she had to lock the door not for security but so an unnamed nit-picker couldn't read her work.

Turning left, she headed towards the main stairs and stopped. Unlit cigarette in her mouth, lighter poised, she turned on her heel back towards the direction she had taken the night before. Desperate to light up but intrigued by Benito's comment that the stairs were *not in use*. She walked slowly along the passageway, past Phillip's door, and Camryn's, and around the curve in the corridor. A plastic sheet was taped across the entrance to the landing and sheets of plywood covered a section of the tiled floor. The space was dark, plywood sheets covering the bank of windows to her right. She looked up. The domed skylight with its insects and flowers was hidden behind more sheets of ply. The whole space was dusty with boxes of tiles standing along one wall, more panels of plywood covered the opening of the spiral stairs. The contractors had been very busy that morning. Alia stepped onto the uneven floor and tiptoed over to the balustrade. She didn't know why she was tiptoeing, but she felt she was trespassing.

She put her hand on the dusty balustrade and looked over. Where, the night before, there had been an elegant, sweeping, polished timber staircase, today was an empty space, a gaping wound where the heart of the house had been. She took the cigarette out of her mouth and peered down into the hole. Her phone-hand twitched. Letting out a low whistle, she walked over to the bank of boarded-up windows. She needed to take a photo. She had to show someone.

Like she had been hit, she reeled back and ran, pulling the plastic sheeting down where it had been taped across the hall. Phillip's door was closed as always, but she bashed on it with her fist, calling out to him. No answer. She ran past her own door, taking the stairs three at a time as she called out an urgent *hello*. The front door was closed and, standing in the middle of the entry hall, all she could hear was her own breath. She had to speak to Benito… or Phillip. He was obviously passionate about this old house and as an employee of the mysterious Whitehall, he would want to know why the contractors had ripped out perfectly good stairs. Perfectly beautiful stairs, windows, and oh, that skylight.

She checked the dining room, but it was empty, and the kitchen door, closed. She ran back to the entry and pulled open the huge front door, walking out onto the terrace. The afternoon air vibrated with heat and the sound of insects. A truck used its air brakes somewhere in the distance but all else was silent.

'Arrghh' she said to the empty foyer, her fists clenched. 'Don't bloody mind my abandonment issues.'

She went back to the dining room and poured herself a large glass of water from the dispenser in the corner. Looking around at the room she could see it was neither quirky nor plush. It had more of a three-star bed and breakfast feel to it. It had been painted and the timber floor had been polished to a high sheen, but the look was more like 'college cafeteria' than the dining room of a stately home. She filled the glass again and went back out into the shabby foyer, slowly taking in her surroundings. She had been so focussed on herself over the past couple of days, but that was nothing new. Surely Phillip could see the contractors were doing the house more harm than good?

She went back to the kitchen door, but it was locked. A note in the same handwriting as the no-smoking reminder was taped to the door.

'I will return at 18:00 to prepare supper. Fruit and cheese in sideboard.'

It was signed with a dramatic signature that probably said Benito but could have said Banana or Bahamas. He'd then printed Don Juan in brackets and added a smiley face. Alia couldn't help but smile and went to the sideboard and opened a door. It was full of water glasses, but the second door hid a cleverly designed cool box that held a small selection of fruits and cheese with a crusty roll and some crackers. Alia smiled and took the plate along with a glass of water back up to her room, the demolished stairs forgotten for the moment.

Phillip

The bright sunlight in her bedroom had turned to gold, so she knew dinner wasn't far away. The trees outside her window hummed with cicadas. Soon, Camryn, if she had returned from her train journey, would pop her head through the door and say something funny. Watermelon would trot in and Camryn would say 'dinner' with her eyebrow cocked. Alia had grown attached to them quickly. She did that.

She took the unlit cigarette from her lips, a habit she had taken up after recalling a friend's mother who did just that. The mother was a well-known writer and Alia could still picture her silhouette as she hunched over her typewriter, glimpsed as the maid pulled the door shut to keep distractions to a minimum.

Limiting distraction worked well for Alia too. Finally, the writing was going well. She wandered over to the bedside and picked up her watch. It was nearly six. Alia counted her words for the day. Twenty more pages of single-spaced lines. She put the cigarette back in her mouth and read the poem she had named 'Stars and Suns'.

'In my galaxy the stars are close...' she read aloud, the cigarette bobbing.

'Burning bright, you bring the softest light
The galaxy, not so lonely after all
Banishing the dark
That was once deeper than night,

You revolve around me.'

It was a tribute to the women in her life, the women who had been there for her. Her grandmother, Star, Mrs P. Maybe she could add Camryn to that list. She read the last line again.

You revolve around me.

That is not terribly flattering.

She wound the sheet back into the typewriter and used a neat row of the capital X to blot out the offending line. She pulled it out again and inspected it.

Better.

The poem needed some stars around it. She rummaged through the box of stationery Phillip had bought but a ball-point pen wouldn't do. She needed a paint pen, or a fountain pen with a calligraphy nib. She sucked in a breath as an idea occurred to her. She went to the bathroom and rummaged through the pile of cosmetics still covering the bathmat and grabbed the liquid eyeliner. Perfect. But first she looked in the bathroom mirror and tilted her head, drawing a practised hand across her eyelid to create the cat's eye effect she loved. She shut one eye. Maybe she would do just one. She looked at herself and laughed, then drew a black line across the other eyelid. It was entirely possible that liquid eyeliner was the thing she liked most in the world. She took the eyeliner to her desk, underlined the word 'Stars' and drew a half a dozen little quirky stars and a sliver of crescent moon.

Crescent moons look more moon-like than a full moon unless you go full Petit Prince on it and draw craters and lines.

The crescent was a lot easier. She liked the effect of the brush-tip and the dark ink, but it would be an expensive exercise to illustrate the books with *Charlotte Tilbury* eyeliner. She pulled the original document box out from under the desk and looked at its dismal contents. Star could have thrown in any and all of the pens and journals littering her desk (and bedroom floor, and kitchen and the yoga room.) Instead, she had grabbed just a couple of journals, printed out what was open on the desktop and, couldn't even be bothered to put a pen in. Alia recalled her agent saying something about her dad not feeling well, but this felt a little like sabotage. Maybe Star had known about the typewriters in the cave. Perhaps she assumed that Phillip, the writing genius, would have some pens.

She shook her head as if to dislodge the thoughts and stacked her pages, plucking a fresh sheet to wind down into the typewriter. 'There we are, ya wee ghosties, a fresh piece of parchment for ye,' she said, but she wasn't sure why she was channelling a Scottish pirate.

She picked up her watch and lay it on her wrist. Once she returned to London, she'd have the diamonds replaced. It was a special piece and although she carried it with her whenever she travelled, she had never worn it. It never seemed to work with any of her clothes and she always worried she would lose it in a mosh or some other over the top situation that seemed to occur all too often in her life.

In the bathroom, she got a fright when she saw her reflection. She had forgotten about the eye liner; for a fraction of a second, she thought she was looking at someone else. She laughed at herself as she did her hair and threw a lace jacket on over her white slip dress. All the time alone was having an unsettling effect on her. Her mind, as Anne Lamott had put it so well, was a place she had always been reluctant to go alone.

She pulled her bedroom door shut and locked it. The old house might have suffered over the years but even the unpolished stairs and stripped back walls glowed in the afternoon light that France seemed to do so well. 'The stairs,' she said out loud and spun on her heel and yelped. Phillip was right behind her.

'Faaaaaark…. you scared the crap out of me.' He smiled and pulled his door shut.

'Why are you always around every time I make a dick of myself?' she said, her hand on her heaving chest.

'My guess is…' he started but seemed to stop and think about it. 'My guess is that you make a bit of a dick of yourself a lot and I am just lucky enough to be around occasionally.'

Alia put her hands on her hips. 'You…' she pointed a finger at him accusingly, 'you would be spot on.' She smiled at him and immediately regretted it. That was her biggest fault; she was too forgiving. Well, that and the selfishness, drug use, and conspicuous consumption.

'Dinner time?' she said.

He nodded. They turned back towards the front stairs and headed down to the dining room, the missing spiral stairs forgotten again as she tried desperately to not make an ass of herself. 'The writing is going well. Who knew all it would take is constant attention on the project?' She grinned at him.

'Why do I have this insatiable need to be liked?'

He simply nodded again, a small smile on his lips.

'It's been a little lonely though,' she said, pouting playfully.

'I'm sure it's a change from your normal day to day but hey, it beats jail.' He said the words so matter-of-factly it caught her off-guard.

She turned to him. 'Yeah, it does beat jail. Were you being an ass just then or are you just socially awkward?'

He stopped walking. 'Um, no, it's the truth. Everyone here has work to do, including you. You could always hold a séance and talk to the other guests if you get too lonely.' Phillip smiled, the thin-lipped variety.

'Stop! One more mention of ghosts and I'll push you down these stairs.'

His shoulders hunched up and down, so she guessed he was laughing. He was definitely a silent laugher. Probably one of those people who weren't allowed to laugh out loud when they were kids, but at least he was smiling. Maybe he never lost control and belly-laughed, but when he smiled, really smiled, the skin around his eyes crinkled. That was a million percent better than his smirks, the ones where his eyes didn't join in. Those awful stiff smiles made Alia want to punch him in the throat, but his trained-killer-vibe stopped her every time.

'You've met Benito,' he said, looking at her from the corner of his eye.

'The cook. Yes, I have.'

He put his hand on her arm, stopping her just outside the dining room. 'Before you embarrass yourself, Benito isn't a "cook". He is chef and head of house. He runs the place. You may have seen the nurses or housekeeping staff who come and go. The owner of the house still lives here. He's elderly and bedbound. He donated the house as part of the scholarship programme run by Whitehall.'

Alia was about to interrupt him, to ask about the work the contractors had done, or undone, but he suddenly looked at her, his hand still resting on her arm.

'I am sorry you've been left to your own devices. I'm busy helping around here and trying to finish my thesis.'

She looked down at his hand and he dropped it to his side. She cleared her throat. Twice.

'Star mentioned you were studying. Thesis, huh?' Alia asked as they entered the dining room. Camryn looked up and waved, chewing. 'Oh yay, you're back,' Alia said, smiling at Cam. 'Dinner smells amazing.'

Camryn nodded and gave her the thumbs up as she finished her mouthful. The table was set with fine white china and silver flatware and a row of candles in neat silver holders ran down the middle of the huge table. Watermelon was eating his dinner from a bowl next to the sideboard. It was strange to see him down there doing something so doglike.

'Isn't this beautiful,' Cam said, waving her arm at the table. 'Benito said we should celebrate my homecoming. I should go away more often.'

Alia and Phillip stood admiring the table and exchanged a glance. Camryn didn't notice, she was already forking the next mouthful in.

'Wow, Benito did all this just for you?'

Cam nodded, beaming.

Alia and Phillip looked at each other again. He gave her another of those smiles that went all the way to his eyes. Obviously, Camryn had an admirer.

'What was that you were saying, Phillip? About your study?'

'PhD. In literature. He's very clever with words,' Camryn chimed in, smiling at Phillip. He nodded slightly and headed to his usual spot at the table. His cheeks flushed pink as he busied himself, tidying his books.

The sideboard momentarily distracted Alia with its variety of dishes, fruit and bread. Camryn finished her mouthful and waved the fake-wine bottle at them. Alia nodded at her glass and turned to Phillip. 'Oh, I remember now, Star said you were studying but wow, a PhD. So, you'll be… doctor Phil…' Alia laughed.

Phillip looked at Camryn and shook his head and she laughed.

'Well, Phil, what did you expect her to say?'

Dancing by Candlelight

They ate together, chatting like old friends across the beautifully laid table. Alia was fascinated to hear Camryn talk about her work, but the challenge was to listen. Star banged on about her not listening so often she played it up just for laughs, but she had to admit she had a real problem. Alia shifted in her seat to look at Camryn while she described her trip up to Paris to buy supplies. She had been interviewed about her new work by a journalist writing for *The New Yorker,* which was brilliant, an anecdote Alia would have missed in the past.

Camryn asked Phillip about his thesis. "Almost done" was all he had offered. Listening was fun and Alia found it nice to not be the topic of conversation for a change. Camryn had mentioned her show a couple of times, but Alia, self-absorbed as usual, had no idea she had been invited to exhibit at the Venice Biennale. That was a big deal. A very big deal. If Star was her agent that news would have been splashed across every billboard in London.

Camryn was a superstar artist and Phillip was a dark horse. He was characteristically tight lipped about his thesis, but he seemed to know everything there was to know about the château, so Alia had assumed it was something to do with architecture or history. She worried she'd missed the part where he'd described his thesis in detail, like the time her friend Andie told her about her grandpa dying, "I'm heartbroken" Andie had said to which Alia had responded "yeah, fuck that guy."

Mortifying.

Alia was shocked from her reverie by Benito standing in front of her, derailing her out-of-control train of thought.

What is wrong with me?

She had met Benito, but he introduced himself officially, and sat with them for a few minutes, his chef hat still sitting high on his head. Camryn poured him a glass of fake wine and Phillip and Alia watched them intently as they chatted about Paris.

She jumped up to clear the dinner plates, eager to slip through into the tiled hallway and see more of the house but Benito followed her to the kitchen as though he didn't quite trust her alone in there. Chattering the whole time as she always did, she wandered over to the glass doors. Through the opposite doors she could see an elaborate electric wheelchair, empty in the corner of the room.

'Benito, where is the room with the Tiffany lamps?'

He walked over and stood next to her. 'Mr Evan lives here. It's not for other guests. It is his house, yeah?' He was frowning slightly and took Alia by the arm and led her back to the dining room. She got the distinct feeling that Benito had just chastised her for being nosey in the gentlest possible way. Apologies tumbled out of her. If there was one thing Alia was supremely practiced at, it was the art of apologising, except this time she realised she actually meant it.

The dining room was empty when Benito shut the kitchen door behind her with a soft shushing sound. Hands on her hips she looked around at the deserted room. She'd been in the kitchen with Benito for mere minutes and she imagined the others creeping from the room to play a prank on her, hiding around the corner. She went to the 'secret door' and pulled it open thinking they might be there, but the empty dark corridor stretched off towards the cave. She couldn't recall where she'd left her torch, but Phillip had said the figures in the mural appeared to be dancing in candlelight.

See…I do listen!

She took one of the silver candleholders and started down the corridor, before returning to the table for a second. There was no way she wanted to be stuck in that cave in the dark with who knows what, or who, lurking. Some light from the dining room spilled into the corridor, providing a very real light at the end of the tunnel to keep her bearings. The corridor was pitch black, but the old double doors were easy enough to see in the candlelight. She put one of the candleholders on the floor and opened the doors, leaving it on the top step as a guide. A breath of cold air swirled around her as she walked down the stairs, holding the candle up to see the fresco. Sure enough, in the flicker of the candle, the figures danced. Alia was hypnotized.

She was in a dream state by the time she followed her nose out to the terrace where she found Phillip in one of the elegant old chairs, smoking, and Camryn on the gravel drive, throwing a little rubber ball for Melon. The sun had dipped behind the house, the shadows growing longer and longer, and the song of cicadas filled the night. Watermelon abandoned the game and trotted off towards the private end of the house standing guard on the terrace. He returned to his ball, only to run down the gravel drive to investigate a bird noise or the crack of a twig a minute later.

'Did you help with the washing up?' Phillip said. He glanced from her to Camryn.

'No, Benito pretty much pushed me out of the kitchen. I took one of the candles into the cave…the fresco… the figures really do appear to be dancing. It's remarkable.' She had completely forgotten the missing stairs but knew in the pit of her stomach their absence had nothing to do with the contractors.

Camryn joined them. 'It's a marvellous sight and it sure beats washing up.'

Alia and Phillip nodded their agreement, exchanging a smirk. It might have been her imagination, but Camryn seemed happy to hear she had left Benito to the dishes.

The warmth of the day was stored in the tiles and Alia was glad she was barefoot; they felt smooth underfoot and the warmth went right through to her bones. She hadn't worn shoes since she'd arrived. Was it really only a few days before? She thought of the ridiculous prank that saw her arrested. She was seriously lucky to have ended up in France, writing, and chatting about art and history with intelligent people. It wasn't completely lost on her that someone without her connections and money would not have been treated so kindly.

Alia strolled along the terrace and picked up the dog's discarded rubber ball.

'Hey, Melon…' she threw the ball a few metres. He trotted over to inspect it but resumed his sentry duty. Alia shrugged and sunk into one of the chairs.

They sat in silence for what seemed like an hour, the two of them smoking and Alia slowly dying inside from nicotine withdrawal. 'For fuck's sake will one of you bastards give me a smoke or do I have to go upstairs and get mine?'

Camryn giggled and Phillip hunched over in silent laughter. He laughed so hard he almost rolled out of his chair. He tossed her the packet.

'You people are hilarious. Seriously,' she said, taking a cigarette. 'Comedy gold, right there.' She smiled at them. 'It's quite alright…I can take a joke.' She took the lighter from Phillip, lit the cigarette and inhaled deeply.

'Do you know how much different shit I take on a regular basis? I had no idea this was going to be a fucking detox.' She handed the lighter back. 'Although it does occur to me that prison would have been something of a detox, too.'

'Do you think they would have sent you to prison?' Camryn asked.

'If I wasn't rich and famous, they would have, any day of the week. Some of the shit I've pulled this year…'

Phillip slowly nodded his head. 'I've seen the videos. Star deserves a medal for what she did for you.'

Alia blew smoke over her shoulder. 'Star has been my biggest devotee, aka enabler, for so long. My guess is she was going to lose her cushy job if I went to jail. Who do you think I did all those drugs with?'

They sat quietly, Alia's words swirling around them with the smoke, as the golden hour gave way to the blue. Alia looked up entranced by the colour of the sky. She had seen *L'Heure Bleue* on many occasions but sitting on that terrace she felt a thrill unlike anything she'd experienced before. It was beauty with no strings attached. She wasn't trying to capture it for her followers, she could just sit back and enjoy it. It might also have had something to do with being sober for a change.

'The sun has set, but night has not yet fallen. It's the suspended hour… The hour when one finally finds oneself in renewed harmony with the world and the light,' she said.

Camryn and Phillip stared at her.

'That's beautiful,' Camryn said. 'Is that one of yours?'

Alia laughed. 'I wish. Jacques Guerlain wrote it about his famous perfume L'Heure Bleue. I did a voice over a few years ago and loved the poem. The rest of it goes something like…the night has not yet found its star. It's lovely, isn't it?'

They sat transfixed as the sky gradually turned to an inky black dotted all over with stars.

'You don't get sky like this in LA,' Camryn said. 'I missed the stars when I moved over there. I missed the sky. And fresh air. I really missed fresh air.'

'Is it that bad?' Phillip asked. He and Camryn continued the conversation while Alia started to think about her own life in London. She loved the country house, her grandmother's house, but she rarely went out there because it didn't fit her life. She would have considered selling it, but it had been in her family for over four hundred years and if there were such a thing as ghosts, she could be sure her grandfather would haunt her until her own dying day if she did. She usually only went out there to throw parties because her London neighbours were politicians and MI5 didn't allow parties in the street. Sex workers and Uber eats were fine but upstanding residents couldn't throw a three-day long "dinner party" without being investigated.

Deep in thought Alia opened her eyes to see her companions looking at her.

'Hmmm?' she said.

'Have you spent a bit of time in France?' Camryn asked. By the tone of her voice, she was obviously asking for the second time.

Listen! Argh, is it that hard to just listen to people?

'Ah, no, actually, I mean, I went to Paris to do stand up at the English speaking clubs a couple of summers ago for a week or two, but no, I usually go to Spain or Greece. More my scene, I guess…' Alia lifted her arms and closed her eyes, miming dancing in a club.

'Ah, right. So definitely not my scene. *This*…this is my scene,' Camryn said then stifled a yawn. On cue, Watermelon was back at her side.

'He's so responsive to you…it's adorable,' Alia said.

'Sometimes he's the reason I get out of bed. On a bad day, I could just hide from the world, but knowing I have to take him out for a walk or get his food…he keeps me alive.' She ruffled his ears and scratched him under the chin. Watermelon went to both Alia and Phillip as if to say goodnight and trotted after his mistress.

'I might hit the sack too,' Phillip said. 'Is there anything you need before I turn in?'

'Yes, a book. I didn't bring anything to read. Are there any books here?'

'There's an entire library but everything is in storage until the remodelling is complete. I do have some books. They're in the dining room which you will have noticed is my favourite place to work.' He got up. 'You want to take a look or do you just want me to give you a couple to choose from.'

'You choose, you're the doctor,' she said. He smiled and went back into the house.

Alia sat back in her chair and blew smoke rings. The silent night settled in around her, interrupted only by the faint hum of distant traffic. She was deep in thought when somewhere in the house Watermelon barked and goose bumps rose on her arms. 'Bloody hell, now I'm getting the chills every time I hear the dog bark.'

'What's that?' Phillip was standing in front of her with a small stack of paperbacks.

She put her hand on her pounding heart. 'If it's not the dog scaring the life out of me, it's you, sneaking up on me!' she said.

Phillip smiled and handed her the books.

'I get this Pavlovian PTSD reaction every time I hear the dog bark… the ghost thing,' she said.

'Yes, he's an uncanny little guy. Seeing how Cam is with him, I'm actually thinking of getting a companion dog. It might help with the actual PTSD I'm dealing with.'

Alia felt her heart sink. 'Oh goddess… I am so sorry, I have bloody done it again, haven't I? Why am I always ramming my foot in my mouth?'

Phillip smiled and sat down. 'It's all good. Most people mean well and pretty much everyone has something in their past that gives them the cold sweats.'

'Yeah… although something tells me you've been through more than your fair share.'

'I'm working through it. My study helps and working for Whitehall. The scholarship keeps a roof over my head. A lot of my buddies aren't so fortunate.' He looked sideways at her. Alia was watching him intently. Phillip pointed to the books in her hands. 'It's amazing how helpful Chaucer was; that guy really speaks to the soul.'

Alia turned over each paperback. Along with Chaucer there was a battered copy of Romeo and Juliet, the collected poems of WB Yeats, and a writer Alia had never heard of, but the cover showed a wounded soldier. It wasn't exactly the light read she was hoping for, but it was better than nothing. She turned it over. The cover had been stuck back together with masking tape which almost completely obscured the title.

'That book, One Defiant Morning, is by Robert Evans. He's 99 now. He can afford the best care, but it wouldn't be the best way to spend the last couple of years, would it?'

Alia shook her head. She had never heard of Robert Evans, but it was difficult for her to comprehend someone that age. Even her Grandmother had died in her 60s. 'No one in my family lives to a ripe old age…' she whispered.

Phillip looked over at her. 'Yeah, I heard about your parents. I'm sorry.'

Alia wanted to make a smart-arse remark like *Why are you sorry? Did you give them the drugs they overdosed on?* but she thought better of it, entirely a new experience for her. She opened her palm and shrugged. 'It was years ago, and you know what? I've come to realise that they were just really toxic people and if you think I'm a nightmare now, imagine what I would have been like if my mother was still putting liqueur on my ice-cream into my teens.' She rolled her eyes.

Phillip nodded.

She could hear him breathing. It had been a long time since she was somewhere quiet enough to hear the breath of another person, in a non-intimate situation. She listened for other sounds in the area. A car in the distance, a dog barking. They sat in silence for a few long minutes and both stood to go in at the same time.

'Night,' they said in unison and laughed quietly. 'Hey, look at that...' Phillip pointed at the moon winking at them over the tops of the trees.

Alia stood transfixed by it. She'd never paid much attention to the sky in London. They walked inside and Phillip shut the door. 'I'm just going to get...' Phillip said, pointing into the dark dining room.

Alia nodded. 'Sure...good night.'

He nodded. Alia watched him go.

There's an enigma wrapped in a riddle right there.

She fished in her pocket for the key to her room and tripped up the stairs as she tried to read the cover of the book. A war story; not her first, second, or third choice of genre. She considered going back downstairs to see if Phillip had any JoJo Moyes but decided it was probably going to be a no.

She unlocked the door and flicked the light switch, leaving the door open. It was a still, warm night. She had been keeping the door closed, the spectre of that line of type on her page hanging over her. Someone had walked into her room and typed that line, but she knew in her gut it wasn't Phillip, not that her intuition was terribly reliable.

She put the books down on the bedside table and went to the typewriter. The page was still blank. She realised she was holding her breath and let it out in a rush. Had she really thought someone would come through her locked door to type a message to her? Someone or something?

She flicked the nightlight on before turning off the main light. There was no way she was going to be in the room in the dark. Crawling into the big bed, she picked up the old copy of Romeo and Juliet and opened to the first page.

'Oh, hell no…' she said, replacing the book on the bottom of the pile. Phillip had said that Chaucer was the goods, but it looked as daunting as the Shakespeare. The battered little paperback, One Defiant Morning, looked grim, but she couldn't judge a book by its cover, surely. She opened the first page. It creaked a little. Alia frowned. It smelled like one of her father's old Ian Fleming paperbacks. She flipped to the first page and began to read.

An hour later she was sitting on the edge of the bed, the nightlight poised over the book, thumbnail wedged between her teeth. She was rivetted by the story of a young soldier who rescued a family from a burning farmhouse in the dying days of the second world war. It was beautifully written. Alia had laughed out loud a couple of times and cried when the soldier thought he would probably never see his father again.

The story felt so real, it must have been a true account, but the cover was so battered she couldn't get any details. She reached for her phone to look up a couple of the dates.

Oh yes, that's right…no phone.

She flicked the nightlight off and listened as the buzz of insects left the room. The bright moon had risen above the trees. She jumped up and grabbed her camera, pointing the lens at it for a better view. She knew there was a special name for the moon when it was changing from full to new, but she had no way of looking it up. The top right corner of it looked blunted, like a cantaloupe that had been dropped. She clicked the shutter of the camera but remembered she had taken the film out after her terrible faux pas with Phillip. She rolled over and buried her face in the sheets.

He will never forgive me for that photo.

She fell asleep wondering why she cared so much.

Braith

Alia woke with a start, coughing, her mouth arid. She had been dreaming she was walking through the château, through room after room, hearing distant laughter but never able to find the party. The bedroom door was shut although she was sure she had left it open. Disoriented, and thirsty, she felt like a hostage. She jumped up and pulled it open. Had she thought, somewhere in the back of her mind, that the door would be locked? That Phillip had shut her in there, Colette-style, to finish her manuscript? Her hand fluttered up to her chest, her heart was pounding so hard she could feel it in her eyes. In the bathroom she drank two full glasses of water and was panting by the time she'd drained them.

'Okay, calm the drama...' she mumbled to herself. Her watch lay across the sink. It was a few minutes after midnight. A few bars of old timey music drifted in through the open door. She calmed her breath and closed her eyes.

Braith might be otherwise occupied again, but at least I can pour myself a drink.

The room was cooler at night, and she shrugged on her favourite kimono. Vintage Chanel, it had cost her a packet. Brand new she had worn it to a function at the Tate, but since then it had been a staple. It reminded her of Coachella, of the retreat she and her friend Connor had been asked to leave in Mykonos, and London, home. She laughed as she wrapped it over her t-shirt and shorts and belted it at the waist.

If this kimono could talk...

'God…I need a drink…' she said to the ceiling.

She rifled through her untidy room (how she missed Mrs P!) but couldn't find her torch. Her eyes fell on the camera. Her cheeks still burned with embarrassment as she put in a new roll of film and tested the flash.

She stood in the doorway, listening to the old music drifting along the passageway. Passing Phillip's closed door, then Camryn's she took the little diversion in the corridor. Up ahead, the contractors had obviously taken away the plastic sheeting she had pulled down in disgust and as she stepped onto the tiled landing, she could see they had taken up the plywood. The corridor was dark, but the light filtered in again from now-uncovered banks of windows and the domed skylight above. She went to the window. The moon hung in the sky, looking every bit as full as it had the night before. Alia shook her head. The excessively angry facilitator at the retreat on Mykonos had been dead right; she really did need to be more present and notice her surroundings. It could be a full moon two nights in a row, right? Alia had no idea.

She lifted the camera and snapped a photo of the moon, the flash bouncing off the windowpane like lightning. She flipped the switch to turn off the flash again and took another just as a large bird flew past the giant white moon. She slowly lowered the camera, staring at the back of it as though she could see through into the film. That would be a spectacular photo if she had pulled it off. She looked back up at the full moon. She really was missing so much of the world around her by being so caught up in the tiny screen on her phone.

She turned to snap a photo of the demolished stairs, carefully returning the flash setting to 'on'. Lifting the viewfinder to her eye she stopped. Her breath caught in her throat. The sweeping stairs once again led the way to the floor below. Slowly lowering the camera, she stared at the rich carpet, the delicate wallpaper and looked up at the insects and flowers caught in a never-ending springtime in the stained glass above.

'Am I dreaming…' she whispered.

She turned in a slow circle, taking in the perfect space, free from dust and boxes of tiles. 'What the fucking fuck…?'

An upholstered chair and an empty plinth stood at the far side of the bank of windows. They had not been there the night before, but then Alia doubted her ability to locate her own nose on her face at that point. She sat on the chair, putting her camera on the empty plinth like an art exhibit. She wanted to say something, but no words would come, and her head was spinning.

A sound from below snapped her back to the present moment.

'Hello?' she said, her voice coming out in a croak.

Taking care with each step, she stopped at the top of the stairs. Were they real? If she was dreaming, would she fall to her death if she stepped out? She clung to the balustrade, perfectly polished and dust-free, and touched the top step with her foot. It seemed solid enough. She pushed down on it and it took her weight. She realised she had been holding her breath again and let it out in a rush. Slowly, she took the stairs down to the lower level, clinging to the balustrade although that too was probably a figment of her imagination as it had been missing only hours before. Safely on the lower floor, she followed the soft hall runner along the passageway. The glass doors stood open and a soft voice could be heard. Someone was reading aloud.

Alia stood in the doorway. Braith was sitting in a chair, cigar in one hand and a bunch of pages in the other. Old timey music warbled quietly from the vintage turntable in the corner. He looked up.

'Thalia…' He said her name the way her father had, his rich voice like a trained actor's.

'Hello…Braith…'

He put his pages down on the little marble side table and laid the cigar in a dish. 'It's marvellous to see you again.' He was staring at her as though he was pinning her down with his eyes.

'It's lovely to be seen.' She hated being called Thalia but somehow in the mouth of this man, it sounded lovely. Comforting. 'You're alone tonight?'

He opened his palms and gestured to the empty room. 'Can I get you a drink?'

'Thought you'd never ask.' Alia winked at him and he laughed softly. 'How is your work going?'

Alia surprised herself with this question. She never, literally, ever asked after anyone's work, creative or otherwise. He held out a tall glass to her, a twist of lemon on the top, beads of condensation forming and dripping as they stood there. 'It's warm isn't it?' She took the drink and sipped it, stopping herself from draining the glass.

She walked over to the open terrace doors, sipping her drink and trying to flap open her heavy kimono that was sticking to her skin. The night air was still. She held the glass up to her cheek.

'This summer has been hot and dry. What we need is a thunderstorm to clear the air.' He stood a couple of paces behind her.

Oh, what the hell, this is just a dream.

She drained the glass and held it out for him. Once again, his eyebrows shot up, but he took the glass and returned to the drinks trolley. Alia unbelted her kimono, letting it hang loose around her, her tiny tank top and denim cut-offs peeking out. Braith reached up and pulled a little tasselled lever and somewhere in the house a bell rang, but he continued mixing her drink. Alia knew that meant someone would be coming through the parlour doors any moment, probably with a fresh bucket of ice. She pulled the kimono back around her and shrunk back into the doorway.

A butler came in and greeted his master. He wore a simple white shirt, open at the collar. He spoke in French and from the few words Alia could grasp they appeared to have an informal relationship. Apart from the fact that the other man moved slowly about the room, plumping cushions as they spoke, he could have been another guest. He didn't appear to notice her, a first for Alia Henry. The butler finished his tour of the room by emptying the ashtray into the empty ice-bucket, then stepped back and saluted. Alia gasped and Braith's eyes flicked over to where she stood as he returned the salute.

The butler didn't react to her. He left the room.

Maybe I am the ghost.

Braith grinned as he handed her a drink. 'It's a Southside, a new drink.'

'The butler couldn't see me.' Alia took the glass and tasted the frosty liquid.

'Romain…well no, he couldn't even if you were really here. He's blind and has lost some of his hearing. It is a shame. He could do with your help. He wishes to be a writer, too.'

Alia looked around the room. The man had moved slowly but methodically, picking up cushions and straightening the drapes.

'He saved my life.' Braith sipped his own Southside. 'He pulled me from a wreck, my car hit a mine, just outside Limoges. His father had been a valet and he worked in the stables, but he dreamed of attending university. The war changed everything. He has a home here for as long as he wishes, but he insists on working.'

'You're a good man.'

'I…' he walked out onto the terrace. '…am a lucky man.'

Alia nodded and followed him outside. The night was sultry, and the full moon hung in the sky like a weather balloon.

'My father would say we make our own luck. He said this all the time. What a privileged beast he was. I believe we can work hard and yes, be ready for an opportunity when it comes along, but it's just the luck of the draw as to whether you are the one blinded or not…or if you are born to wealth or not.'

Alia could only nod her head. She would be in the lock up if it wasn't for wealth and privilege.

'You asked me about my work,' Braith said.

Alia found her voice. 'I did. Tell me everything.'

The Studio

Alia woke with a pounding head and a desperate need for food and water. She needed to talk to someone. Something very odd was going on and it was probably related to her being cut off from the recreational drugs and unrestricted access to booze she had enjoyed since her early teens. She peeled herself off the bed. She had fallen asleep wrapped in the heavy silk kimono and she woke drenched in sweat.

Standing in the shower, she opened her mouth, letting the water run in. The night before had been memorable to say the least. She and Braith had talked until the sun peaked its fiery head over the tops of the trees. After hours of talking and laughing they had enjoyed the sweetest of kisses, just a gentle touching of his lips to hers. After much consideration they decided the kiss was weird. As gorgeous as he was, Braith reminded her of her father. He was stylish, intellectual, literary…and a very big drinker. But he looked at her as though she was the most interesting person he had ever met. He asked her opinion on everything from war and politics to the New York art scene. It was clear from his physicality that he wasn't exactly a ghost, but from his words and his manner she knew he wasn't a resident of 2019. She had no idea who he was or how he and the château of times gone appeared at midnight, but she never had been the kind of girl to ask too many questions when she was having fun. And Braith was a lot of fun.

'Ah, my camera…' she said, remembering she had left it sitting on the plinth above the stairs.

The stairs…

She shut off the water and dried herself. Her stomach growled. Forgetting her camera and the stairs in typical fashion, she wiggled into a pair of denim cut-offs and pulled a t-shirt over her still-wet skin. There was no way she was going to miss breakfast.

Watermelon ran out to greet her in his usual low-key fashion, trotting over to her and staring up as though trying to recall where he'd seen her before.

'Hey little guy…' she said, scratching him behind the ears.

A 'yoo-hoo' came from inside the studio. Melon trotted back in through the vine-covered doorway and Alia followed him. The interior seemed far too big for the exterior.

'Hello there.' Camryn was walking towards her wearing a heavy apron and eye protection that made her look like a steam-punk cosplayer. She removed her gloves and put her hands out to welcome Alia. 'Come in, come in, you look like you could use a cool drink.'

'I'm glad Watermelon didn't bark; it's really giving me the shivers.'

'What because of the ghosts?'

'Abso-fucking-lutely,' Alia replied.

'You don't want to be here in the morning when I first open up. Little guy dashes in first, barking and running about chasing them out for me,' she laughed but Alia didn't.

She followed Camryn to the back of the orangery. There was a small kitchen area and even a table and chairs, and a door off to the right that Alia assumed was a bathroom. At the thought of the bathroom, she suppressed a giggle at her conversation with Braith the previous night. It had been a well lubricated party for two and the look on his face when she asked to use the bathroom was hilarious. *What?* She had said…*let me guess. You're one of those men who think women never need the bathroom? Women, yes, but goddesses? The man certainly had a way with words.*

He'd led her through the dark house by moonlight so as not to wake the staff, both of them giggling like children, to use the facilities on the other side of the spiral stairs. They'd returned to the parlour circuitously after a full tour of the wide terrace. The château was enormous, she had only seen a tenth of it, by day or by night. She had to admit she didn't remember much of their discussion after he pulled out what he referred to as an *ace*, a slim, well-rolled joint, and asked her if she wanted 'a blast'. The house and its occupants were full of surprises. And then there was the newspaper, The New York Times, dateline July 12, 1950. His book was on the Best-sellers list, but he could only show her the blank space where he had sliced the list to send to a great-uncle in Cardiff.

1950.

Cam was standing in front of her looking at her fingernails. Alia spluttered an apology. She really had to stop zoning out.

'What brings you to my neck of the woods?' Camryn was red in the face, hair stuck to her neck in wet curls. She went to the little fridge in the corner and pulled out a carafe of cold water and offered a glass and a seat to her visitor.

'Well, you weren't at breakfast and Phillip said you were really busy.' She looked around the space. It continued along a small glassed-in terrace that had a high timber bench set into it.

That would be a perfect place to write.

'That heavy apron looks hot.'

'What this old thing?' She posed like a model and giggled. 'Ha…yes, but very necessary when you're blowing glass…as are these…' She put the goggles down on the table and sat heavily in a chair. Alia had no idea glass blowing was such hot work but the more she thought about it, it made sense. Watermelon jumped up and sat on the chair next to his mistress. Alia chose the one at the other end of the table with the view of the garden.

'What an incredible space this is.' She looked around the room, taking in the architecture but then seeing the projects Camryn was working on. She sat upright, her eyes moving from piece to piece.

'Camryn, these are incredible.' Alia wanted to move among the stunning glass panels and sculptures lining the room but there was a white rope dividing the space. One of the pieces stood over six-foot-tall in the centre of the huge room, a figure of a woman in the palest green, like sea-glass. She appeared to have been dredged up from the sea floor. Alia's phone hand twitched. She groaned inwardly.

'The pieces along the wall are for my show, the art movers are collecting them tomorrow. These here...' she indicated three huge panels of stained glass and a large piece hidden from view, 'are for the house. Original stained glass that was here before the war and before the vandals and squatters moved in. I can't let you in there. One false move and it's all gone. Like that.' She snapped her fingers making Alia jump.

On the closest table, twenty or so small panels of glass stood on edge and one lay on a platform raised a few inches above the table, waiting patiently for attention. Alia had seen them before.

'These were from the door to the...what do you call it, that living room behind the kitchen...'

'How did you know that?'

'It super weird but I've been having these really realistic... ah... dreams and I saw them...but they are a little different. There are different scenes with birds on them, like...' Alia looked at the vaulted ceiling of the orangery. 'Different birds in their habitats. Herons and ducks. I am so surprised I could remember that. I'm usually very keen to get to the b...' She was going to say 'bar' but stopped herself. Not only was Camryn sober and it is probably a bit rude to talk about drinking in front of a person in recovery, but it also came across as a bit sad, Alia realised. 'Bed. Sleep. I'm usually keen to get some sleep so I can write. The dreams have really interrupted my writing schedule.'

Camryn went to the table holding the panels. She lay each small sheet of glass out onto another table and signalled to Alia for her to follow. 'Oh, hairy goddess, no, there is no way I am stepping foot in that enclosure. I am the most accident-prone person I know.'

Camryn laughed. 'I'll give you the drawings and you can give me your feedback then. I like them how they are, but I know they are missing something.' She came back through the rope enclosure and went to a shelving unit that was made up of dozens of flat planks of wood with only inches between. She reached in and pulled out a bundle of papers and laid them on the lunch table. They were the ink preparation drawings for the glass panels.

'Take a look, what do you think I need to change?' Camryn seemed genuine.

'Are you seriously interested in my weird dreams?'

'You knew they were from that room and I don't know how you knew unless you had somehow seen it, so yeah, tell me everything. My options are limited at this point. Deadlines looming. Listen, I have to get back to my furnace. Do you want to take these back to your room and give me feedback at dinner time? I feel bad asking because you're also on a deadline…'

Alia accepted the challenge immediately. It was nice to be needed.

'And perhaps tomorrow you could come and look at the other pieces for the house? I know the large one is a mural, it's blue and green mostly, but I have no idea what it is…and I'm having trouble with the dome.'

Alia turned her head to follow Camryn's pointing finger, jumping up, her water spilled on the floor. 'The dome?'

Camryn nodded enthusiastically from behind her own glass, water sloshing down her apron. She gestured for Alia to follow. Alia put her glass down, took a deep breath and followed the artist through the maze of exquisite glass to a large wooden box that looked like a fruit crate from Waitrose. Alia's hand went to her mouth.

'This is the stained-glass dome from over the stairs…' Despite the water, her throat felt dry. Camryn let out a slow whistle. 'Oh, you are a marvel…I'll give you this drawing, too. I really have to get back to my furnace. Let's talk. I just knew when I saw you, you were here for a reason.'

Alia followed her out in a daze. Camryn pulled her into a quick hug.

'You are meant for greater things than you know…' she said.

Alia laughed awkwardly. Somewhere a phone rang. Alia hadn't heard a phone in…well it felt like weeks. Had it only been a couple of days?

'Gotta get that, thanks, chicky, I'll see you at dinner,' Camryn said as she pushed open the door Alia had assumed was a bathroom. She could see equipment and the warm glow of the furnace through the open door. Watermelon trotted back in and followed his mistress through the door, but not before giving Alia a good long stare and the door shut behind him.

Alia propped Cam's drawings around her room. The large one, a full-sized render of the dome lay on the floor and she stood over it. They were exquisite as they were, but Cam was right, they were missing something. Art Nouveau was over the top, decorative, pretty even, but these had a modernity to them, they were pared back, austere. The pieces Cam had made for the Venice show were ornate and feminine and Alia wondered why she wasn't bringing the same energy to the pieces for the house.

After poring over the drawings, she felt inspired to write. For hours she hunched over the old typewriter and as the sunlight dimmed the pages stacked up. When she could no longer see the type well enough, she sat back to admire the twenty-five pages from her efforts. It was a personal best and something to celebrate.

She stood up and stretched. *Where is a bottle of bubbles when you need it?*

After turning the light on, she stood over the dome drawing again. There were changes she would recommend but there was no way she could take a pencil to Cam's work. It felt wrong, scrawling all over what was essentially a work of art in itself. She could direct Camryn to make any changes herself; Alia's skills just weren't up to the task.

The house was in darkness by the time she went down for dinner. No one had tapped on her door with a friendly *yoo-hoo* and the dining room was empty except for a place set for her, a note tucked into the napkin. She couldn't remember spending so much time alone, ever. At home, her life was one continuous party, with friends coming and going at all hours of the day, the ever-patient Mrs P on guard to makes sure she ate the occasional apple and didn't drown in her own vomit.

The note, from Benito, informed her of the whereabouts of her meal, inside the multi-purpose sideboard, but not the whereabouts of her housemates. She took her platter to the terrace steps and ate, listening to the night sounds of the house and its surroundings, the moon hanging in the sky looked like a half-deflated football.

There are worse places I could be eating dinner right now.

She forked another mouthful in and chewed, eyes staring up at the odd-shaped moon. The food was delicious, everything Benito prepared was top-notch. She was lucky, she knew, but the company, her own, left a little to be desired.

Although the note had told her to leave the used plates on the table, she tried the kitchen door, on the pretence of washing up. It didn't budge. She leaned her forehead on the cool painted surface, those vodka bottles she'd spied in the fridge calling to her like sirens.

She'd been floating on a bit of a high after her successful writing day, but the solo dinner had done her in.

Where in hell are they and why didn't they take me?

She knew why they didn't take her. She was under house arrest and couldn't risk being seen in public. Knowing it and being okay with it were two vastly different things.

They could have at least told me. Left a note under the door.

At least if she'd been at home, she would have certain comforts and friends who could pop round to visit, hopefully with various substances. She climbed the stairs and wandered down the hall to the dusty building site that was the spiral stairs, the sheet of plastic she had torn down had been re-taped across the hallway. There was nothing for it but to go to bed and hope she woke up in 1950.

Total Eclipse

Scratchy gramophone music roused her from another dream. Relieved to be awake, she lay staring at the ceiling. In the dream, a party was being held on the terrace, but try as she might, she couldn't open the doors or attract the attention of any of the revellers. It made her sad.

Her bedroom glowed with a strange light. She half-expected a UFO to be hovering outside the windows, but it was just the moon. A full moon. Again. Even the most committed city dweller would know that a full moon three nights in a row was not natural, and the moon was an odd colour. Something wild was going on. She reached for her watch but knew it would read a few minutes after midnight. The music stopped for a moment before starting up again. If Braith and his gramophone were ghosts, then so was the full moon. He had said once that the full moon was his favourite time so somehow it always seemed to be full in these dreams or whatever they were.

She shrugged into a long silk wrap dress and ran her fingers through her hair. A slight smile on her face, she opened her door and turned right, the hallway glowing in the strange moonlight felt magical. She shivered all over, the evening was cool. The music drifted up from downstairs, the same music she always heard. She wanted to pinch herself but then if this was a dream, she didn't really want to wake up.

The landing above the spiral stairs was luminescent, the moonlight flooding in through the open windows and the glorious dome above. She peered down the stairs and closed her eyes. How could any of it be real?

After testing the stairs with one foot, she took them slowly, her hand on the balustrade for safety. It was the only part she knew still clung to the central axis of the staircase in her time.

Is that what this is? Time travel?

Her head felt light and her bare feet sunk into the plush runner on the terracotta passageway below. The hall was dark except where the light spilled from the beautiful etched glass doors leading to the room she called the Tiffany Parlour. A door further along opened and Braith appeared, a newspaper in one hand and a bottle of whiskey in the other. He looked up; a broad grin crept across his face.

'My dear Thalia…how good it is to see you.'

She smiled. 'You say that like it's been a while. I know we were blasted but it was only last night.' She made air-quotes when she said blasted. They met at the parlour doors and Alia ran her hands over the woodwork dividing the glass panels.

'Just last night? We were blasted, weren't we?' He laughed, head back and mouth open.

This man knows how to laugh.

He handed the newspaper to Alia. 'You are just in time for the eclipse.' He went to the bar and took down two glasses.

She read the date on the newspaper. *September 12, 1950.*

Breakfast with Phil

Phillip was seated at his end of the dining table surrounded by neatly stacked books and piles of paper. He was shirtless. Alia stood in the doorway, unsure of her next move. He looked up and greeted her brightly. 'How was your day yesterday?' he said as though he wasn't at all sitting there naked for all she knew. Did she have everything she needed, he wanted to know? How's the writing going?

Alia cleared her throat.

'Someone's chatty today.' She headed straight to the sideboard and loaded her plate with pastries. Benito came in and asked if she'd like anything from the kitchen. She winked theatrically at him. "One of whatever you've got.'

Taking her usual seat rather than using the empty upholstered seats favoured by Camryn and Watermelon, she looked around the room as she munched on her croissant. She looked at the ceiling. Anywhere, but at Phillip.

'I…am…chatty…' He spoke the words in staccato as he peeled, one by one, coloured Post-it Notes from his stacks of paper. 'I am chatty because my thesis is…complete.' He peeled away the last of the bright flags from his manuscript and rolled them into a colourful wad. 'I can box it up today and post it off to London.'

Alia had an unexpected reaction to the word "London." She had only been in France for a few days but felt like she'd been away from the city for a year. It threw her. She had meant to pepper Phillip with questions about the stairs or who the mysterious nightly visitor might be, but he wasn't wearing a shirt and she was famously easy to distract.

'Congratulations,' she said, as Benito brought her a pot of yoghurt and a bowl of granola. She smiled up at him. 'I'll be healthy by the time I leave here.'

She ate as Phillip used a contraption to bind his thesis papers.

'Why can't you just email it?' she said.

'I have to send a hard copy and a file separately. Once my tutor has proofread, I will have it printed and bound in navy leather.' He grinned up at her.

'I have to admit I am pretty bloody impressed that you're doing a doctorate. I was surprised.' She licked the yoghurt off the underside of the lid.

'You think I am stupid because I have muscles?' He reached across to pick up a pen and flexed a smooth bicep.

She blushed but ploughed on. 'Do you know James Blunt? He was in the army?' She smiled at the wall just above his head.

'Why did you mention the army?' He fixed her with his blue eyes.

Alia's gaze dropped to his face and felt her ears burn red. She had never blushed so much in front of a man in her whole life. 'Cam said…I'm sorry…I shouldn't have mentioned it.' She expected him to skulk away to brood on the driveway over a cigarette, then carefully tuck it into his little weird portable ashtray.

'It doesn't matter. I was just trying to get a rise out of you.'

Alia smiled at him. 'Oh well done you! You did get a rise out of me when I saw you sitting here. Well, Bravo. So, is this the real you? I have to admit I'm happy the uptight-weirdo-you is just you-on-a-deadline. You are actually more normal than I thought. You are wearing pants?'

'Um, yeah, of course. Sorry. I apply a gel to the, aah, scars to make them softer and I have to let it dry. I normally do this in private but I'm trying to beat the post-collection.' He looked up at her and smiled. 'I promise to be a better host. This whole thing with you blindsided me. I had no intention of coming out here. I had to pack up and go within an hour of Graeme's call.'

She was taken off guard by his apology. 'It's funny, but I don't even know Graeme. So, you just jump when he tells you to jump?'

'It's not that funny when you consider he's the guy who signs the cheques. And yes. I don't even ask how high. I just jump because I am not an heir to a fortune, and I have to pay for my tuition somehow.'

'Fair point. So, what do you do for them when you're not guarding wayward writers?'

Phillip shrugged. 'Anything they ask me to do.'

'Have they asked you to do anything illegal? Have you killed anyone?'

He rolled his eyes. 'It's nothing like that. I pick up writers and celebs at the airport, take them to their hotel, get them to film sets or interviews.'

'Ah, like Jonah Hill in Get Him to the Greek?'

Phillip looked confused. 'Sorry, pop culture references are pretty much wasted on me.'

'Right then, we probably haven't got much to say to each other…' She lifted her coffee cup to him and smiled.

'I'll have time to watch some movies once this thing is in the courier's hands. I might as well enjoy myself a little if I'm here for the rest of the month, so any suggestions would be great. I could read some of your work if you like.'

Alia laughed. 'Pretty much my whole body of work is pop culture references so it's probably not something you'd even understand enough to proofread. But thanks.'

Phillip nodded. 'So, I might start my movie marathon with…what did you call it? Get Him to the Greek? As in the Greek Theatre? In L.A.? I had to make sure a well-known pissy singer got there once. It was a right laugh.'

Although he said it had been a laugh, she still couldn't imagine him laughing. Alia put her cup down. 'So, you are Jonah Hill, but hotter. Ha!'

The words hung in the air between them. Phillip looked away and down, his lips were parted as though he was about to say something. He shook his head as though he'd thought better of it.

Alia put her hands on her hips. 'So, who cares if I think you're hot? You know you're hot, look at you? You're fit as fuck and you know it.'

'Well thanks, I'm not used to being told in such a frank manner.'

'Just say "thank you, Alia" and let's move on.'

'I just said thanks.'

'Right, well I'm embarrassed so I say ridiculous things when I'm embarrassed. Anyway, where's Camryn?'

'Had to go to see the space in Venice. For her show. Check out the pics.' He slid his phone along the table to her. She recoiled. As much as she wanted to see the photos, she was afraid if she touched the phone, she'd never give it back.

Phillip watched her. 'It won't bite.'

'I just need to stay away from the screens. I need to detox.'

He nodded and stood to retrieve his phone. He was indeed wearing pants. Denim jeans. The angry red scars ran across his chest.

'Wolverine, right?'

He stopped mid-lean, reaching towards his phone.

'Pardon?'

'It's just, the…' she mimed a claw slashing him across the chest but ended up looking more like a kitten batting at a ball of wool.

Phillip chuckled softly.

'Oh, come on. That's comedy gold.'

'Yeah, I met Hugh Jackman in a bar. We fought over who'd pay for the bourbon.'

Alia laughed and clapped her hands. 'Nice effort at banter. Bravo.'

Phillip picked up his phone. Alia could smell him, he smelled of soap, and cigarettes, but mostly soap. He sat in Watermelon's upholstered chair.

'Umm… These ghosts you and Camryn keep talking about. It's a joke, right,' she said.

'It's not a joke. It sounds a bit nuts, I know. Why?' He looked at her. He had blue eyes with a deeper blue ring around the iris. How had she never noticed his eyes before? Probably too busy looking at his arms.

She smiled and looked down. She felt her ears burn again. She'd never been attracted to anyone who wasn't a complete anarchist or a complete arse. Here was Phillip; presumably a war-hero, apparently intelligent, obviously thoughtful, probably a decent human being. Who knew good guys could be appealing? She was learning something new every day in France. When she looked up from the floor, he wasn't looking at her, but a smile was twitching at the corners of his mouth.

'I've been ah, having some weird dreams.'

'I'm no expert but it could be something to do with drying out?'

'Ha, yeah, it probably is, because I've been dreaming about... Oh, goddess, you are going to think I am an old soak!'

'I already do, but hey, been there. Three hundred and twenty days sober. I should probably halve that due to all the extra ciggies.'

Alia laughed. 'That's amazing. Really great. I guess you could say I am…what? Three days sober. Dream cocktails don't count, surely?'

'You're dreaming about drinking?' If he'd tried to keep the mocking tone out of his voice, he wasn't successful.

Alia nodded, her face burning with embarrassment. 'Believe me, if I am dreaming about booze, the sex dreams are mere days away.'

'Are you planning to keep going? Do you think you have a problem with alcohol?'

Alia wasn't sure if she had a problem specifically with alcohol, but her life was one big party. 'Maybe, I do. I love a drink. It's my favourite food group.'

Phillip put his phone on the table. 'If you want to talk about it, I'm here, Cam's here, well she will be tomorrow or the next day. We've been through it. Still going through it.'

Alia nodded and tried to say thanks, but her throat was dry. She picked up her coffee and gulped the last few mouthfuls. 'Back to the ghosts…have you seen anything?'

'Yes, I have actually. Some really odd stuff. Not really a ghost as such, but I've had things go missing from my room, even though I keep the door locked. A razor my dad gave me, an old one, something of a family heirloom. Benito gets upset because good utensils disappear. The neighbours say lights are seen at night sometimes, when no one is in residence upstairs, so, who knows really. Maybe someone lives in the roof and only comes out at night.'

Alia had been hanging on every word and shot up out of her seat after his last sentence. 'Oh, goddess, don't say things like that. That's far worse than a ghost.' She shivered dramatically.

Phillip smiled at her; his blue eyes sparkled.

Oh, goddess!

'So…how is the writing coming along?'

Alia plonked down into her seat. 'Thanks for changing the subject. Yes, writing is happening. I'm on a roll.'

He smiled again, eyes crinkling. She wanted to keep saying things to make him smile. 'I have to admit I am a bit freaked out when I can't find you guys. When you go off and don't tell me. And the dreams. I'm dreaming about cocktails, yes, but also about the house. I'm walking through the house, looking for people then I wake up…in the dream… and there's a man. He feels like the ghost of Christmas past.' She looked downed and inspected her fingernails. 'I don't know…perhaps I can incorporate him into my story…' She sighed and sat back in the chair. 'Maybe I'll make him into a female character who inspires a young writer who is struggling for inspiration. I like a little bit of the mystical in my work.'

'Right then, no time like the present? I'll bring you some lunch.' It was a statement, not a question and Alia felt a little buzz that Phillip would be bringing her food. He was on his feet, his shirtless torso tucked neatly into the jeans. Alia was staring.

'Will you be wearing a shirt? It could be like the painting, le Déjeuner sur l'herbe and you can be the half-naked one…' Her voice trailed away.

'I'll dress for lunch.'

He smiled again and wished her a pleasant morning. He picked up his neat pile of bound documents and went out via the kitchen door. Alia stared after him. She had never met anyone as confusing as Phillip. Annoying, frustrating, gorgeous, and clearly not the slightest bit interested in her. She wasn't used to being rejected but she also didn't want to seduce him. *Seduce. Such a weird word.* No, she didn't want to hook up with him. She wanted him to like her.

She jumped up and followed him into the kitchen, but Phillip had disappeared. Benito was nowhere to be seen either. She went over to the glass doors dividing the kitchen from the tiled hall and the set of doors that led into the bland sitting room on the other side. Curtains had been pulled across the doorway opposite and an intravenous drip stand stood in the otherwise empty passageway on the faded terracotta tiles.

Stranger and stranger things…

The next couple of days flew by in a pleasant haze of writing and meals taken with Phillip in quiet conversation and even laughter. Cam had stayed longer in Venice than she had planned, waiting to see her works safely stored. Phillip said she was excited about the space for her exhibition.

He ran so many errands, she often felt she was the only person in the château. She was under strict instructions to stay-put so she avoided asking if she could go with him, but one day she intended to dress up in one of her floaty kimonos and run, slow motion, down the hall. What else does one do in an abandoned castle?

A touch of boredom aside, she was enjoying her daily routine of writing and sleeping, quiet meals with Phillip, along with her nightly adventures with Braith.

She'd asked Phillip to pick up and alarm clock on one of his errands. She didn't want to risk sleeping through the night and missing out on running down the spiral stairs to drink Braith's newest cocktail creation and hear about his recent triumphs and tragedies.

The day before Camryn was due back, Alia flicked through the stack of pages she had assembled. Being surrounded by Cam's divine drawings had had an energising effect on her work.

Although he wasn't in her demographic, Phillip had read her work that day at lunch. He especially enjoyed the story about the mysterious stairs appearing just in time to save a young woman's life. She turned over the afternoon's events in her mind. The only disappointment was he had worn a shirt to lunch.

Oh, that and managing to get her talking about her family.

The bastard.

She was sick of the whole story but somehow, Phillip had pried it out of her over lunch as though there was truth serum in the sandwiches. Everyone knew her sad tale. Her parents had died tragically young. It was all very dreary and boring, and she was fed up with therapists telling her she chose bad boys because she was looking for her father. That made no sense. If she wanted a Daddy, surely, she would have fallen for an older guy. She thought of Braith. He reminded her of her father, but she certainly wasn't falling for him. He was just too nice. She didn't do nice guys, apart from the fact he existed only in her dreams.

Benito had prepared a picnic lunch, but the afternoon had turned stormy. Phillip said the picnic was his way of keeping her focussed on her writing, didn't want her to be distracted by something shiny, or a butterfly. She had laughed it off but wondered how she'd missed the ulterior motive. She was normally so cynical and something of an expert in all things passive-aggressive. Captivity was dulling her edge.

But she'd had the last laugh because he didn't realise, *he* was the distraction.

Alia had convinced him to picnic along the hall, on the landing where the stairs… should have been. They took turns describing how they thought it would have looked in its glory days. Phillip told her he had seen a few grainy photographs.

'Your descriptions are pretty detailed,' he said, staring up at the ceiling where the stained-glass dome should have been.

Alia took a big bite of her sandwich. She chewed slowly, not sure how to explain how she knew what the space should look like, even to herself. She was desperate to tell him, but knew it sounded completely bonkers. Eventually she swallowed and shrugged, chattering about the houses she'd grown up in. As though this explained anything.

Phillip had started to pack up the picnic things at that point, as though he'd heard quite enough about her childhood, or been stung by a bee.

He'd nodded goodbye and said, "Happy writing," and she'd called after him to remind him about the alarm clock. He'd promised to pick one up in Tours before collecting Camryn from the train. She could still see him, hurrying off down the hallway, leaving her to lean against her door for ages after closing it, wondering if it was something she'd said.

Despite Phillip's distracting presence and the aftermath of it, her afternoon's work had been successful, and she'd finally stopped when the light was gone. Phillip had told her he wouldn't be at dinner, so she ate her meal in her room before writing for a few more hours. It was her most productive day, well, ever. Literally.

Her mind went back to lunch again. Sitting in the half-demolished space was strange. Sitting there with Phillip, having a civil conversation was stranger still. She was lucky to be surrounded by such decent people. Lucky indeed considering she should probably be out on bail awaiting some kind of public nuisance charge. The stormy afternoon had given over to a windy, rainy night. She had to pull the windows shut to stop the rain pouring in and she fell asleep, reading, with all the lights blazing.

Waking from another strange dream, she rolled over in bed and reached for her watch. She blinked at the bright room, wondering why the lights were all on. She ran her hands through her hair and checked the time. Once again it was a couple of minutes past midnight. The rain had cleared, and another bright full moon hung in the sky. Throwing on a kimono she pinned her hair on top of her head and painted her eyes with a winged effect. She rummaged around in her vanity and found the perfect shade of lip paint to match the orange suns on her dress. Braith wasn't a ghost and she knew he wasn't a guest. If he was living in the walls and only coming out at night, as Phillip had joked, he was a master craftsman who seemed to be able to conjure an entire set of stairs, stained glass, and could mix a great cocktail.

She took the gently curving passageway around to the stairs, the polished timber floor glowing in the light of the full moon. She didn't bother testing the stairs anymore, she swept down following the sound of music. The evening was warm, and the terrace doors stood open, lace curtains billowing in the breeze.

'Anybody home?' Alia said as she wandered into the room.

Braith was standing at the terrace doors and threw his hands up when he saw her. 'My aren't you a vision tonight, my muse. Where have you been? I could have used some of your help today. I thought you had abandoned me.' He walked over to her; arms wide as if to embrace her but instead put his warm hands on her arms and looked into her face. 'I had to make do with my memories…and my broken heart.'

'Just make me a drink, you dreamer.' She went over to the terrace. 'Who broke your heart?'

He raised an eyebrow and went obediently to the bar. An elegant marble countertop had replaced the old-fashioned trolley. 'You did, I needed inspiration and you were nowhere to be found.' He handed her a drink. 'Is it possible you get lovelier every time I see you?'

'It is entirely possible.' She laughed.

It was a shame this was all in her head somehow; she felt more comfortable in this room than almost anywhere else in the house. Alia took her drink to the silk-upholstered sofa and draped herself across it. Braith sat in an armchair and set his drink on the tiny marble table.

'What kind of creative pursuits do you have your hand in just now that keeps you too busy to see me?' He steepled his fingers and smiled slightly. In his tweed jacket and pressed slacks, he looked like her third-year tutor and sounded like her father. He seemed more intense, even a little manic. He had never asked about her work before.

Alia explained her poetry, her stand-up shows, her legion of followers she liked to refer to as the *Hot Mass*. She always got excited when she talked about her work and when she eventually stopped talking and looked over at him, Braith was gawking at her, mouth open, eyes wide.

'Are you okay? You look like you're having a stroke…'

'This is your work? In London?' his voice trailed away. 'No wonder you haven't been here. How do you have time to help other artists?'

She was shocked at his accusing tone. 'I try. I always have a couple of local comics to open my shows, wherever I go.'

He looked confused. He picked up his drink and threw his head back, draining the glass. 'This isn't really what I was expecting.'

In all the nights they had sat drinking and talking, he had never shown any interest in her work, preferring to talk constantly about his own. He walked over and made himself another drink. Alia waved her glass at him, but his eyes seemed to be glazed over, seeing but not seeing her. She sat up, annoyed and uncomfortable so she did what she always does when she feels nervous and out of her element; she talked. She explained her presence in the house, the arrest, the contract, and the deadlines. He appeared to be listening but wasn't looking at her. Then he spoke. From everything he said, he seemed to have always believed she was there to help him, as though her presence was entirely to inspire him. He stopped talking and sat heavily on the end of the sofa, shaking her from her own thoughts.

'You have truly taught me something new about the world this evening. I know who you are, but I am stupefied that an established publishing house would give a young… girl… such a contract.'

He waved his hand at her as though he could sum her up and dismiss her in one gesture.

Alia's hands slapped the sofa. 'Wow, you are just like Phillip! One minute telling me how great I am and the next laughing at me, ridiculing me. I'm not at all surprised by your response. A lot of men these days are having problems understanding that we are not in the dark ages any more what with 'time's up' and the 'me too' movement.'

He was staring again. 'I have been living here in luxury for too long after the deprivations of war and have become soft. This, this is what I need. To be nervous again, on edge. I need to tap into this confusion. I should go back to New York.'

He sat back and steepled his fingers again saying the last words softly, as though to himself.

'Tell me, what are you writing about?' He sat back against the sofa and sipped his drink. 'I will give it my professional opinion.'

He looked down his nose at her, literally and it seemed, figuratively. Alia sat up and pulled her expensive silk dress out from under his backside. 'Thank you, but you're not exactly my demographic. I am writing for 6 to 16-year-old girls.'

He looked at her, laughing. 'Can girls even read at that age?'

Alia was accustomed to men who thought they knew more than she did, about everything.

'What are you writing then, smart arse?'

Braith stared at her. 'That is fine language for a lady,' he said.

'I am a Lady by title only.' Alia stuck out her tongue at him and he laughed heartily but there was an edge to his voice now.

'Oh, you certainly are what my American chums call a fire-cracker,' he said and shook his head. Braith picked up his glass and described the plot of his novel between sips. He seemed nervous.

Alia allowed her face to go blank. His story was the exact plot of the old novel Phillip had given her. She wasn't sure how you tell someone that another writer has beaten them to the punch. She cleared her throat and wished there was liquid in her glass. 'I am actually reading a book like that now. You might want to do a little more research because it's a very similar storyline. They even teach it at university, Phillip told me.'

Braith stood up as though he'd been slapped. He turned to look out into the dark night. 'Who is this Phillip you keep going on about?' He sounded annoyed.

'He's…. I have spoken of him before. He works for my publisher. He's a driver. Well, he drove me here. He can be a little bossy.'

'And this bossy driver knows what is taught at university?'

'He's a student, studying his PhD in literature. He knows a lot about it…'

Braith was frowning, looking into his glass. He said nothing for a few minutes. Alia felt like running from the room and finally plucked up the courage to interrupt his brooding and say goodnight when he turned to her. He spoke softly and she had to lean in to hear.

'Everyone's voice is different. I'm sure my story is unique because I lived it. It is true and honest. Regardless of what this Phillip says, I will write my story.' He put his empty glass down with a smack against the marble table. 'Will you excuse me?'

He was gone before she could respond. Alia stood up and looked around the empty room. She knew he was terribly upset by the news that his story was old news, but he would thank her later. Star had warned her that the worst thing a writer can do is be boring. The second worse thing is to copy someone else's story. She gathered up his glass and placed both on the bar, then went to the French doors and leaned against the cool glass. There was not a light to be seen, not a sound anywhere. Even the moon seemed to have disappeared. She went out onto the terrace and looked down towards where she had seen the hospital bed. She shivered. Going back inside, she pulled the French doors shut. Star also told her, far too often, that she took her youth for granted. To this, she usually responded with something like *d'uh, that's youth for you.*

She locked the doors and pulled the lace curtains closed. The room was so beautiful. She rested her hand on the smooth marble of the table as she bent to turn off the Tiffany lamp. She knew none of this was real, but it felt real enough. She knew Braith was somehow real and not real at the same time and that he thought that of her too. She flicked off two more lamps then went to the internal glass doors, standing ajar where Braith had fled the scene. She ran her hands over the images, committing to memory the tranquil pastoral scenes that Camryn was recreating. She looked down the hallway. Braith was standing there crying like a fourteen-year-old schoolgirl.

'Braith…I…'

He turned and walked away.

'What a drama queen…' she muttered. She might be fairly new to writing but if there was one thing Alia Henry was good at, it was taking criticism. She'd had a lot of practice. He would have to learn. But then they didn't have social media back in these days, whatever days these were.

She flicked the old-fashioned light switch off, plunging the room into darkness and groped her way along the darkened hall, reaching for her phone once again, for the torch app. She grunted in frustration. She would bring the torch Phillip had given her next time if she could find it.

If there is a next time.

Braith had been devastated by her words, and for some reason Alia cared. She was used to telling people what she thought; her friends just laughed it off. People knew that was her thing. She was a truth teller, or maybe she was just an arse.

'He's going to have to harden up a bit if he wants to be a serious writer…' she mumbled into the darkness.

Praying that the stairs would still be in place, she took small steps, one hand resting on the wall as she went. She could still feel the wallpaper under her fingers, the rough and smooth of the striped pattern comforting in the dark. After what felt like an age, her bare toes found the bottom step and she peered upwards towards the glass dome. The sky was a void, no moonlight shone through the stained glass or the bank of tall windows above on the landing. She prodded the bottom step with her foot and rested her weight on it. Braith might have left in a huff but whatever weird stuff was going on seemed to be hanging about. She leaned heavily on the balustrade as she started up the stairs but was running when she made it to the landing above, counting the steps as she went to calm her hammering heart.

She tripped on the last step, sending her sprawling. Her knees scraped along the hard flooring. The tears that had been just behind her eyes finally broke free from their moorings. It had been a long time since Alia had cried. She brushed the tears away with the back of her hand, almost punching herself in the face. Maybe they were tears of frustration, but she had to admit she was a little scared. She knew that Braith wasn't a drifter living in the walls. That wouldn't even go close to explaining the stairs, the tiles, the house in all its glory night after full-mooned night. She sat up slowly and rubbed her eyes like a small child as the space around her transformed back into the dusty, half-demolished shell she knew during the day.

She pulled her knees up and scrambled away from the gaping hole in the floor. She felt tired suddenly and her knees were stinging. She pulled herself up using the wall for support and slowly walked back to her room.

In the bathroom she stared into the mirror. Tears had made tracks on her cheeks but her winged waterproof eyeliner was as good as ever. She perched on the side of the bath and gently bathed her skinned knees.

Would she see Braith again? He had been pretty upset.

Alia Henry had a knack for opening her mouth and saying the wrong thing to the living and dealing with the Other Side or whatever he was, seemed to have similar consequences. New tears ran down her cheeks. She had been enjoying herself, as strange and uncertain as the whole thing had been. As Braith said, a little bit of fear can be good but the last thing she wanted to do was piss off a ghost and have an Exorcist situation on her hands.

She patted her knees dry and swung her feet back over onto the bathmat. This time, she switched off the lights and sighing heavily, went to the windows to peer out into the now-stormy night, willing a full moon to appear. Giving up, she crawled into bed, wincing as her raw knees met the sheet. Her hand fumbled on the bedside table for her watch, but it wasn't there, and she fell asleep reaching into the darkness.

Camryn

The next morning dawned hot and bright and her bedroom glowed with morning sun that felt like a laser beam. As she did every morning, she jammed the pillow over her eyes and staggered to the bathroom. Tossing the pillow back into the room, she flipped the water on in the shower and stood under it with her mouth open, still wearing her silk kimono from the night before.

She covered her eyes as the tears came again. This was another new feeling, and she didn't like it any more than she liked embarrassment. It was regret and sadness mixed together, and it was not a good feeling. She had offended friends before without feeling a thing so it made no sense at all to feel bad about telling the truth to someone she barely knew, someone who may or may not even exist.

'Snap out of it,' she whispered to her reflection in the bathroom mirror.

She wound a towel around her wet hair and wrapped the other around her slim body and tucked the corner between her breasts, jiggling them at herself in the mirror. No old-time, ghostly hipster was going to make her feel bad about herself just because he had thin skin. *Speaking of skin, mine looks amazing.*

She turned her head from side to side admiring her smooth, clear cheeks and smiling, went in search of clothes. The room was almost pulsating with sunlight. She pulled on cut-offs and a tank top and glanced at her typewriter as she bit the nail on her thumb. She had to find a new place to write, her room was an oven.

Out in the corridor, she looked towards the spiral stairs, or at least where they should be. As though in a dream, she wandered past Phillip's room and Camryn's. She stopped and listened outside Cam's room, but all was silent. She took the little bend in the corridor and the half-demolished landing of the day-light hours revealed itself. Little dark patches of blood and scrape marks in the dust revealed her landing strip from the night before. The stairs must have disappeared the second she reached the top. She looked over the edge at the dusty floor more than twenty feet below and shuddered, her heart thudding in her chest.

Her stomach rumbled and her hand flinched towards the pocket that would normally hold her phone. She had no idea of the time and the house, deeply silent, seemed empty again. She hesitated in front of Camryn's bedroom again but didn't knock and, pulling her own bedroom door shut, went in search of breakfast.

She found Benito and the nurse she had seen reading to the old man sitting at the at the vast dining table. Both looked up and smiled, with bonjours all round. Benito asked if she wanted an omelette or anything else, but she shook her head and told him she was more than happy with the pastries and coffee. She sat quietly eating and watching them work. They were creating menus, a task she had seen her grandmother do with her own cook.

'Monsieur Evan is having a party,' Benito said, looking up from his paperwork. 'He is having a birthday. One hundred. Such a great age. You will be invited, an honoured guest as a writer-in-residence.' He smiled broadly at her.

'I'll be there. I'll dance with him on a table,' Alia said, grinning at them.

'We 'ave been working with him, to get him ready for the party. I don't think he will be dancing on the table,' the nurse said, in her heavily accented English, 'but a party will be nice.'

Yes, a party will be nice, so why are you two so grim?

Alia was nodding and smiling but imagined a party where they all sat around a hospital bed taking turns to read aloud and eat pureed vegetables.

The coffee was a balm to her jangled nerves and Alia only half listened as they finalised their plans. They spoke in rapid-fire French, but she caught enough to know the party was still few weeks away, on Bastille Day, or *Quatorze Juillet* as it is known in France. Still, it gave her a little thrill to think there would be an event to look forward to before… Before she returned to London and to her normal life.

She sipped her coffee and closed her eyes. She missed her life. She missed her freedom. She could walk out of here today and even if she had to pay the ridiculous fees Phillip hinted at, at least she would be free to do her own thing and free of the cranky old ghost named Braith. But then she would miss Camryn and Benito and the crazy old house. And Phillip.

A noise in the room made her jump and when she opened her eyes Phillip was standing beside her as though thinking his name had summoned him. Alia nearly jumped out of her skin. Camryn was behind him, smiling, gliding in, holding a bag aloft and Watermelon stood and glared at Alia. She was sitting in his seat. She stood and the dog claimed his rightful place before she was fully upright.

'Yeah, I missed you too, bruv,' Alia said, laughing.

Camryn chuckled heartily and handed Alia the bag. It was heavy and Cam kept her hand under the bag until she had a good grip on it. Alia had her fingers crossed for a bottle of Prosecco. She pulled out a cardboard cylinder and placed it on the table as Camryn sat in her usual spot and Benito and the nurse watched on with interest. Alia carefully opened the top of the cylinder and slid out the inner package, wrapped in bubble wrap, and lay it on the table. She could see some colour through it, blues and greens.

'It's a maquette.' Camryn said, as Alia peeled away the wrapping to reveal a glass sculpture, a miniature of the sea-glass woman in Camryn's studio. 'I wanted you to have it.' Alia picked up the tiny green woman and ran her hands over the body, which was rough and smooth somehow, at the same time. She looked up at Camryn with tears in her eyes.

'This is…the most beautiful gift I have ever been given…'

Without warning the tiny dog stood on his chair and barked at the kitchen door. Alia almost dropped the sculpture. Camryn shushed him and Alia stood the sea-glass woman on the table.

'I'm sorry, I'm just so jumpy,' she said. 'Thanks Camryn, it's divine.'

'It's a sample I made very early on for my submission and when they gave it back to me yesterday, odd as it sounds, it made me think of your visit to my studio and how fortuitous it was.'

Alia made sure it was secure on the table and stood up to hug her friend. Benito offered to cook a big brunch for the returned travellers as Camryn regaled them all with stories of her whirlwind trip to Venice. Alia relented and took Camryn's iPad to look at the photos. Her allocated space at the Biennale was, fittingly, an ancient Glassworks and her show inspired by the sea, the history of glassmaking in Venice, and the art nouveau pieces she was working on for the house.

Phillip had a surprise for her too. He placed a little silver carriage clock on the table and stood back. 'It has an alarm. I checked.'

'It's perfect, exactly what I would have bought myself.'

He smiled and nodded. 'Technically you did buy it yourself, Whitehall… expenses.'

Alia grinned at him. She didn't care that the clock had gone on her expense account, he had chosen it and it was perfect. They enjoyed a long breakfast and as the men were clearing the table, Alia took Camryn aside and asked if she could spare a small place in the studio for her to set up her typewriter. Her bedroom was too hot. Camryn loved the idea and offered to help her carry her work things down to the studio after she had freshened up.

'It will be wonderful to have you there. It's so empty now that everything has gone to Venice. I know just the spot for you,' Camryn said, hugging Alia.

Again, Alia felt tears prick in the corner of her eyes.

Writer in residence

An hour later, Phillip carried the old heavy typewriter while Alia and Camryn followed with her boxes of what she called her writerly stuff. The sun was almost at its zenith, but inside the orangery it was cool. It seemed so empty without the lines of sculptures and the 7-foot glass woman.

Watermelon ran in and barked at the empty space. 'You could rent him out to bored Notting Hill housewives. They're always getting space clearings. You know, people come in with gongs and incense and wave it all about to clear the bad juju away…can I say that? Is that cultural appropriation? Yes, it is, please forget I said it.'

Camryn and Phillip were waiting for her. 'I'm sorry, I talk when I'm excited.'

'And upset, and happy, and embarrassed.' Phillip said sotto voce, turning his head to Camryn and putting on a face.

'Ha…ha dee har,' Alia said to his back.

Camryn showed them to the hidden alcove. Alia looked around the cosy space, beaming. 'This is perfect,' she said.

'Where do you want it?' Phillip stood in front of the desk with the typewriter.

'That looks perfect, what a great outlook,' Alia said.

'Your bedroom has an amazing outlook…and pedigree. Benito thought you would love it. It's called the Writers' Room because so many have slept there over the years. It was the favourite bedroom of the owner of the house too, although he worked down here. I've seen an old photo of him sitting around about here…' Phillip gestured to a spot a little further along the built-in desk. He ran his fingers over the pitted timber surface.

'Let's put the typewriter there, I need all the help I can get at this stage.'

She dumped the reams of typing paper onto the floor and took the box from Camryn and set it on the desk. She flipped open the lid, took out the sea-glass lady and sat it in a pool of soft sunlight at the far end of the desk. She stood back and looked but thought better of it and put it next to the typewriter. 'She will inspire me, she can be my muse,' she said, and pretended to tweak the statue's nipples.

'See, that's what I like about you; you don't take yourself too seriously!' Camryn laughed.

Alia reached back into the box and pulled out the drawings Camryn had given to her.

'I have a lot of ideas for these when you're free.'

Camryn sucked in a deep breath at the sight of the wad of papers. 'I'll get some thumbtacks and we can put them up. I have to get moving on those, so yes, any ideas would be helpful. The big boss wants them installed before the party. There's going to be a big push to get some work done…the French minister for the arts is coming. Now that Venice is in the can, I can concentrate on the glass for the house.'

Camryn went to a filing cabinet in the corner of her office space cum tearoom and brought back a packet of thumbtacks. She took the drawings one by one from Alia and after lovingly reacquainting herself with each design, tacked it to the wall. They all stood back and admired the new wall decorations.

'So, it will be a big party?'

Phillip nodded. 'Absolutely. He's famous. Well, he was. How are you enjoying his book?'

The two women stared at the drawings, lost in thought. Phillip cleared his throat.

'I'll go and get a chair out of the cave and then you can work on your own words.' He set off at a trot. Watermelon followed him which Alia found quite surprising.

'He's taken quite a liking to Phil. He's such a nice guy.' She stopped and Alia looked up. Camryn's eyes were full of mischief.

Alia frowned at her friend. 'He is…' She nodded her head in agreement.

He is a very nice guy. Maybe a little too nice…

'He'll be a good teacher. He's got such a nice manner,' Camryn said, taking the rest of the stationery items out of the box.

'Teacher? I thought he was doing a PhD?' Alia turned as he disappeared along the path. What had he said, just before he took off? Was it something about the paperback she was reading, the old war story?

Camryn was talking. 'Yes, and he will no doubt write, but he'll have bills to pay, rent, and the like. Not everyone is as lucky as you, Alia.'

Alia was about to ask Camryn what Phillip had said about the old novel but hearing Camryn's rebuke, looked away, her cheeks burning with embarrassment. 'I didn't mean anything by that…I meant it in a nice way. He's obviously really clever, he could do anything.'

Camryn walked over and stood close to Alia. She spoke softly as if to a small child. A small, stupid child who needed to be taught to mind her manners.

'Yes, he can do anything. He's excited about his future, and will have his pick of schools, but my guess is he will go where he is most needed. He will be able to do something really good.'

'But…a teacher?' Alia scrunched up her nose. The two women stood looking out onto the garden. Camryn didn't say anything for a few moments and when she did, she spoke softly.

'Nothing wrong with being a teacher, it's a very noble, very necessary profession and he'll be such an asset to any school especially once the kids find out he was in the Special Forces. There'll be no playing up in sir's classroom.' Camryn laughed as she leaned back against the wall.

Watermelon didn't bark this time and Phillip plonked the chair down startling both women. 'No there will not.'

Alia yelped at the sound of his voice.

'…and I will contrive to show them my scars on the first day and they'll be little angels all year. It worked with you.' He grinned at Alia and winked. She gaped at him.

Alia stood back to allow Phillip to lift the heavy old leather chair into place and sat down. She was still confused about his comment about the scars, but she worried he had heard her derision about his chosen profession. He couldn't have heard, she told herself as she watched him play with the dog. Not even Action Man Phil could have run that fast carrying a heavy old chair. Camryn bent over and gently clapped her hands at the dog. He spun in circles, barking.

Alia clapped her own hands and ushered them from the writing nook. 'Okay, hush you lot, writer in residence here, work to do…'

'Are you ready for lunch? Benito's brought a picnic,' Camryn said, poking her head around the corner. Benito stood behind her, peering at the space Alia had made for writing.

Alia nodded eagerly and typed a few more words on the page. She sat back in her chair and stretched her arms, admiring the pile of papers she had to show for the morning's efforts. She had even used one of the marker pens Phillip had bought to begin on the illustrations for the book. For the first time she felt she had a chance of getting the work done. As to whether it would be good enough for Whitehall and the mysterious Mrs Grant and Graeme the bogeyman-slash-lawyer they kept talking about was another thing altogether.

'This is better than your bedroom?' Benito looked at her with one eyebrow cocked, his arms spread wide to show how narrow the space was.

'It's perfect, Benny, but the commute is a killer,' Alia said.

Camryn laughed and Benito followed suit once Cam had explained the joke. He was still chuckling under his breath as he set up the picnic lunch on a blanket outside the studio. A few low clouds scudded through the blue sky and a light breeze played with their hair as Benito presented them both with filled half-baguettes and watched them expectantly as they took a bite.

'It's really good,' Alia said, nodding at his eager smile. Camryn nodded in agreement and Benito patted her on the arm. Happy with the review, he bit into his own sandwich.

After devouring the meal, Alia realised she was keen to get back to her typewriter. It was wonderful to finally have a cool place to write. Benito packed up the lunch things.

'Phillip said I can't stay long. I am not allowed to distract you,' he said. Alia assumed the message was for her, but Benito was looking at Camryn. Alia smiled at them as they stood shyly looking at each other.

'Oh, Cam? You know who else is a nice guy?' she said.

They both stood back as though she had splashed them with cold water. Benito turned on his heel and bustled up the path with a hurried wave goodbye and Cam turned to Alia.

'What?' she said. Her hands were on her hips, but she was grinning.

'Don't you mean who?' Alia replied, smirking at Camryn. She walked into the studio.

Watermelon ran past her and sped around the empty studio barking, until he stopped at the entrance to Alia's writing nook, fur bristling, growling under his breath. The exchange between Benito and Camryn forgotten as Alia jumped in fright but doubled over in a fit of giggles at the sight of the serious little dog. 'What is it, Lassie?' she said.

'Don't encourage him. He was so naughty at breakfast, barking like that at the secret door.' Camryn spoke in that voice parents use when speaking to small children about how clever and wonderful they are.

'Oh, come on, you and Phillip think it's hilarious,' Alia said rolling her eyes.

Cam followed her into the studio, clapping her hands and shushing Watermelon who was still growling at the empty space.

'Hey, are you still having those dreams?

Alia nodded.

'Can I pick your brains again? The deadline for the party has really put the pressure on. The skylight will be a piece of cake now that I have a direction. The doors, too. Tell me, have you seen a mural with a blue and green pattern? I've no idea what it is because it was smashed and only features in the corner of a few photos. It's in what we call the office.'

'I haven't been into an office yet; I only see the domed stairs and the parlour. I guess I stop there because that's where the bar is.'

Camryn laughed softly and Alia's cheeks burned. She put her hands up. 'Cam, I don't know if they are dreams or not, but every night I wake up… it's always a little past midnight. I throw something on and hightail it down the stairs. There's a guy there, Braith. He makes the best G and Ts. It is so real but then in the morning the stairs are gone and so is he.'

'So much for the detox, then.' Camryn smiled. 'The front stairs? To the foyer?'

'No… Oh, it's so weird. I want to show you, but I don't know if the magic extends to others or if it's just me…' Alia stopped talking. Camryn was staring at her.

'Magic?' Camryn's expression was indecipherable.

Alia cleared her throat. 'You think I'm mental?'

'No,' Camryn started slowly.

'Oh, Cam I so wanted to tell someone about this crazy shit. You've got no idea what I've been doing every night. It's affecting my writing… but in a good way. It's made my stay here bearable at least.'

Camryn smiled and patted her arm.

'Oh, and you, I love being here with you, even if you think I'm crazy!'

'Honey, I do believe you. It sounds amazing and I'm jealous,' Camryn said. 'I don't really know what to think. All I know is you've been very helpful with the glass pieces so however you're getting that information is okay with me. And no, I don't think dreaming about a G and T is unusual, considering. So, we'll talk about the mural. Later?'

Alia nodded. Camryn finally convinced Watermelon to stand down and they disappeared into the furnace room. She wasn't convinced Cam believed her but then she didn't know what to believe herself.

Standing alone in the studio she felt the hair on the back of her neck stand up.

It's just the breeze.

Suddenly, the last thing she felt like doing was writing but write she must. As usual, she had left a blank sheet of paper in the typewriter and on the fresh page was a line of type.

The full moon is a time of quiet contemplation, the new moon is the time for action. The waxing moon, for writing, and while it wanes, we make our words sing. B.R.E.L.

'Huh,' Alia said in a rush of air. She sat back in the chair.

She wound the barrel of the typewriter up and took a closer look at the words.

B...for Braith?

She felt tiny goose bumps rise and suddenly felt like writing.

My life is a Black Mirror episode

Alia was exhausted by the time her writing day had finished. She yawned as Benito presented them with a wheel of cheese he and Phillip had picked up from a trip to a local farm that day. Benito wanted to place an order for the party, and they had collected samples from all the different cellar doors and farm shops in the area. Phillip passed his phone to Camryn to show her the photos he'd taken of the area. Despite the industrial parks and residential developments, it still had its natural spaces and quaint villages if you knew where to look. Alia put her hands up to refuse the device. 'You've been doing great work. It's not going to hurt if you use the internet for five minutes.'

Alia looked down at the device and shook her head. 'I just need to completely detox. Digital detox,' she said.

'So, you're not dreaming about posting on, what do you call it? TikTok?' Camryn said, grinning.

'No, I am not. Just the booze.'

Phillip laughed and got up to take the phone. 'You're still dreaming about cocktails?'

Alia looked up at him. She didn't think he was being rude, it sounded like a genuine inquiry. She nodded, a sheepish grin on her face.

'Totally normal,' he said and sat back down, flicking through the photos again. 'You're wise to stay away from social media. Star is handling all that.'

She bristled at the mention of her agent. 'She'd better be. I've hundreds of thousands of followers who are probably wondering where the hell I am.'

Phillip looked up at her. 'Didn't she tell you?'

'Tell me fucking what? I've been here in purgatory with you. Did you think she was sending carrier pigeons, or do you think we communicate telepathically?'

Camryn reached over and rubbed her hand. Alia smiled a thin-lipped grimace at her friend. Phillip got up and walked over again, holding the phone in front of him. 'Star and Regina have it all under control.'

Alia reluctantly took the device. 'What's Mrs P got to do with any of this?' Phillip squatted down beside her as she scrolled through the feed of her own Instagram account. There she was in front of the townhouse carrying flowers. Another shot showed her from behind, shopping at a store in the village near the country house. Another post showed her reading to a small child in a hospital bed. Alia glanced at Phillip.

'I have literally never visited a children's hospital, other than after that unfortunate incident at Coachella.'

Phillip reached across and kept scrolling. In the next photo Alia was walking a puppy. Then came a video of clouds scudding over the hills behind the country house. Then an arty shot of the night sky. The photos were interspersed with snippets of her writing and occasional quotes from famous women.

'How the hell did Star get these photos? Is it Photoshop?' Alia spoke very slowly as though she was having trouble forming words.

'It's Regina. She's the best body double I've ever seen and as long as they don't show her face…' He leaned over and scrolled to an image of her arriving at the village church for a wedding.

'Oh no, I've missed Harper's wedding.'

'No, you haven't,' Phillip said. He laughed softly.

She stared at the screen. 'My followers have… gone up…' She put the device on the table as if in a dream. 'Well, there you go… they've got a ghost writer waiting in the wings and Mrs P to do the location shots.

It's like an episode of Black Mirror. Do you think Whitehall or whoever are going to really terminate me?' She drew a line across her throat.

Camryn looked from Alia to Phillip and he put his head down and chuckled. 'Of course not. It's damage control. I've told Star you are pumping out the work and she's more and more relieved every time I talk to her. She wanted me to courier some pages over, but I told her I had to talk to you first.'

She could feel her hackles rising again. 'Damn straight you need to talk to me first.' She stopped and took a deep breath. Phillip was sitting calmly, his face neutral. He had just said he told Star he had to get permission first. She counted to three and leaned back in her chair. 'Thanks. I appreciate that. Come down tomorrow and I'll let you take some photos of my pages but I'm keeping my originals with me. I've gone old-school.'

'I'll be down tomorrow,' Phillip said. 'I understood that Black Mirror reference because I've been watching the shows on the list you gave me, and yes, you're right, I am hotter than Jonah Hill.' He laughed again. 'Shall we retire to the terrace and smoke too much?'

'Sounds good to us,' Cam said. She clicked her tongue at Watermelon and picked up her unfinished glass of non-wine. Alia grabbed her own glass and followed; certain she should be upset about being replaced so easily but gratitude felt like the more appropriate emotion.

Very A-musing

Alia's new alarm clock buzzed at midnight, but she was already drifting somewhere between awake and asleep. A bright full moon hung in the sky again. She stared at it for a few moments, seeing it but still not believing it was real. Shaking herself awake, she threw her legs over the bed and ran to the door, pulled it open and stood in the hall which glowed in the moonlight. She looked down. Alia Henry knew herself well. She was the sort of person who didn't check she was wearing shoes before going to the supermarket, or check she was wearing pants before answering the front door.

Her white silk vintage kimono shone like a pearl. She had wanted to be prepared, wrapping herself in it before falling asleep. She didn't stop to check her hair but after dashing down the hall towards the spiral stairs, she hesitated on the landing. She put one foot on the top step and rested her weight on it, before plunging down.

She could see the glass doors to the parlour standing open, the same one she had helped Camryn design that afternoon.

Braith was standing at the terrace doors, a bottle in one hand and a glass in the other.

'What are we celebrating?' Alia said, a little breathless as she entered the room.

Braith smiled slowly and poured himself another glass. 'You know very well, Lady Thalia.'

He placed emphasis on each of the syllables of her name. She took a glass from the bar which had seen the addition of overhead glass racks and a marble bench top.

'Humour me.' She winked as she held out her glass to him. Obviously, he had recovered from his hurt feelings.

'My second manuscript has been accepted. Sales are steady with the first book. I am the darling of the London literary scene, or so says my agent.'

Alia touched her glass to his and threw back the dark liquid. It hit her throat and slid down, burning as it went. She gasped.

Braith laughed, head back, mouth open. 'Ouzo…in your honour,' he said, lifting his glass to her.

She raised her eyebrow at him and held out her glass for a refill. 'Aah, yes…'

She walked around the room aiming for the sofa. Another new addition to the room loomed on the far wall; a huge gold-framed mirror. She stood in front of it, admiring both its sinewy, art nouveau style and her own reflection. Her hair hung loose around her shoulders, and the deep V-neck of the kimono made her appear taller than she was somehow. Even she thought she looked other-worldly in the outfit and could see suddenly why Braith regarded her with something not unlike reverence. She shifted her gaze in the mirror to see he was staring at her from the other side of the room.

Ouzo, in my honour?

She swirled the dark liquid in the heavy-bottomed glass. He thinks I'm a…muse…She lifted her gaze, taking in her whole reflection from the bare feet and up.

'How very a-musing…' she said under her breath. Lifting her glass to his reflection. It all made sense and answered her ego's question as to why he hadn't tried to sleep with her. Although there were definitely men who would have tried, even if they thought she was the daughter of Hades himself.

She turned back to the room and walked slowly to the sofa, propping herself on the back of it while he settled himself in his favourite leather chair.

'Tell me about your new work,' she said, lowering her voice to sound like she thought a muse would, breathy and low.

His eyes lit up and he smiled and began to speak. He had been working hard, he assured her. Since her arrival in his life, he had been diligent, writing hours every day, attending events that would further his career even if he didn't wish to. He was pressing the flesh when he must, he said, a phrase which always conjured unpleasant images in Alia's mind. She had never been a great listener, but she forced herself to hang on his every word. For whatever reason, each night she was visiting this man and he was inspired by her presence. As much as that offended her as a feminist, it was nice to know she was doing something for someone else for a change.

She blinked at him.

Is he still talking? So much for being a good listener.

'...so, I just began to write any old thing and found I was writing every day, so very much. I saw myself as a miner, like the men who worked for my father but instead of descending into a pit and digging for gems or coal, leaving heaps of rock behind, I created mountains of words, piles of dross and rambling sentences to get to the fleck of gold. There are times I write all day, to salvage just one sentence the next. The rest goes in the fire.' He shrugged and smiled up at her. 'I have you to thank. You brought me to life when you came to me.'

She opened her mouth to speak but found she couldn't, and a couple of tears sat just under her eyelids. She walked to the bar and placed her glass on the marble top. Aware he was watching her, she walked to the terrace doors so she could be out of his vision. Her hand went to her throat and at first, she thought he had poisoned her. Her throat was tight, and she felt a burning sensation behind her eyes. She went out on to the terrace into the cooler night air as a sob escaped from her throat. She wanted to call out but couldn't speak. Tears ran down her cheeks, her shoulders heaving as she cried.

She felt his hand on her shoulder and turned to him.

'I am sorry, I simply wanted to thank you.'

She still couldn't speak but put her hand to her lips and then on to his, something she had seen her grandmother do a million times. She laughed though the tears were still coming.

'I think these are happy tears,' she said, smiling and taking the handkerchief he was holding up to her. She dabbed her eyes and cheeks taking the glass of water he had fetched from the bar.

They stood on the terrace and talked, laughing and sipping ouzo until the rooster across the fields began to crow. Her feet were cold, and she was more than a little drunk, but she felt alive and awake despite having only a few hours' sleep. She put her arms out to Braith, pulling him into a hug. As much as she was attracted to him, (he was a man after all), it was obvious that he viewed her not as a woman but as an ideal. She tried to imagine any of her friends believing a muse was visiting them. Maybe if they were at Burning Man at the time…

'Goodnight, Braith,' she breathed in his ear. 'I will see you tomorrow night…'

He pulled out of the embrace and looked down at his shoes like a little boy. 'You always say that, but then it's months until I see you again.'

She was surprised. 'For me, I see you each night…but somehow, yes…it's always a full moon.'

He laughed. 'I am always surprised to see you but somehow you are here when I need you the most. The first time I saw you was early in '47, when I was beginning. I had written pages and pages but nothing of worth, no gold mined from those piles of slag. Then, you came to me many times in '48 when I was feeling terribly uncertain and you felt my story was unoriginal. In '49, my writing was yielding gold and silver. You remember the eclipse? That was 1950, and yes, you came to me when I was first on the list, the Times, remember?'

She was nodding her head, tears streaming down her face. To her, the visits hadn't followed a strict timeline.

'…and yes…the full moon is my favourite time. I feel…'

'Potent?' she said. She remembered him saying that, in…1948? A slow smile crept across her lips. She had somehow travelled to 1948,

1949…and '50. She put her hand to her face. She was grinning like a loon. 'What year is it now?'

'It's 1954,' he said, taking her hands. 'April. Tomorrow is Good Friday. Perhaps I am harking back to my ancestors who had rituals for the full moon.' He looked away, clearly embarrassed.

'Why are you embarrassed about that?' she said, rearranging her face into something more normal, she hoped.

'It's not terribly manly to admit such a thing, is it?' He was laughing.

'It's human,' she said emphasising the word by placing one palm on her chest and the other on his, 'to be honest about your feelings, and your process as a writer. It is human to pursue a goal with such dedication as you have.' Alia wondered where such wise words were coming from.

'And now it's '54 and every dream I have is coming to fruition. Thanks to you.'

'Pfft, you're doing the work. I just turn up every night…every few years, apparently …to drink your booze.' Alia laughed through her tears and Braith had tears welling in his eyes.

They stood face to face for a few moments. This moment, Alia thought, was where she would normally reach across and brush the curl out of the boy's eye, or the boy would reach across and playfully tug on her fingers, but Braith wasn't a boy. Braith nodded formally and checked his elegant gold watch.

'I'm afraid my current deadline involves a driver and a train ticket.' He gently took her elbow and led her into the house, and pulled the doors shut behind him. He drew the heavy drapes across where lace curtains had been on her last visit. 'I will be in Paris by breakfast time tomorrow, bound for New York in the evening. I am so very pleased to have seen you again. I fear… I never will again.' He brushed away a tear on his cheek.

'I'll see you tomorrow night,' she said, that lump in her throat again.

He stood behind his favourite chair and leaned down to switch off the elegant lamp on the tiny marble table. He seemed to be waiting for something.

'Goodnight, then,' she said and turned to go. She was almost at the glass door when he spoke.

'Do you know what the future holds for me?' He spoke quietly, staring at the floor.

She looked back at him. 'No, I don't...I can tell you things, general things, about... history, but I have to admit I don't...know you.'

'So, I am no Orwell, then. No Hemingway...'

Alia didn't know what to say. 'Who cares about those old guys. You're so young and already a success. Keep writing, who knows the gold you will unearth?' She smiled and he appeared to be satisfied with the response.

Boys…

The next morning Alia ate breakfast with Camryn and Watermelon. Phillip and Benito were nowhere to be seen. After her emotional meeting with Braith, the words flowed from her. All day she hammered away at the typewriter as the sheets stacked up. She was mining for some gold of her own.

The orangery acted like an enormous sundial and as the sun shifted, so did the quality of the light. In the afternoon it changed from a bright white, bouncing off the limewashed walls to a warm, burnished glow making the stained glass in Camryn's workshop look as though it was lit from within. Alia stretched. She felt she had been writing for hours. A nice stack of typed pages sat next to her, all smug and proud of themselves. Phillip had bought her a ring binder and she punched holes in the sheets and added them to the steadily growing pile.

'Yoo-hoo… dinner? The boys are back, I've had a text.' Camryn held her phone up.

The sun was still high in the sky, but they had missed lunch and Alia was famished. She stretched her long legs. 'After dinner, can we have another little meeting about the glass work for the house,' Camryn said.

Alia nodded her head. 'It would be my pleasure. You've made my time here actually enjoyable. I can't imagine what the place would be like if you weren't here. I probably would have ended up in bed with Phil.'

Camryn nudged her as they trudged up the path to the house. 'Would that be so bad?'

Alia laughed. 'Not bad…but also, not good because that's what I do. I make a fool of myself all the time. I get my kit off in stupid places. I…I…jump into bed with people who don't like me, just to see if I can win them over.'

'What makes you think he doesn't like you?'

'Well, most boys who like me are all over me, buttering me up, you know, trying to impress me.' She lowered her voice as they walked into the entry hall. 'He's not interested, believe me, I know.'

Camryn leaned in and whispered in her ear. 'Maybe, that's what boys do.' She used air quotes when she said "boys." 'Just don't dismiss the idea completely that men who are kind and serious are not interested just because they're not trying to shag you on the stairs.'

They erupted into laughter as they walked into the dining room.

...and so, to Cuba.

Alia was walking slowly through the château wearing the gown she'd worn to the Met Ball the previous year. The dress was heavy, wet, weighing her down. She dragged its sodden train behind her over the sumptuous hall runners and polished floors, feeling weary and unable to take another step, as though walking through honey. She woke to heavy rain and thunder and she was wet alright, but that was because the rain was coming in.

'Bloody stupid dreams,' she muttered, shaking herself like a dog. She pulled the windows closed and ran to the bathroom.

She peeled off her clothes and wrapped herself in fluffy towels and walked back to the windows to watch the storm. Lightning flashed and for a second, she could see the hand of the little silver carriage clock. It was a few minutes after midnight.

Of course, it is...

Lifting the clock to her ear, she checked if it was still working and with the ticking still in her ears, she stared out into the rain. A pool of light appeared downstairs. Someone was awake. Could it be Braith, even on this evening with no full moon in the sky? She pulled a long kimono from the armoire and wrapped it around herself, freeing her hair from the towel, she let it fall, dampish, around her shoulders. She grabbed the newly unearthed torch, opened the door, and walked slowly along the corridor. In her bare feet, her kimono dragged, reminding her of her dream. The corridor was dark but, even in the gloom, she could make out the bank of tall windows and the dome overhead.

We're on.

She flicked the torch on and shone it down on the spiral stairs and up into the domed skylight. She was glad she had the torch even though the dome seemed to glow with otherworldly light. The doors to the parlour stood open but the furniture was covered with heavy dust covers and the stunning Tiffany lamps nowhere to be seen, presumably boxed up somewhere. Braith stood at the open terrace door staring out into the heavy rain.

'Does this rain make you homesick?'

He turned his head halfway, his eyes still on the pouring rain. 'It does.'

'Are you going away?' She waved her hand at the covered furniture.

He nodded. 'Drink?' Already walking towards the trolley, he didn't look at her when he said, 'I've missed you, where have you been?'

'Actually, nothing for me, thank you. I'm trying to drink a bit less.'

He'd already taken two glasses down from the shelf and picked up a bottle of whiskey. He shrugged and filled both glasses, gulped down the contents of one and carried the other over to the terrace door.

Alia stood awkwardly in the doorway. 'It's sheeting down. Normally I see you at a full moon.'

He shrugged again and stared down into his drink. She walked over to him. She could feel the light spray on her arms, and she shivered, but it was the coolness from Braith that made her feel cold. He turned slowly, as though he too was moving through water, Braith looked up and seemed to see her for the first time.

'Cold?' Once again, pre-empting her response, he took his jacket off and put it around her shoulders, murmuring as he did, 'I wrote to Hemingway. He knows how to write from a place of deep unrest.' He was speaking more to himself than to her. He continued on, enthusing about Hemingway like he was practicing the man's eulogy, mumbling and again slightly manic.

The rain had let up a little, but a breeze lifted the curtains and she shivered again. He bustled her out of the doorway, pulled the doors shut with a bang and flicked the curtains across. He stalked across the room, poured whiskey into both glasses and held one up for Alia. She knew if she declined the offer, he would simply down it in one gulp before starting on his own, so she accepted it. Apparently, he thought drinking like Hemingway might help.

'I'm going to Paris tonight, then on to America again, and then to Cuba, to write, and perhaps to see the great man himself. I am desperate, Thalia. Desperate to make a name for myself.'

She nodded and sipped her drink. He had been so focussed and happy the last time she had seen him, but perhaps she had gone to a previous time in his life. 'Braith, you can't rush brilliance…'

He necked his own whiskey and returned to the bar. 'Do you know the year?'

Alia shook her head.

'It's '56. I have been writing for 10 years and after a dalliance with the best-seller's list I lost my way. A failed writer with an inherited fortune is still a failed writer.'

She wondered where he'd gone wrong, where he had lost his way…

'Sir?' A young man, holding a chauffeur's hat and driving gloves, appeared at the door.

'Oh, you're here…are you here early?' He looked at his watch, frowning. He turned to her. 'I hate travelling in the rain.'

'Beg pardon, sir?' Braith turned back towards the driver and shook his head. 'Has the rain cleared? The car, packed?' He seemed to be barking orders, distracted by the journey ahead.

'The rain is clearing, sir.' The driver gave a small bow.

'Right you are, then,' Braith said. He drained his glass and tucked the whiskey bottle under his arm. 'Time to go.'

'Hiya,' Alia said to the driver to no response. The young man hovered in the doorway waiting for directions. She shrugged and opened the neckline of her kimono, showing the driver her breasts, but he stood solemn, his hat in his hands. He nodded to the man of the house and left them alone. She turned back to Braith who was doubled over with silent laughter.

'Oh, you have cheered me on my way. I was maudlin and now, thanks to my little trickster, I am refreshed.'

'And you got to see my boobs,' she said, taking his jacket off and handing it to him. 'Bon voyage.'

'Turn off the lights on your way out, will you?' he leaned over and kissed her gently on the cheek and shook his head, laughing, as he left.

She flicked the light off and followed him, fumbling with her torch as she went. She pulled the parlour doors shut and saw him disappear around the corner at the opposite end of the corridor to the stairs. What would happen if she walked out the front door and told Braith she wanted to go with him? Did she really want to go back to the 50s?

The answer was a resounding no! As much as she liked Mad Men, she most certainly did not want to go back to the 50s. Was that even how this whole thing worked?

She wandered along the passageway towards the spiral stairs, running her hands along the wall. She loved her life. She had always sucked the marrow out of every moment, but suddenly there was something new in her life. She was a writer. A real writer. She wasn't trying to get likes and follows, she had found an unknown side of herself in this rambling old house on the edge of an industrial estate.

She ran up the stairs, lifting her heavy dress over her knees and kept running to her room, feeling as though she had made some kind of decision, although she wasn't sure exactly what it was.

A sleepover?

Working in the orangery was always eventful and could be distracting if she wasn't careful but as the pieces for the house approached completion Alia struggled to stay focussed. A magnificent chandelier had grown almost overnight, hanging from a gold chain just inches from the floor. The glorious dome for over the stairs was complete but sitting in its wooden framework didn't do it justice. Cam placed lamps beneath it and the two women stood gazing at the delicate glass butterflies and dragonflies, forever frozen, swooping through space. It was a shame. It would be months before it was installed as the new stairs had yet to be built.

With all the other pieces complete and awaiting installation, the large panel for the back office was taking some time. Even though the famous Mrs Grant had assured Camryn the piece wasn't essential and didn't need to be in place in time for the party, she was determined. Alia felt terrible watching her friend pace around the studio. Each night she had gone to bed reminding herself to ask about the panel, but she kept forgetting.

As she watched Cam standing back, scowling at her iPad for inspiration, she had a brilliant idea. 'You should come for a sleep over tonight.'

Camryn looked up at her, a grin on her face. 'Oh…cheeky.'

'Lol, no sorry, not like that. But then, it has been a while…' She winked at Cam. 'Where was I? I think we should see if you can… meet Braith. See the house. See the mural.'

Cam walked slowly towards her. 'Do you think it would be okay?'

'Why not? I mean, he'll be so excited to see two of us!' Alia shrugged. Cam laughed, nodding her head, her eyes scrunched tight.

Alia jumped up and clapped her hands, making the dog bound with excitement. 'Great, we'll have a sleep over in my room, I think. Dress for cocktail hour…You don't have to have any cocktails, just dress for it.'

Camryn sat in a chair, looking relieved. 'You can just knock on my door if you like? Melon snores.' The little dog looked up at the sound of his name.

'Umm, we could try that, but to be honest, I would wonder if you'll be there at all. See… the whole house somehow… transforms…' Alia went over and sat with Cam. 'It goes back to how it was. I've seen it in the '40s and early '50s. I've walked along the terrace, but I'm embarrassed to admit I've never been curious about what exists outside the parlour. I've never asked, although I keep meaning to. I'm distracted by the booze, I guess.'

'And the good-looking man?'

'Yes, but it's not like that. He's intelligent and funny and he reminds me of my dad which is weird, but he…' Alia stared at the tabletop.

'He…?' Camryn prompted.

'He thinks I'm a…' she stopped and laughed. 'Cam, he thinks I'm a muse. He thinks I'm Thalia, *the Thalia*, the muse of comedy.'

Camryn's eyes widened and she grinned. 'You are funny, and you dress goddess-like with all your floaty kimonos, oh and… and…you are about seven feet tall…' the words spluttered out between giggles. 'I mean…sorry, I can see why he would. You're magnificent.'

Alia stuck her tongue out at her friend. 'I've been called worse things…'

Cam nodded her head and the two women sat quietly for a moment. 'Do you think it's…time travel? God, I can't believe I just said that.' Camryn laughed.

'I don't know. I think I told you it's always a full moon… oh, and I found this on my typewriter when I first moved down here.' She ran into the writing nook and flipped through her file. She grabbed the sheet of paper with the poem about the full moon. Camryn had followed and she nearly bumped into Alia on her return. Alia was puffing. She read the poem to Camryn.

'It's about the moon. I know it's him.' Alia looked around at the space. 'He's your ghost,' she said to Watermelon, flapping the page at him.

Camryn sat back down at the table. 'He probably wrote that quote about swearing, remember, when you first got here?'

'Yes,' Alia said, and pounded her fist on the table. She startled the dog and he bolted from the room.

'So, it wasn't Phil after all…' Camryn said softly.

'So, it's settled,' Alia said flopping onto a chair. 'You'll come with me tonight.'

Camryn nodded. 'It's a deal…' she said.

Alia woke with a start as Watermelon jumped up onto the bed. Her new alarm clock was chiming softly. Camryn had fallen asleep in the easy chair and looked peaceful in the bright moonlight. Alia patted Melon on the head and got up to use the bathroom, gently waking Camryn as she walked past.

'Cam look at the moon,' she whispered, pointing at the orb in the sky. 'Let's go.'

A thin crescent had hung in the sky as they sat talking for hours before falling asleep, Alia telling Camryn everything she could remember about Braith, the house and the whole crazy experience. Camryn sat upright and stared at the moon, stretching while Watermelon jumped off the bed and stationed himself at the door, growling. 'Shush now, little man,' Camryn said to the dog as she headed into the bathroom. He lay down, head on his paws.

'It's okay guy, you get to see your big scary ghost tonight.' Alia scratched him behind the ears.

Camryn came out of the bathroom, smoothing her silk dress. 'Is this okay?'

'You look gorgeous. Let's go.'

Camryn grabbed her sketch book and phone, carefully checking it was set to silent. 'Now, Melon you need to be quiet, got it?' she said in a soft voice.

'I swear he just nodded his head,' Alia said.

They made their way along the corridor, Alia using her torch to show the way. Camryn pointed at her own bedroom and they took the bend in the corridor arriving at the landing. The tiles seemed intact underfoot. Alia shone the torch on the floor and nudged Camryn, but she was preoccupied with the view above. The moonlight coming through the domed skylight was something Alia had seen most nights, but Camryn stood transfixed by the sight.

'It's divine,' she said, dropping her sketchbook and taking a dozen quick photos with her phone. 'I might just leave the sketchbook here and take my phone.'

Alia looked around at her. 'I wouldn't leave it there. I left my camera here a few weeks ago and haven't seen it since.'

'What a shame.' Camryn kicked the book to one side. Alia almost laughed at Camryn's tone of voice. Her words said, "what a shame" but her tone said, "don't talk, I'm busy having my mind blown."

Camryn turned in a full circle, taking in the incredible sight of the beautiful landing, tall windows, and spectacular domed skylight over the stairs, almost a perfect match for the one that she had made. Watermelon stood at the top of the stairs sniffing the air. He ran back to Camryn, letting out a little whine, then hid behind her leg.

'Oh, you big sook,' Alia whispered to him. 'You talk a big game barking at nothing, but when it comes to the big league you run and hide behind your mummy.'

Camryn chuckled and waved her hand around at the vision before her. 'This is just spectacular.'

'You ain't seen nothin' lady.'

Alia led the way down the stairs and the two women were halfway down before they saw Watermelon cowering at the railing. 'C'mon boy,' Alia said, slapping her knee gently. Watermelon turned around and dashed back along the corridor towards the bedroom.

'What a wuss,' Camryn said. 'Tally ho.'

They continued down the stairs arriving in the long corridor, the flagstones on the floor glowing warmly in the light.

'He must have had lights installed here. I've never seen these before,' Alia whispered, pointing at the elegant wall sconces, long gone in the present-day house. Camryn snapped away taking shots from every angle. Alia pointed at the parlour doors up ahead and Camryn set off towards them. Braith's favourite old-time music started up and Alia found herself smiling.

'It's him, Cam, he's always playing this song.'

'Billie Holliday. It's…yes, *Easy to Love*, I think. My grandfather loved this song.'

Camryn had stopped a few steps behind her. She was gazing at the design in the etched glass doors, a mixture of vines and flowers with the occasional animal or shepherd. She lifted her phone without taking her eyes off the door and snapped off a dozen photos.

Alia smiled and pointed into the room. 'Ready?'

Camryn nodded and followed.

'Good evening, monsieur,' Alia said as she entered the room. Braith was standing next to the record player. The old gramophone was gone and in its place was an updated model. A section of the bookshelf had been modified to house a collection of records.

'My muse is here, just in time to choose the music.' Braith threw his arms wide and embraced her. She grinned at Camryn. 'And who might this be?' he said, extending his hand to Camryn.

She blushed and held out her own hand. 'I… it's… aah…a pleasure.'

'Braith Robert Evans-Lewis. And you are?'

'Braith Robert Evans-Lewis?' Camryn said, gripping his hand.

Braith looked at Alia and back at Camryn. 'We have the same name.' He laughed and gently lifted her hand to kiss the air just above it.

'Oh God, lol… Camryn Brentwood.' Camryn's cheeks flamed and her free hand fluttered up to play with the bow on the front of her dress.

'Camryn. You're Welsh?'

'I am.' Camryn was staring at him.

'Which one are you?' He was still holding her hand.

'I'm not. I'm an artist, a glass artist. Ali…ah, Thalia is helping me, too.'

'A glass artist. I adore glass, I have Tiffany pieces, Lalique, mostly European. I prefer Art Nouveau. Would you like to see my collection?'

Camryn was smiling at Braith, nodding her head. Alia could see her hands were shaking.

'But first a drink?' He looked over at Alia.

'I'm okay for now. Let's look at glass.' She smiled at Camryn.

Braith took the needle off the record and put his cigar in a small marble dish on the shelf. They followed him back through the parlour doors and along the corridor, Camryn gripping Alia's hand. Braith opened an ornate set of double doors and they were in an elegant dining room. An enormous crystal chandelier dominated the room. Braith flicked the black Bakelite switch on the wall and the chandelier began to slowly light up. 'I've just had it wired,' he said.

They all stood looking up as the room began to glow.

'Remarkable,' Camryn whispered.

'Cam, this is the dining room.'

Camryn looked around, her forehead creasing and smoothing as though she was trying to understand what Alia had said. Suddenly her mouth formed an 'O' and she drew a sharp breath.

'Oh my god, the dining room. Such a shame…' It was the space they sat in daily to eat their meals. The enormous table was still in place, but the rest of the room was very different. Twelve matching chairs surrounded the highly polished table and a pair of ancient looking sideboards stood where the cheap Ikea one stood during the day. Camryn ran her hand over one of the richly upholstered chairs and smiled at Alia. Only two of the chairs still sat at the table, a little tattered and faded but she and Watermelon used them every day. And of course, the magnificent chandelier was long gone.

An array of glass objets d'art stood along the tops of the sideboards, gleaming in the light from the chandelier. The walls were bare as ever but squares and rectangles of darker paint told the story of missing artwork. The secret door leading to the cave corridor was no secret. A heavy timber door with iron hinges stood in its place.

Camryn walked slowly in front of the glass pieces. 'I have seen examples of many of these before but to see them grouped this way is marvellous. So much better than in a museum, and this chandelier. Is it Italian?'

'It came from Rome, yes. You have a great eye. I am told the table was built right here two hundred years ago. I have had a restorer from Paris to polish it and the chairs have been remade according to a style seen elsewhere in France. According to the former owner, the walls here were stripped bare by the Nazi's. He and I have managed to trace many of the pieces that were stolen, but some remain lost.' He looked sadly at the walls. 'Through here, ladies.'

Braith turned right towards the door to the present-day kitchen. Instead of the vast commercial-style kitchen, the space was divided by a corridor with an old-style scullery on one side and a pantry on the other with plain glass and timber doors separating them. They reached another door and realised they were back on the flag-stone walkway. If they turned right, they would have eventually found themselves back at the spiral stairs.

'I have saved the best for last,' Braith said as he opened another set of double timber doors. He left them standing in the dark. They could hear his footsteps crossing the room. A clicking sound on the opposite side of the room was followed by a small light glowing on the ceiling. As Braith returned to them the light became brighter until the space revealed a huge indoor swimming pool. But what lay between them and the pool beyond was the star attraction. A glass mural of two peacocks stood in the middle of the room, flanked on either side by glass doors etched in the same manner as the parlour doors. A true Art Nouveau treasure.

'Oh Cam, now you know,' Alia whispered. 'I'll distract him, you get some photos.'

Camryn's hand went to her bra where she had hidden her phone. Alia had suggested earlier that they shouldn't show Braith the smart phone or things could get very weird.

'Braith, show me the swimming pool and tell me about your current work.' Alia looked back and winked at Camryn as she and Braith walked arm in arm into the huge conservatory. She was thirsty but she didn't want to leave Camryn alone. The thought that her friend might be lost in the past horrified her, so she kept an eye on Camryn as she snapped her photos.

Braith had news. His third manuscript had been released to great acclaim and his second novel had won prize after prize.

'I believe it was the uplifting nature of the story that captured the imagination of the public and the judges. Who else has written such a story? Not your friend Phillip I am sure.' He was grinning at her.

'You, sir, look like the cat that got the cream,' Alia teased.

'I am my dear, and I have you to thank. I am preparing a great tribute to you; I will show you next time.'

'Tomorrow night?'

'Yes of course, Tomorrow night and one year when I shall no doubt see you again.' He feigned a huge sigh and looked at her with puppy dog eyes. 'Is your friend finished? I could do with a drink.' He nodded at Cam who had entered the pool conservatory and was staring at the reverse side of the peacock mural.

'Ready to go, Cam?'

'No…'

Alia went to her friend's side. Camryn took her hand and hugged it to her chest.

'Thank you,' she said.

'You are welcome. Now come with me because I don't want to leave you here in the past or whatever it is.' She turned, dragging a reluctant Camryn behind her.

'Have you captured enough information with your little spy camera?' Braith asked as he flicked the lights off, plunging the room into darkness. Camryn let out a yelp and clung to Alia's arm.

'Ah, yes. Thanks.'

Braith chuckled in the dark and a door opened through which they could see the parlour. They both took off at a trot, tumbling into the parlour like puppies.

'Do you mind if I have a drink?' Alia said quietly to Camryn as Braith made his way to the bar area, now a fully kitted out space.

'I have whiskey or bourbon and no ice.' He didn't sound hopeful but was already taking glasses down from the rack. 'I'm leaving again. Thalia, you always come to me on the cusp of something monumental in my life.' He poured the amber liquid into the glasses.

'I'll take a glass of water, please,' Camryn said.

Braith stopped briefly, looking from Camryn to Alia.

'Oh, whiskey for me,' Alia said, winking at Camryn. 'It doesn't count if you dream it?'

Braith topped up one of the glasses with a dash of water from the little silver tap behind the bar. After handing it to Alia, he lifted one of the other glasses and saluted Camryn with it before swallowing the whiskey in one gulp, then rinsed and refilled the glass with water.

'I could handle a cigarette if you have one?' Camryn said.

Braith immediately produced his elegant gold case and held it out for the two women.

'And what is this monumental change you have coming?'

Braith picked up his glass, which he'd refilled twice. Alia watched Camryn as she watched him.

'I am moving to New York. Just for the winter. I could never live anywhere but here. My agent asked me to choose between New York and London.' He took another sip and looked at the two women.

'You say that as though London would never be an option for you. What's wrong with London?'

Medusa herself would have been proud of the glare Camryn directed at Alia. 'What?' Alia said, returning what she hoped was a glare of equal force.

'I would never live in England,' Braith said, softly. He went back to the bar and refilled his glass.

Camryn sipped her water and then said something Alia didn't quite catch. Braith raised his glass to her again and Cam raised hers. Alia looked into her glass.

'I will be leaving in the wee hours of the morning. Will you visit me abroad?' He refilled his glass again. Either he was nervous about the trip or he had really stepped up his drinking in the months since she had seen him. Or had it been years? The silver streaks in his hair suggested years.

'Who knows how this thing works?' Alia said finishing her drink.

Braith took the glasses from them. 'As much as I have missed your company, I must get some sleep. The driver will be here at an ungodly hour.' He turned to Camryn. 'You should come to New York with me, I would enjoy showing you the sights.'

Camryn blushed and looked over at Alia. 'As lovely as that sounds, I'm due in Venice for the biennale in about,' she looked at the quirky aqua-coloured watch on her arm, '60 years…'

Braith laughed and clasped her hands in his. 'This is a most remarkable thing. Shall I see you again?'

Camryn smiled and nodded. 'Who knows what life will bring?'

He drew her into an embrace. Camryn put her arms around him and had tears in her eyes when he released her.

'*Hwyl fawr,*' he said.

'*Hwyl fawr,*' she replied, wiping the tears from her cheeks.

'And my muse, Thalia. Shall I behold your spectacular beauty again?'

'Oh wow,' Camryn said. 'And I was feeling all special.'

The trio laughed as Braith released Alia from an embrace and took both their hands. 'You have both given me the most incredible gifts. If I survive six months in New York City,' he looked at Alia and she nodded to reassure him that he would survive. 'Then I will think of a way to repay you.'

'Just keep writing,' Camryn and Alia said at the same time.

Braith clasped his hands and smiled. 'I will see you in six months?' he took Alia's hand.

She leaned across and touched his cheek. 'I'll see you tomorrow night.'

Camryn and Alia left the room and walked slowly along the flagstone hall. As they went, one by one the sconces on the wall behind them went out. 'Let's go,' Alia said in a harsh whisper and dragged Camryn up the stairs. They made it to the top and Alia turned to look back down to the lower floor.

'Why would you make me run up a flight of stairs. Are you the muse of Personal Trainers now?'

'I saw the lights going out and I thought the stairs were going to disappear? It's happened before.' She lifted the hem of her dress and turned the torch on her legs to show Cam where the old scrapes had healed. The two women linked arms and walked back along the hall.

'What did you say to Braith?' Alia whispered.

'*Cymru am byth*, it means Wales Forever. And when we left, *Hwyl fawr*. It's how we say goodbye, but also something like *all the best.*'

They reached Alia's bedroom where Watermelon sat waiting.

'You are the worst guard dog. I was almost tempted away to New York.' Camryn scratched her little dog's head.

Alia shut the door behind them and crawled onto the bed. Camryn sat next to her while Watermelon curled up on the easy chair.

'I think I know who he is.' Camryn put her hands on her cheeks and forehead as if feeling for a fever. 'It makes sense. He used a nom de plume and no one knew who he really was. Phillip said this house was an artist's colony at some stage. He must have stayed here, written here. Every Welsh high school student reads the poems of B.R.E.L.'

'Oh goddess, the poem I read you today, about the moon. It was signed B.R.E.L. It must be his typewriter. No wonder Watermelon barks his fool head off every morning when we open the studio. But I'm not sure. Braith has never mentioned poetry, just novels. Did B.R.E.L. write novels, too?'

'If he did, I've never read them. He was a mystery, like the Banksy of poetry before Banksy existed.'

They sat quietly for a few moments. 'Camryn, I think we've totally ignored the fact we had a drink with a ghost tonight, that I've been visiting a ghost every night for the past few weeks.'

Camryn took Alia's hand. 'That's just the thing. Because no one knew who he was, I didn't know he had died. He was reclusive and I guess he would be really old, so it makes sense. I feel like a bad Welsh person for not knowing he had passed.' Alia heard Camryn sigh in the darkness.

Alia squeezed her friend's hand. Watermelon jumped onto the bed and curled up next to Camryn. The two women lay looking up at the faint outlines of rosebuds on the ceiling until they fell asleep.

Camryn's phone

'Alia…. Alia…'

She rolled over just in time for Watermelon to jump onto the side of the bed and lick her cheek. Alia groaned and covered her face. 'Why?' she mumbled through her fingers.

'Hen, I can't find my phone. It's probably in the bed.'

Alia crawled out of the bed and curled up on the floor. 'It's all yours.' Eyes open a fraction, she watched as an increasingly frantic Camryn pulled the bed apart.

'I've been up and down the corridor. The stairs are…' She mimed an implosion, a collapse. I can't find my phone. You don't think it's…'

'Back in the 50s?'

'Oh God,' Camryn groaned, burying her face in her hands. When she lifted her head, she was laughing.

'Oh, that's a relief, I thought you were crying.'

'No use crying over spilt milk. I should have used the sketch book.' She held up the unused book.

Alia sat up, shielding her eyes from the morning sun. 'Phillip said things go missing all the time. They must kind of slip through. It's probably with my camera.'

Camryn glanced about the room, frowning. 'I'll have to rely on my memory. I'll see you at breakfast. I have to go and get some sketches down or I'll forget everything.'

Alia lay back down on the floor and grunted something she hoped Cam would take for agreement.

Alia ate breakfast alone after Camryn grabbed a plate to go and bolted for the studio with Watermelon leading the charge. Phillip was nowhere to be seen. After the night with Cam and Braith, Alia felt a little let down. She drank her coffee slowly, wishing the day away so she could see Braith again. It wasn't as though she wanted to shag him, she just enjoyed his company. It was a complicated situation and Alia didn't usually like complicated. Alia liked easy. She liked silly boys with floppy hair and neck tattoos. She liked cute bikinis and cocktails. She preferred her relationships to be like shooting stars. Burn bright then fizzle out, never to be seen again. Braith was none of these things and yet she wanted to spend time with him.

She refilled her coffee and wandered slowly down to the studio. Cam was hunched over huge sheets of paper, mumbling to herself like a mad scientist.

'It's good. I stared at them enough and it's all here. I got it…' Camryn said more to herself than to Alia.

Alia muttered some encouraging sounds and headed into the nook. Watermelon was sitting on her chair. 'Hey buddy. What's your deal?'

'He's been there all morning. Barked his silly head off at the ceiling and bolted in there.' He jumped down as Alia approached and ran to Cam as she strolled over.

'I thought so…' Alia wound the barrel of the typewriter up. 'It's him. It has to be.' She pulled the sheet of paper out and handed it to Cam.

'He's critiqued your work. Oh….' Camryn read through the page of suggestions. 'You know in terms of calibre of writers you've got line notes here from the Welsh equivalent of Eliot or Bertrand Russell or Lessing.'

Alia took the sheet back. 'There's more. He's gone through my whole manuscript.' Alia flicked through the sheets. 'I mean he's not exactly in my demographic, but I like what I see here. I can work with this.'

'Is my phone in there?' Cam said.

Alia looked around and shook her head. 'No, and my sculpture is gone now, the cheeky sod.'

Camryn let out a sigh. 'My head is spinning.' She went back to her work area and sat at the table with Melon at her side.

'Do you think it's cheating?' Alia held the sheets of paper to her chest.

'Of course not. If I could get him to come here right now and remind me which way the peacocks were facing, I'd dance a jig.'

'Want to come again tonight?'

Camryn nodded and smiled.

Camryn and Alia both managed to work through lunch, and looked up, surprised to see Phillip standing in the studio, hands on hips.

'I have a surprise for you two, but you didn't come up for lunch. Cam I've been phoning you all day. Have you lost your phone?'

Camryn laughed. 'Aah, yes.'

'It's not lost, it's in 1959. Did you bring food?' Alia called from the writing nook.

Phillip looked down at his hands as though he was surprised to see they were empty. 'Er, no. I didn't think of that. Um, what's she talking about?'

'I think our ghostly friend has purloined my phone.'

'Interesting. Can we talk about this in the car? I'll ask Benny to make you a snack for the road.'

'Where? We have work to do you know,' Alia called.

'Are you going to make me tell you? Come on, it's a surprise.' He sounded genuinely disappointed.

She came out of her nook and felt a little jolt at the sight of him. 'You don't look terrible...' He wore blue pants and a white shirt with elegant tan shoes and was freshly shaven.

'Um...thanks?' He laughed. 'So, are you going to let me surprise you?'

The two women looked at each other.

'Seriously?' He was smiling but he sounded a little annoyed.

Alia and Camryn started talking at once. 'It's just that we were working, and…we had plans.'

'What plans? Are you telling me you don't want to go and stay in a fancy hotel for the night?'

The two women looked at each other and began tidying up their workspaces. Alia stashed the marked-up pages in a document box, placing the new work in the binder should her ghostly mentor decide to show up again.

I'll see you tomorrow night.

If she slept somewhere else, she wouldn't see Braith. But then the idea of a night away was tantalising. Shaking off a tinge of guilt, she recruited Phillip to pull the windows shut and was panting by the time they'd finished. 'Phillip, is this okay? I mean, will it violate my agreement?'

He shook his head. 'It's all been arranged.'

Camryn waited for them, with Watermelon in her arms.

'Pack for overnight. Do either of you want to know where we're going?'

The two women looked at each other and shook their heads. 'I don't mind as long as Melon can come too,' Cam said.

Phillip nodded and scratched the dog's ears.

'Out is good enough for me,' Alia said and gave a little squeal of excitement. 'Give me ten minutes for a quick shower.'

'I'm going to need a little more than ten,' Camryn said as they locked the studio door and dashed off towards the house.

Paris

Alia was waiting by the car when the others emerged from the house. When she'd unpacked the vintage Elsa Schiaparelli dress, she'd wondered why Regina had thought to put it in but, as always, she'd been right on the money. Alia completed the look with her standard over the top eyes and little other makeup and pulled on the black patent pumps Mrs P had packed. Camryn was gorgeous in a body-hugging snake-print dress and Phillip was carrying his jacket over one shoulder. Benito made up the foursome and looked dashing in a black suit and shirt, a pinstriped waistcoat for extra quirk. The trio stared at her.

'How did you manage this,' Camryn swept her arm up and down, 'in the what? Twenty minutes since I left you? And you've had time to pack an overnight bag.'

'Too much?' Alia said. She struck a pose.

'Always,' she replied, smiling, and reaching out to touch the hand-finished lily pattern running across the bodice. 'Exquisite. You are beautiful, as always. And tall. Beautiful and tall.'

'You are beautiful, too,' Benito said from the other side of the car.

Camryn blushed and grinned at Alia and climbed into the back of the car.

'You've gone the full Statham tonight, I see,' Alia said to Phillip as he opened the passenger side door for her. Benito was in the back with Camryn, Watermelon strapped into the seatbelt between them. Camryn leaned forward and ran her hand over the leather seat. 'There's something hard stuck here, where the backrest meets the seat.' The others watched as she freed a pair of oversized black sunglasses from their hiding place.

Alia squealed and held her hand out for them. 'I was wondering where they'd got to,' she said. One of the arms was missing but she put them on. Phillip made sure her dress was inside the door and smiled at her as he walked around the car to the driver's side.

'Driver…' Alia said, staring straight ahead, the broken sunglasses sitting crooked on her face.

He started the car. 'Yes?'

'Can we stop at the offy for a couple for the road?'

Phillip rolled his eyes and Camryn snorted in the back seat as the car rolled slowly down the gravel drive.

The first three hours in the car seemed to fly by, even with a couple of rest-stops for the dog. To the obvious relief of all her fellow passengers, before Alia could announce the beginning of the 41st round of I Spy, the exit for Versailles came into view.

'Are we going to Versailles?' Camryn piped up from the back seat.

'No,' Phillip said, smiling in the rear-view mirror.

'Where are we going?' Camryn said.

'I was wondering when one of you would ask,' Phillip said but drove on in silence.

'Right you are,' Alia said. 'I'm not going to lie; I really don't care where we're going. It's nice to be out of the house for a while. I feel like a '50s housewife.'

'So, you really don't care where we're going?'

Alia shook her head.

'Benny, can you whisper in Camryn's ear and tell her where we're headed. Alia doesn't want to know apparently.'

There was a hush in the car, and she could just hear Benito mumbling something to Camryn. The sound Camryn made suggested they were headed somewhere good enough to make a normally sensible woman squeal like a schoolgirl.

Alia watched the traffic and the urban sprawl build as they drew closer to Paris. She had never spent time on a car ride watching the world go by. If she were conscious, her head would be down, staring at her phone.

She was vaguely aware of the conversation in the car as they talked about current events. Phillip turned left and crossed the Seine. She smiled to herself as the Eiffel Tower slipped by on the other side of the river, unnoticed by the other occupants of the car, busy as they were discussing Phillip's thesis defence. It was scheduled for the Monday after the big party, in less than a weeks' time. He didn't want to reschedule but he didn't want to miss the party.

He looked over and smiled at Alia. 'At least you're awake for this arrival,' he said as he pulled the car into traffic on the Place d'étoile. Had it only been less than a month since her arrival at the château? She smoothed her stunning vintage dress. It was hard to believe she had been arrested just weeks before for public indecency.

'I am much better dressed, too.'

He glanced down at her dress and smiled as he pulled the car up beside a boutique hotel and put the hazard lights on. 'Here we are. Jump out, I'll park the car. Just follow Benito,' he said to Alia. Benito and Camryn were already climbing out.

She threw her tote over her arm and followed Camryn and Watermelon, who were following Benito, who was grinning like a lottery winner.

L'Ecrivain

Benito had handed a key to Camryn and held one out to Phillip as he walked through the door.

'We are sharing. Hope that's okay? The ladies are in one of the front rooms. Put your things in the room and meet here in five minutes.'

They headed to the lift. Phillip was smiling at her, but his eyebrows suggested he was confused about something.

'Are you okay? Your forehead looks as though it wants to say something.'

'Do you truly not want to know where we're going?'

'Are we not already here? This is pretty good.' He stood back and let her into the lift.

'Yes…and no. Whitehall owns this hotel. It's called L'Ecrivain, *The Writer*. We're having an early dinner meeting with Mrs Grant. You remember her? She's here on business and wanted to meet you.'

Alia pulled her shoulders back. 'Oh dear… I will need a stiff drink before any such meeting can take place. I'll be in the mini-bar if anyone wants me.'

'You'll be fine. I'm meeting her for the first time too,' Camryn said.

'She will love you,' Benito said, looking at Camryn.

Alia and Phillip exchanged a glance. Oblivious to their raised eyebrows, Camryn handed a brochure to Alia. 'Check out those spiral stairs. They look familiar.' The last words were a whisper. Alia's eyes widened as she took the brochure. The lift door opened, and they filed out into a plush hallway, dark navy-blue doors with gold numbers lined the ochre-coloured walls.

'Five minutes. In the foyer,' Benito called over his shoulder as he and Phillip unlocked their door.

'Benito's excited,' Alia said.

Camryn drew in a breath. 'It's incredible. The restaurant opens to the public next week and they're using his menu here at the hotel. It's a big deal.'

'Why doesn't anyone tell me anything?' Alia whined. 'Jokes…' She grinned at her friend. 'That is exciting.'

Camryn unlocked the door and Watermelon raced into the bathroom. Alia cocked an eyebrow and pointed at the dog. 'Cam. Does he…'

Camryn shook her head. 'No, he doesn't use the bathroom. He's just investigating. I'll take him out for a wee-walk around the block.' She pulled out his leash. He bolted to her side at the sound of its jingling. 'Do you think it's a coincidence? The stairs? Oh, by the way, dibs on the window.' She put her bag down next to the bed.

The view from the window captivated the two women for a moment, the right-hand leg of the Arc de Triomphe dominated the view. The room had a generous desk complete with a lamp, power outlets, and a large notebook and pen, embellished with the elegant hotel logo. 'Ah, Alia…look.' Camryn was pointing at the wall where a group of tastefully framed black and white photos hung. Braith Evans-Lewis hung there along with an artistic grouping of other famous writers. 'It can't be a coincidence.'

They stood staring at the younger face of the man they had spoken to only the night before. There was a knock on the door. The two women grabbed each other's arms in fright and laughing went to the door. Benito clapped his hands like an excited little boy and pressed the lift button. 'Let's go eat, ladies.'

'And that's why commas are important,' Alia said, winking at him.

Benito turned to look at Phillip. He laughed and said, 'I'll explain it later.'

Alia nudged him. 'You may need Cam to draw some diagrams.'

The lift door slid open. 'We're going to take the stairs, Melon needs the exercise,' Camryn said. The men were already in the small lift.

'Don't be late, we have an appointment,' Benito said, showing the women his watch.

The door of the lift closed on Benito's concerned face. They followed the richly patterned carpet runner to the end of the corridor where it met a landing. High above, a dome of silver-grey glass allowed an almost incandescent light to flood the dramatic spiral stairs below. Camryn took Alia's arm as they descended, taking on the filtered glow of the Paris sky. They were giggling by the time they reached the first floor but stopped laughing as Phillip bounded up the stairs to meet them.

'Mrs Grant is running late, but she'll be here in a moment.'

Cam let Alia's arm drop and hurried down the stairs and out the door, Melon running along beside.

'What is it with this woman that's got you all aflutter?' Alia said following as quickly as she could in her patent leather spike heels.

Phillip shrugged and held out his elbow for her. 'She's the boss.'

Alia matched his shrug and took his arm. A little buzz of static electricity passed between them and they both looked up and blushed in unison. 'Oh lol…' Alia said and instantly regretted it. 'Isn't it amazing,' she said, 'how I will say literally anything rather than say nothing. It's a talent, I think. My true talent.'

'I'm sure there are plenty of things you're good at,' he said, the blush deepening. 'I didn't mean anything, I just meant things like writing and…'

'Oh no, it's catching,' she teased and squeezed his arm.

In the foyer, an elegant woman in a blush pantsuit, matching coat draped over her arm, and gold-rimmed sunglasses, seemed to glide into the room on rollers. She smiled up at them.

'That's her,' Phillip whispered.

'She's not that scary,' Alia said more to herself than anyone else.

Phillip rushed forward to take her coat, air-kissing the cheeks offered. The famous Mrs Grant might dress like a Parisian, but she had a New York accent and an Ibiza tan. Benito went in, greeting and kissing.

Alia wasn't used to feeling socially awkward. She stood to one side waiting for the right moment to introduce herself. She didn't have to.

'And this must be our little trouble-maker?' Mrs Grant extended her hand for Alia to shake. 'But you're not so little, are you? How tall are you? Six? Six one?' She was body scanning Alia like a TSA agent. 'Oh, you are like Regina, aren't you? Younger though… You were right, though, Hobbs. You are gorgeous, aren't you? That dress…divine… Vintage?' She stood back for a better view.

Hobbs? Phillip's cheeks were pink again.

'It's lovely to meet you finally. I've heard nothing at all about you.' Alia hoped her comment hadn't been received as snarkily as it had sounded in her head.

She was worried for nothing. Mrs Grant didn't appear to register anything that was said to her. It was as though she was two steps ahead of everyone else. Camryn and Watermelon joined them. Benito made the introductions.

'Good, good. Let's eat?' Mrs Grant said, and turned to Phillip. 'Ah, Hobbs, I need to be at *Gare de l'Est* at twenty-one hundred. This place came up a treat.' She stood in front of Benito and smiled. 'Lead the way, maestro.'

Benito cleared his throat and guided them to a line of staff waiting at a double door upholstered in silver leather, black studs making subtle diamonds.

'Bievenue a L'Ecrivain,' he said. The small group clapped and smiled. Benito introduced Mrs Grant as she shook hands with each member of the kitchen staff.

Hobbs…Phillip Hobbs thinks I'm gorgeous, eh?

Alia fell in beside Camryn. 'Who does she think she is? Aunty Liz?' Camryn's eyebrows did the thing they always did when Alia said something she didn't understand. 'Q.E Two,' Alia whispered.

'Aah, oh I see' she nodded. '…yes, you're a Lady with a capital L, I keep forgetting that. No, really, she's a bit of a powerhouse but you have to be, don't you? To do what she does. I'm hoping she will mentor me, for the business side of things. She helped with the submission to the

Biennale and she's been good to you, remember?' Cam whispered the last words as they took their seat in the empty restaurant.

Camryn seemed nervous. Did she think Alia would make a scene? She smiled at her friend in what she hoped was a reassuring manner. The company she hadn't even known existed a few weeks before had indeed been good to her. It also appeared to know intimately every aspect of her life and had controlled most of it.

The restaurant décor was in keeping with the rest of the hotel, understated luxury with a hint of eccentricity, a writerly theme but understated. Antique mirrors lined the walls making the intimate space appear to go on forever. Luxurious, yet simple furnishings filled the room. Overhead, chandeliers made from pages of books cast a muted golden light over the space. Benito disappeared into the kitchen while a waiter filled their glasses with sparkling water.

'Got anything harder than that?' Alia said, grinning at the waiter.

Mrs Grant skewered her with her blue eyes for three long seconds. When the eyes flicked away finally to the waiter, she smiled, talking to Alia even though she wasn't looking at her. 'What's your tipple, pet? I heard you like a drink. You don't mind, do you?' She turned her head, directing the question at Phillip and Camryn, her hand closing over Phillip's.

Things were getting weird. 'An Aperol Spritz, thanks?' Alia smiled up at the waiter.

Mrs Grant put her finger in the air. 'One here, too, Paul. Lovely.' She smiled at Alia. 'How are you finding things at the château?' That piercing gaze again. She could not get a read on the woman.

'It's wonderful. Cam and Phillip are wonderful. The food's...wonderful...'

'They said you had a way with words.' Mrs Grant chuckled to herself. 'Did any of you hear about the meeting with Alia? The first one. I wasn't there but it's legendary at Whitehall. You remember?' She fixed Alia with that gaze. 'She's offered this deal, six books. It's unheard of in the current climate. Three books for young girls aged 8-11 and three for 13-16.' She looked at the others to see if they understood the rarity of the situation. Alia was getting nervous. She had a vague memory of the meeting, but it was entirely possible she had been there in body only.

Mrs Grant continued. 'So, Alia interrupts this meeting of about twenty people in suits… she was apparently wearing a long dress with no shoes, and… Alia you tell it. Tell them what you said.'

Alia froze and stared at the floor. She felt Cam's hand on hers under the table. She couldn't recall saying anything at all.

'Tell us, Pamela,' Phillip said, smiling at Alia from across the table.

Without missing a beat, Pamela leaned forward. 'She gets up in front of all these suits and says, "What about the twelve-year-olds?" Confused the shit out of everyone but she was one hundred percent right.'

Cam laughed and squeezed her hand again. Mrs Grant seemed to think the anecdote was the funniest thing she had heard for a while. Alia was still trying to work out if Mrs Grant loved her or loathed her.

'If you think that's funny, you should see one of her shows. Brilliant!' Cam said.

Pamela took a sip of water. 'So, I hear. Has she met Himself yet? Robert?'

No one spoke. 'Hobbs?' Mrs Grant prompted.

Phillip jumped in his seat. 'Ah, no. Umm, things have been busy. Alia's writing and he's not been well, as you know, and with the party and the big birthday, everyone just wants him to be well.'

'How's your thesis proceeding?'

'Complete, sent. I defend in a week. Then start my new post in September.'

'Congratulations,' she said, a little warmth seeping into her voice for the first time. Paul returned with their drinks and Mrs Grant sipped hers. 'Another, when you can, Paul.' Mrs Grant's eyes met Alia's with a smile over the edge of her glass. 'It's been a long day. I had a breakfast meeting in LA and here I am. Then breakfast in Cologne tomorrow. I am looking forward to coming down to see you all.'

Camryn didn't react to the news of Phillip's new job so she must have known about it. Alia wondered if someone had told her. She had been trying to be a better listener. The waiter brought another drink for Mrs

Grant as Benito brought platters from the kitchen, placing them on the table with a flourish. He sat and rubbed his hands together.

'Bon Appetit, my friends. Enjoy,' he said, using a set of small tongs to lift morsels onto Camryn's plate. 'You must try one of everything, so I have made the portions very small. Everything is the best, just eat.' He placed three or four pieces on Mrs Grant's plate.

Phillip handed a small set of tongs to Alia and chose pieces for himself. The diners were silent for a long time, each lost in their own thoughts and by the sounds coming from each one, enjoying the food.

'Benny, it's incredible,' Phillip said.

'It's wonderful,' Alia chimed in, winking at Mrs Grant, who laughed.

Mrs Grant tapped her glass lightly. 'The next surprise for the evening involves the incredibly talented Ms Camryn Brentwood.'

The news was a surprise for Cam judging by the expression on her face. She looked up and smiled at Mrs Grant. 'Did I…?

'Yes, Cam. You have been nominated for the Hepworth Prize.'

Cam's hands went to her face and she made a little squealing sound. 'Fuck, yes, I did.'

The group laughed. 'Is that your acceptance speech?' Alia asked.

Cam nodded and pumped her fist. 'I have been working my bum off for nearly twenty years and finally it's all coming together.'

The rest of the meal was exquisite, and Alia and Mrs Grant bonded over vodka martinis before Phillip, *Hobbs*, declared it was time to go to the train station. Mrs Grant, Pamela, kissed their cheeks and promised to see them at the party.

The morning after...

Alia rolled over in the plush bed and eyes squeezed closed, stumbled to the bathroom. Camryn was still snoring softly, the covers pulled over her head.

She didn't have her watch but the light pouring into the north facing windows suggested it was around midday. She jumped into the shower and let the warm water run over her body. The night before had been... *surprising* was the word she settled on. After the formidable Mrs Grant had disappeared into the first-class lounge at the Gare de l'Est, they had toured the city, Phillip at the wheel. He knew Paris well, another surprise for Alia. She had asked how he knew his way around so well and he'd said cryptically, *it's my job to know the fastest route,* earning him anew the title *Transporter*.

The city had been merely a backdrop to their tour, the fun was all in the company. She couldn't remember the last time she'd had that much fun or that little alcohol. By the time they'd arrived back at the hotel, Camryn and Benito were deep in conversation, Watermelon asleep on Alia's lap. She noted Camryn's hand clasped in Benito's as the sky began to lighten. After arriving back at the hotel, they had quietly walked up the spiral stairs as Phillip explained his new position, but he hadn't told them the name of the school.

'Jason Statham can play him in his biopic...' she giggled to herself. She flicked the hot water off and stood in the jet of cold. Imagining Jason Statham as a decorated, returned soldier was easy, but a teacher at a posh public school?

She shut off the water and grabbed a towel, winding it around her hair. 'Cam,' she called in a soft sing-song voice. She grabbed another towel and wrapped it around her wet body. 'Cam, what's the time?' She sat on the edge of the bed and gently nudged her roommate. 'Where's Melon?'

A grunt came from under the covers. Alia whipped her hand back. 'Cam?'

'Nope.'

She was on her feet, gripping her towel. The top of Phillip's head appeared as he pulled the covers down. His eyes met hers. 'Cam's…ah, in my room.'

Alia dived into her bed and pulled the sheet up to her chin. There was something about Phillip that made her nervous and it wasn't that he would be inappropriate. She wished he would. That would make things less confusing.

'In your room? Why? Oh….' she said and threw herself back, laughing at the ceiling. 'Cam, you sly dog.'

Phillip was laughing too.

'So…breakfast? I'm starving,' she said as she took her overnight bag into the bathroom. 'I'll be out in a minute and you can have the room.' She slid the door shut and threw on white jeans and a black tank top that somehow felt too revealing with Phillip in the next room. 'I'm coming out now,' she called although she didn't know why.

Phillip was sitting up on the bed, the sun shining on his muscular back. 'Great view. Our room faces the other direction. Nothing much to look at.'

'Cam put dibs on that bed for the view, so I hope she's enjoying herself…' she laughed and rolled her dress from the night before and stashed it in her bag. She picked up her shoes, her hands were shaking. *I must be really hungry…* She looked around the room checking to see if she had forgotten anything. 'I'll see you downstairs?'

Phillip nodded.

Alia's eyes settled on the framed photos on the wall. 'Phil, is that Braith… Evans-Lewis?'

Phillip looked up and nodded. 'It is. He was a great writer, a great man and a good-looking man. He looks a lot different now. Time can be cruel.'

Alia spun on her heel to face him. 'What do you mean? I thought he was dead?' Her voice was louder than she'd intended.

Phillip's forehead creased. 'Er, no. I told you. He lives in the château. He donated the house to the philanthropic arm of Whitehall, his daughter's company. The man himself was a bit of an enigma. I have very little information on his early life. It was as though he appeared from nowhere, became a war hero, then began writing literary masterpieces. I gave you his Nobel-prize winning novel. He went by Robert. Robert Evans. Had to change his name for the American audiences. Braith was too foreign, apparently.'

Alia's mouth was opening and closing but no sound was coming out.

'Mrs Grant. Pamela. She's his daughter. He's the subject of my thesis. Hey, are you okay?'

Alia sat on the edge of her bed.

How can he still be alive and a ghost?

She had to talk to Camryn. 'Phil, I'll see you downstairs. I... really need to eat. I'm feeling a little lightheaded.'

She was puffing by the time she reached the foyer. She'd taken the stairs, half expecting them to have disappeared with the sunlight. Cam and Benito were sitting with the staff in the restaurant and called her over. Alia took a seat next to Cam, nudging her gently under the table. Cam grinned and squeezed Alia's hand. A selection of breakfast items appeared on the tablecloth like magic as Alia was staring at Camryn. For her part, Cam seemed to be avoiding eye contact with her, preferring to hang on every word the restaurant staff said.

Phillip joined the group for a quick bite before retrieving the car. Benito said his goodbyes to the staff, giving them last minute directions. They would be catering the party at the château, the party for Braith. Alia tugged Camryn towards the elegant ladies' room in the foyer as one of the staff returned Watermelon after his walk.

199

'She's his daughter,' Alia said too loudly as the heavy door shut behind them.

'Who?' Cam looked worried. 'Benito?

'What? No, Mrs Grant. Get Benito off your mind, you saucy minx.' She gently punched a blushing Camryn on the arm. 'Oh, my hairy goddess, you guys are so cute together.'

'I know, right? I've been playing it cool because, Phil said something early on that you and Benny…partied one night…'

Alia laughed and leaned on the marble sink. 'That was Braith. I'd met him that first time and I was confused. I tried to ask Phil about the man in the house…any way, we're off topic.' She took a deep breath. 'Mrs Grant is his daughter. Braith's. B.R.E.L. He's the old writer who lives in the house. Mr Evans. He's not a ghost.'

Camryn stared at her. 'How?'

'I have no fucking idea. It's hurting my brain.'

Camryn nodded. 'If I hadn't seen it with my own eyes, I would have thought you were nuts. Maybe there's a gas leak in your bedroom. Co2 or something. Makes you hallucinate.' The two women grinned at each other.

'Cam? How was it?'

Camryn squeezed her eyes shut. 'Alia…it's amazing. I'm walking on air. He told me he *knew* the minute he saw me.'

'*Knew* what?'

Cam looked down at her hands. 'That I was *the one*. No one has ever said anything like that to me. Do you think he was just saying that to get me in bed?'

Alia shook her head. 'No Cam, I don't. I'm cynical. A. F.' She punctuated the letters with her pointer finger in the air. 'But yeah, I don't think Benny is a player. He's sweet.'

'I hope so. It's nice to be…liked, you know. Wanted…'

'It is…' Alia hugged her friend.

'Plus, I bloody love Whitehall and the château, and I don't want things to be awkward.'

'It's not going to be. Even if things don't work out, so what? You had a great time together. What's it matter?'

Camryn smiled and nodded towards the door. As Alia followed, she wondered how much experience Camryn had with relationships. The night before she'd said she'd spent twenty years on her career. Alia shook her head in wonder.

Imagine what I could do if I spent a bit more time on mine.

Three hundred. Sixty. Five.

She wanted to huddle in the back seat and talk to Cam about the entire past twenty-four hours, but she could see Benito wanted her to himself. She couldn't deny Cam that after she divulged how worried she was Benito was only there for one thing. Alia watched them from the corner of her eye as they sat together in the middle of the back seat while Watermelon rode up front. They obviously had various important topics of conversation themselves.

After the first hour, apart from the occasional gentle laugh from the back, the car ride was quiet, unlike the raucous drive north the day before. Cam and Benito soon fell asleep, his head on her shoulder. Phillip looked over at Alia every ten minutes or so and smiled but didn't seem interested in conversation. He seemed to be stuck in a loop of 'about to say something, then deciding against it.'

The sun-baked fields blurred into a corn-coloured haze as the car sped along the Route Nationale. Phillip had plotted the course to avoid roadworks on the autoroute with the bonus of a view of rolling farmland, interrupted only by the occasional sunflower field or village. Alia was delighted to watch France unfold before her. Apart from the previous day, she couldn't remember ever having looked out a car window before.

They stopped for late lunch in a tiny hillside bistro. Benito had woken as they approached Chambord, perfectly timed to direct them to the old vine and cliché covered building. After lunch Benito said he had a surprise for them. Leaving the car in the restaurant carpark, he took Camryn's hand and led the way. Cam looked over at Alia and fluttered her hand in front of her heart. They took a narrow, winding footpath through a surprisingly dense forest which after ten minutes opened on to an enormous park. A couple strolled past with three or four scruffy dogs who ran joyfully in and out of the undergrowth on extendable leads. Watermelon watched them but except for the occasional excited "yip", didn't join in.

'Just a little further…' Benito said, rounding a bend. 'Et Voila.'

They stood shoulder to shoulder admiring a spectacular château. 'What?' Alia cried. 'Oh, this is some kind of fairy tale.' She covered her heart with her hands.

'Château de Chambord,' Camryn said in a hushed tone.

'Would you like to visit the château?' Benito asked the group.

Alia was keen to get back to their own château. She was so accustomed to churning out a few dozen pages each day, she was missing it, but Camryn looked as though she really wanted to go in. 'As long as Melon can go in, I'm in.'

Alia grinned at Benito and nodded. Phillip looked at his watch. 'Let's do it.'

They followed the path as it wound its way past the manicured gardens and ran alongside the moat. Dozens of children dressed in medieval costume darted past, cardboard swords raised shouting at the sky. Once the mini melee had passed, Benito and Phillip pulled out their phones and began snapping photos of the château, its chimneys in sharp contrast to the deep blue sky. The visitor centre was empty, and the staff stood in a huddle near the desk, their heads swivelling as the foursome walked in. They were all young women, Alia's demographic. The chance of one of them recognising her was high.

'I'll wait here,' Alia said, hanging back and pretending to admire the souvenir t-shirts. The last thing she needed was exposure this late in the game. She pulled one of the embroidered caps on and let her hair fall around her cheekbones. 'Can I buy this?' she said to Phillip as he approached.

He cocked his head to one side and held up the receipt. 'I thought it might come in handy, so I told her to add a hat to the bill. They were craning their necks arguing about whether or not it was Alia. Funny how kids always assume the adults in front of them can't understand what they're saying.'

Cam and Benito came up behind Phillip, laughing. 'He was brilliant, threw them off your scent,' Cam said as they left the visitor centre. Once they were outside on the flagstone walkway she filled in the blanks. 'It was great. He told them, in French, "oh no, please don't tell my sister she looks like Alia. She hates it…happens all the time. She'll get really upset and the drive home will be a nightmare".'

Alia stopped. 'Gee, thanks, bruv.' She punched him gently on the arm.

Cam and Benito walked ahead, their little fingers hooked together as Alia and Phillip watched them go. She turned to Phillip, startling him. 'Do you think he will be at the party?'

Phillip's head snapped back a couple of inches. 'Who?'

'Braith.'

'Mr Evans-Lewis? …er, he will make an appearance, I suppose but he is 100 so he probably won't be dancing on any tables. Why?'

She walked a few paces. 'It's hard to explain. I guess reading your thesis and his novels, I feel like I know him.'

'I could ask. He doesn't really like meeting new people.'

'Could you just ask?'

Phillip looked as though he was thinking for a few seconds but nodded his head.

'Now, in other business, it really annoys me that I was your…'

Phillip stared at her.

'What I mean is, when you, said… the thing…' Alia pointed back towards the visitor centre. 'The girls in the…I don't want to be.' She stood, hand on her hips, looking up at the ornate stone ceiling.

Phillip looked down at the flagstones. 'I'm not… sure…I mean…' There was a moments silence and they both laughed.

'Wow listen to us, the Insta-poet and the soon-to-be doctor of words struggling to string a few together. I like you. I like the look of you, and

I like who you are, and I think you might like me, too. I didn't like it when you told those girls I was your sister because I want to kiss you and that would be a bit creepy, even for minor-aristocracy.'

Phillip grinned. 'That would be a bit creepy… sis.'

'Oh, hairy goddess, will you stop?'

'Okay, let's visit this magnificent building… sis.'

Alia let out a sound of disgust that seemed to echo around the huge space and he smiled at her. She felt a little flicker of energy pass between them, but he continued through the room. He turned back to her nodding his head in the direction he was going, a question in his eyes.

'Come on,' he said, and put his hand out to her. A joke crossed her mind, something about not wanting to hold her brother's hand, but she swallowed it and took the few steps towards him, taking his hand. They walked through the cavernous rooms, joking and trying to count the fireplaces. They had lost sight of the others and Alia had lost count of the fireplaces because all she could think about was her skin touching his.

'Do you miss your phone?'

Alia was surprised not just by the question but by her response to it. 'No. I mean, I wish I had my camera right now.' She pointed at the intricate ceiling, 'But no, I don't miss the whole content-creation thing.'

'You can borrow mine if you like.' He held out his phone with his spare hand, but she shook her head.

'Thanks. I'm good. You know there aren't many men who can walk with me like this. Most guys aren't…'

'Man enough?'

They both laughed. 'I was going to say tall. Tall enough, but yeah.' She stood facing him. He leaned in, his lips touching her ear, for just a moment. He was saying something. 'What?' Alia said, her eyes closed.

'Three hundred. Sixty. Five.'

She could feel his breath on her neck. 'What?' she whispered.

'Fireplaces.'

'Oh, you are an insufferable nerd,' Alia said, squeezing his hand. 'Let's go find the love birds, bruv.'

The short drive back to the château included stops at the bank, the post office, a hardware store, and an enormous supermarket on the outskirts of Blois, but Alia chose to stay in the car with the dog. She was itching to get back to her writing but was distracted by both the nearness of Phillip and the desire to go straight to sleep so she could run down those spiral stairs again. Would Braith still be there? What year would it be? The 60s?

The others interrupted her thoughts as they piled into the car with their grocery bags. Camryn dropped a shopping bag in Alia's lap. She squealed and blew five kisses which Cam caught and held close to her heart. The bag was full of Alia's favourite things, chocolate, and cigarettes. The car passed through Blois as the famous château on the hill glowed in the late afternoon sun. Alia picked up where she had left off watching Phillip in the window reflection. Occasionally, he looked over at her as he had on the trip from Paris, but she didn't want to meet his eye. She was afraid of what she might say or do, a new feeling for Alia Henry.

He was completely unlike anyone she had met; let alone anyone she'd fancied in the past.

Hobbs. She's gorgeous, Hobbs.

Past-Alia would know what to do with a hottie like Phillip Hobbs. She stifled a giggle. Past-Alia would take him by the hand the minute they returned to the château and lead him to her room, but each time she thought of what might happen next, she found herself blushing. She wasn't sure what was happening to her but sleeping with Phillip was both the last thing on her mind, and the first. He was exquisite and fragile like her grandmother's Fabergé egg. The combination both scared and intrigued her. Like Grandmother's precious Russian egg, she didn't want to break him; she was too afraid of the consequences. But she really wanted to touch.

The crunch of the gravel under the tyres snapped Alia from her thoughts. She had to push Past-Alia far from her mind if she had any hope of carrying on a conversation with Phillip. Never mind Dame Judy, or Dame Helen. *What would Thalia do?*

The thought wound its way around her head. She needn't have worried. An urgent phone call pulled him away as they unpacked the car. Benito and Camryn wandered off, deep in conversation and Present-Alia was still standing on the driveway, her bag of goodies clutched to her chest.

'Right…well I'll just…' She shut the car doors and wandered slowly into the foyer.

In their absence, the contractors had done wonders. The walls had been painted a warm cream and Camryn's exquisite chandelier hung from the vaulted ceiling. Each crystal was shaped like a leaf, some clear, some etched and some opaque like the sea-glass woman Camryn had given her.

'Isn't it perfect?'

Alia jumped and her hand went to her chest, dropping her shopping bag.

'I didn't mean to frighten you,' Phillip said.

'It is perfect. I was mesmerised. I want to see each and every delicate piece up close. I want to touch it and feel the rough and the smooth.' Exquisite and fragile seemed to be the theme of the day.

'Sorry I took off. Important business. The meetings in Cologne went well. Mrs Grant has offered me a position in the company in Germany.'

A broad grin edged across Alia's face but stopped halfway. She wanted to jump up and down and congratulate him but from the expression on his face he looked as though he needed condolences instead. He shook his head. 'I've already accepted the position with the Department for Education.'

'Oh no,' Alia said, picking up the sweets that had rolled from her bag.

'No, it's not a bad thing. I'm excited. It is flattering to have two jobs to choose from, but I made my choice. I'll be fronting up to some of the more challenging schools in the country over the next few years and I'm looking forward to it.'

Alia was nodding. It all suddenly made sense to her. 'You know, you are changing the way I look at the world. You, Cam, this house. My life is unrecognisable in, what, a couple of weeks, so yeah, who am I to deny that to the kids you're going to teach. You've got a gift and it's better to share that with the next generation rather than driving spoiled celebrities to the airport.'

Phillip chuckled softly. 'You are lovely, you know that?'

Alia unwrapped a chocolate and popped it in her mouth. She had to process the comment as she chewed. She swallowed the sweet and cleared her throat. 'Actually, no I don't know that at all. This is what I am talking about. No one would have said I was lovely two, three weeks ago. I was an arse. Twenty-four, seven, three-six-five. The number of fireplaces at Chambord. That's how much of a spoiled brat I was.'

'Was?'

Alia threw the sweet wrapper at him. 'Have you thought any more about whether I could meet Braith… I mean, Mr Evans-Lewis?'

He furrowed his brow. 'I can ask.'

'I'd really like to meet him before the party.'

'I wouldn't get my hopes up if I were you. He's not well.'

They stood under the chandelier. A breeze found its way into the foyer, winding its way through the crystals, casting tiny rainbows around the room. They both stood, mouths open in wonder, as rainbows chased each other across their faces.

He bent to pick up the wrapper she'd thrown and pocketed it. He pointed into the dining room with his elbow. 'I have, things. I'll see you at dinner?' Phillip turned towards the dining room.

Alia was a little shocked by his abruptness. She had hoped they were having a moment. She shouldered her overnight bag and started up the stairs. 'Of course. Me too. See you at dinner, bruv.'

'Alia. Sorry, I…' He took out the sweet wrapper, looked at it and put it back in his pocket. 'I don't know how to deal with this.' He pointed at her then at himself.

The lump had returned to her throat and she had to hush Past-Alia because *she* definitely knew how to deal with *this*. 'You could walk me home?' She smiled down at him.

'I'll watch from here.'

He was still standing under Camryn's elegant chandelier when she got to the top of the stairs. He smiled up at her and her heart threatened to burst from her chest, *Aliens* style. 'Haven't you… things to do?'

'I just wanted to make sure you got home safe.'

She smiled and felt lightheaded. She felt like a character in a book. She lifted her hand and waved because once again, she couldn't trust herself to speak.

Thalia

Like a family, they sat in their usual seats at the dining table, enjoying a light dinner whipped up by Benito who took one of the wooden chairs so Melon could have his usual spot. Alia could almost read Camryn's mind as she looked at Benito. *That guy is a keeper.*

Benito picked up the fake wine and filled Camryn's glass, then took her hand and kissed it. He said "Miss Camryn" managing to make her name sound like a song.

'Isn't it amazing,' Camryn said, 'when the right person says your name it takes on a special quality.' She turned to Benito and they beamed at each other.

Alia was pleased the new couple dominated the conversation; she really wasn't up to talking. She let their voices wash over her. Occasionally Phillip responded to one of them and when he spoke, she was pulled back into reality by the sound of his voice. Eventually, Cam commented that she was unusually quiet. She cleared her throat. 'Speaking of names, which Cam did ages ago.' She nodded at Camryn. 'I have an announcement to make. I'm going by Thalia from now on,' she said. She bit into a dinner roll.

Camryn smiled conspiratorially in her side-eye.

'Well it is your name,' Phillip said from the other end of the table.

She nodded. 'It is, but I've always hated it.'

Phillip looked from Camryn to Thalia a slight frown crinkling his forehead. Thalia looked at the happy couple.

Phillip wants to know who has been saying my name.

'Anyway, it doesn't matter what you call me, and I'll probably still be Alia for my followers, but yeah, I'm Thalia. It just feels right.' She finished her roll and grinned as she chewed. The others nodded and murmured their agreement.

Cam stood up as Benito cleared the table. 'Alia… ah… Thalia, before it gets dark, can we pop down to the studio for a chat about the mural?' Her eyes were flashing. As the two women left the room, Watermelon looked up at them from his chair, sniffed the air, and curled up again.

'I guess he wants to be one of the boys, tonight,' Thalia said.

Camryn looked from Melon to Benito. 'See you later, gentlemen,' she said.

They walked out under the new chandelier, Thalia congratulating her friend on her success. She wanted to stand underneath it, but Camryn had other fish to fry. She dragged Thalia out across the terrace and down onto the gravel path to the orangery. Thalia yawned. She was keen to do some writing, but she couldn't wait to get to bed, too. She looked up at the fading light; it would soon be time to see Braith again, although Thalia guessed Camryn would be more interested in visiting another man that night. They were giggling like little girls by the time they unlocked the doors, and both started talking once they were inside.

'Oh Thalia, I think I'm in love.'

Thalia threw her arms around her friend. 'I don't think you're alone there. Benito is head over heels.'

'You think so?' Camryn said into her shoulder. Thalia nodded enthusiastically.

When they pulled themselves apart, they were both crying happy tears. It had been a momentous few days, and Thalia wasn't sure if Cam was more excited about her blossoming relationship with Benito, the trip to Paris, or her new-found knowledge about the stained-glass mural. Then there was the whole matter of Braith. If he wasn't a ghost, what on earth was he?

Cam offered no theories on how Braith came to be there every night; fixated as she was on her mural, repeating the words "Peacocks, Thalia…" like a mantra. Camryn went to a table topped with the huge sheet of drawing paper that had been her focus for days, the incomplete concept for the mural. She began to sketch the peacocks with thick, bright pastels.

Thalia was impressed at Cam's professionalism once again. At some stage over the past day, she had ordered the necessary glass from Italy and while she waited for it to arrive, she would make the drawings and begin the delicate silvery framing. Thalia left her mumbling over the drawing like one of Shakespeare's witches over a cauldron.

In her rush to leave for Paris, Thalia hadn't left any paper in the typewriter barrel and was disappointed to see no comments on the work left in the binder. She ran her hand over the typewriter keys feeling a spark of inspiration but there was no artificial light in the writing nook. She grabbed one of her journals and a pen in case the inspiration should strike later, and she yawned as she wandered back over to Camryn.

Good morning, Braith

Thalia woke to her bedside alarm. She'd fallen asleep reading Phillip's thesis and snippets of Braith's second novel *The Peace and the Pilgrims.* She felt like she had only just nodded off, but sunlight was streaming through the windows. She picked up the novel and turned to the author photo, the face of the young Robert Evans, *Braith Robert Evans-Lewis,* looking out at her across the years. As for the man himself, he seemed too good to be true. According to Phillip's thesis he was a war hero, a famous writer, and a generous philanthropist. Thanks to Camryn they could now add cult-poet to the list of achievements. His charitable work only started with the château he had given to the Arts Council of Britain.

She looked up at the blue sky, not believing she had slept through the night, missing an opportunity to see him. A tear ran down her cheek and she rolled back into the blankets. She would be leaving in a couple of days. Would she see him again?

She lay very still while a dark thought bloomed in her mind. Perhaps the elderly writer, Braith, had died in the night. Absentmindedly, she reached over and picked up her grandmother's watch and stared at it. It had been missing for weeks and suddenly it was lying on her bedside table, its elegant little hands both pointing at the twelve. If it was twelve midday, she had slept for over twelve hours. Either that or the watch had stopped at midnight. She flicked up the little wheel on the side and began to wind it and then stopped. She sat up and looked outside. Huge trees blocked most of the view but between their branches she could see tracts of lush, green farmland. If her watch had mysteriously appeared, could it be midnight in her time and daytime in Braith's?

She wrapped the watch around her wrist and fastened it as she moved from the bed to the door. She felt like she was on autopilot as she pulled it open and immediately knew the stairs would be there. In her time, the hall had recently been painted duck-egg blue with white trims but now stood gleaming with multiple deep colours and stunning artworks lining the wall. The floorboards polished to a sheen and a sumptuous runner guided her to the spiral stairs. The sun, streaming through the domed skylight and the huge bank of windows, reflected off elegant gold framed mirrors she had not seen before. The whole space was pulsing with light. She looked out over the garden and the rolling hills beyond and could not see another house let alone a lorry depot and the neon sign for a service centre.

She turned and ran down the stairs. Braith was in the hall, a clipboard and pen in his hands. Two men were carrying the sofa from the parlour. He looked up and smiled broadly at her.

'Going somewhere?' she said.

'Of course, you are here on this most momentous of days.' He might have been overseeing removalists, but his attire suggested he was having lunch at the Ritz. His linen suit pressed, his shoes, polished, his dark hair sprinkled with grey. When he smiled at her, the tiny lines around his eyes crinkled. He had aged into a sexy Pierce Brosnan clone although in 1968 Pierce was probably running about in short pants somewhere. Braith pulled her into an embrace. He smelled lovely. He nodded at the bar; its shelves were bare.

'I'm afraid I can offer you nought but my company today. Oh, perhaps a cigarette.' He put his hand on his pocket, the top of the elegant gold cigarette case was showing.

'Perhaps later,' she said and looped her arm into his. 'What's happening?'

They walked through the parlour, the terrace doors stood open and tea chests waited along one wall for the removalists.

'I am moving. New York has wooed me and won. My agent was right.'

'They usually are,' Thalia said.

'How is your friend, the artist, my country woman…Camryn?'

'She is fantastic. She's making incredible art, and she's in love. Tell me, are you B.R.E.L?'

He stopped walking. 'I am, but you understand, I am two writers. A poet of simple words and a novelist of complex thought.'

Thalia nodded. She understood what it was to be two different people. They stood in the near-empty parlour. 'How is your wife? Fiancé?'

'Marvellous. I am a husband and a papa now. My little girl is an American like my mother. She is already a force of nature.' His eyes shone.

Thalia nodded. He was right. His little girl had grown into a powerful woman. Two removalists marched through the room and each collected a tea chest on his trolley. They were grizzled old men with huge moustaches, and they spoke to Braith in French, not looking in her direction once. Thalia giggled and danced about the room, while Braith laughed. The two men looked at each other, eyebrows raised in confusion. They left the room with the last two chests and Braith closed the terrace doors.

'I know you,' Thalia said as he bolted the doors.

He stopped what he was doing and slightly bowed his head.

'Camryn knew you because you're Welsh, but Phillip, he's an Englishman. If I tell him about B.R.E.L, he will know all there is to know. You are known. At least you will be if you keep writing.' She was whispering by the time she finished.

He turned to look at her with tears in his eyes. 'It matters, of course it does, but I am going to America for love. My family is there. I will continue to have success…you say…but even if you tell me I will never sell another paperback, I will still go.'

The usual lump had taken up residence in her throat. She moved towards him and put her arms around him. 'I'm very happy for you but I'm sad because I hoped we might fall in love.'

217

He laughed softly and smoothed her hair. 'We are in love, my dear, but you are my dream and I am yours.' He stood back and put his hands on her arms, holding her gaze.

Thalia felt shivers up and down her spine. 'I'll never meet anyone like you in my time.'

Braith laughed and held out the cigarette case to her. 'But you already have. You speak of him at every opportunity.'

Thalia furrowed her brow in confusion for a few moments but then looked down at her bare feet. 'No, Phillip and I are just friends, he's far too good for me.'

'My wife is far too good for me, also. That is the beauty of being in love, it makes you want to be a better person.'

Thalia laughed, surprised by the idea. 'I actually do want to be a better person around Phillip. He's actually kind and intelligent. These are not qualities I find attractive…usually and I find him very…attractive…actually.'

Phillip. Kind, funny, intelligent, sad, Phillip.

He brought out all the good there could be in her. She had been a better version of herself away from her manic existence in London, away from the people who encouraged her mad behaviour because there was something in it for them.

'Wonderful,' Braith said as he lit her cigarette. 'You can start by dropping the word actually from your vocabulary. The word actually is superfluous, actually.'

Alia laughed mouth open and loud. Braith took her hand and kissed it. 'Apart from the fact we exist only in each other's dreams I could never marry you. You scare the living daylights out of me,' he said.

She threw her arms around his neck. 'And you, sir, would bore me to tears…actually.'

'I have a surprise for you.' He took her arm again and led her down the hall to the dining room, the room bare except for the enormous table and two chairs which sat off to one side in an alcove. Thalia wanted to mention the chairs so the removalists wouldn't forget them. They must have been the two chairs still in use in the dining room. How they had survived the destruction wrought on the rest of the house was a mystery.

The large wooden door was gone, and the secret entry of Thalia's time stood freshly made in the wall. The door stood open as the removalists went to and fro, ferrying larger items into the cave. He explained he was only shipping the essentials to New York. Everything else would be stored in the cave, the door hidden from intruders. Thalia desperately wanted to warn Braith against leaving anything in the house but knew the cave had remained largely untouched except for a small flood in the 90s. They walked arm in arm down the corridor she and Camryn had run along weeks before, laughing hysterically, probably running from the echo of this gentle, quirky man. The cave seemed much smaller, stacked as it was with tea-chests and furniture wrapped in canvas. Braith stood under the mural painted on the domed ceiling. He was smiling. No, he was grinning.

'A tribute to you.'

Thalia looked up, then back at the grinning man. She was lost for words.

'I had a painter come over from Italy. It's my way of saying thank you for all you have done for me over the years.'

Thalia stared up at the nine muses dancing on the ceiling. She finally found her voice although it was only a whisper. 'By candlelight, it looks like they are dancing…'

'Aah, so you have seen this in your time?'

Thalia nodded. 'They think it's old, like as in ancient. Like Renaissance old.'

Braith laughed softly. 'The painter will be chuffed to hear that, although I am not entirely sure how I will explain it to him. If you look closely, you'll see it's quite a good likeness.'

Thalia stood on her toes and peered at the faces. She finally found her face there, well, a pretty good likeness of it, on the body of a toga wearing goddess dancing with her eight sisters. She smiled at Braith. Unsure of how to thank someone for spending a huge amount of money to paint a mural on their ceiling in your honour, she did something she had never done before. She said nothing at all. The tears wouldn't really let her.

She put her arms around him and hugged him until he was laughing. When she released him, she looked up again.

'I wish I had my camera.'

'Oh, yes, I have been meaning to tell you…all these years… I,' he seemed to be trying to recall something long forgotten. 'It's 1968, my dear. Many years since I have seen you and yes, I have your camera. I found it on the upstairs landing one morning. More than a decade ago.'

'My Canon?' Thalia clapped her hands and jumped around.

Two of the younger workers in denim overalls appeared at the door with a desk. Braith nodded his head towards the door and she followed him up the stairs as the young men waited. He gave the men some instructions and Thalia stood behind him pulling faces. Neither man reacted and they started down the stairs with their load. Thalia whooped with laughter and the echo whipped around the cavernous space. One of the men kept his head down, but the young man at the top of the stairs nearly dropped his end of the table. His workmate looked up at him, obviously annoyed, as he stopped and turned around to see the source of the sound. His eyes met Thalia's for a second and he balanced the table on one arm and crossed himself with the other.

Thalia ran along the corridor in silent peals of laughter, bursting into the dining room and doubling over. 'He saw me. He heard me,' she said while trying to catch her breath.

Braith followed at a more sedate pace, the way Phillip had done…would do…? 'I am not surprised he saw you. He is the son of the local mayor and while his father wishes for him to become a doctor, he dreams of being a painter. He has an artist's soul.'

Thalia shook her head and laughed. 'Perhaps I truly am a muse.'

They walked through the kitchen where more staff were packing away copper pots and pans in wooden tea chests. There was a platter laden with grapes, cheese and bread on the tiled bench top, a large pitcher of water and anodised mugs. Braith picked up a bunch of grapes and poured two cups of water and kept walking. Once they were out of earshot, he handed the cup to Thalia and offered her the grapes. She took a sip and admired the bright yellow cup. Her grandmother's housekeeper had dozens of the bright cups and refused to let Thalia drink from a glass until she was thirteen. Thalia smiled at the memory but also remembered breaking a glass just to see what the reaction would be. It wasn't that she was a mean-spirited child, she'd just always had trouble with impulse control.

Braith pushed open the double glass doors to the conservatory. The pool sat empty, the white tiles gleaming in the sunlight. The breathtaking Tiffany stained-glass peacocks still held court in the magnificent space. They kept walking, turning left rather than to the right, towards the parlour. She had no idea how any of this was real, but she munched on very real tasting grapes as she followed him. He took a small bundle of keys from his pocket and unlocked a plain wooden door that Thalia would have missed if he hadn't stopped in front of it.

'Another secret passageway?'

'My office,' he said, pulling the door open to reveal a small but elegant space, still fully furnished unlike the rest of the house. 'A place for me to hide away from the world.' He ran his hand across the top of the desk.

'I wish someone would look at me the way you look at that desk.'

He laughed. 'Oh darling, I am sure everyone looks at you that way, you're simply too busy to notice.'

Thalia shrugged. He pushed the chair out and bent under the desk. Thalia couldn't see what he was doing down there, but she heard a popping sound and a low bookcase moved slightly. Braith stood and brushed his immaculate clothing free of non-existent fluff and went to the panel, opening it up to reveal a safe. Thalia laughed. 'Aah the ol' hidden wall safe behind the bookcase trick, huh?'

He grinned at her again and fiddled with the dial.

'My birthday,' he whispered and winked at her, and the door of the huge black safe swung open. Braith reached in, coming out with her camera in one hand and Cam's iPhone in the other.

'Oh, Cam's going to be so happy.' She reached for the phone but Braith held it tight.

'This… Now this is very interesting. I wanted to see how it functioned and I did manage to take a few photographs I believe but eventually it went blank. It is a marvellously small camera.' He held it up to the light.

'This isn't just a camera. It's a phone… a telephone, and believe it, or not, it's a super-computer, more powerful than the rooms full of computers NASA is using to get men to walk on the moon.'

His brown eyes locked on to hers. 'Really? The moon?'

She nodded. She couldn't wait to see the photos he'd taken, probably in 1959 but she would have to wait until she was back in 2019 to charge the phone. She lifted her own camera and snapped a photo of him against the backdrop of the bookcases. He was still an elegant and attractive man, at…she did the numbers in her head. He was nearly fifty. He handed her the phone with a reluctant sigh and turned back and peered into the safe. 'I have all kinds of treasures in here.' He emerged with a large silicone spatula in one hand and an old safety razor in the other. He turned the razor to show engraving on one side.

Phillip Gordon Hobbs.

Thalia snorted as she took the razor and the spatula. 'Gordon. I am going to give him heaps for that.' She then remembered her own middle names and decided she might go easy on him. Braith once again leaned into the mouth of the safe and surfaced with her sea glass woman. 'Oh, my goddess, you're light fingered!'

Braith laughed and carefully put the sculpture down. Thalia explained it was Camryn's work. She stopped herself, once again, from explaining the long hours the talented sculptor had spent recreating the damaged glass panels and chandeliers.

'These items have appeared over the years. I have simply collected them.' He started to pull out books (a first edition Harry Potter), kitchen utensils, and jewellery, and lay them all on the desk.

'I can't carry all this stuff.'

'You can always come back tomorrow.' Braith winked at her.

Tomorrow…

Thalia felt the air go out of her lungs and sat heavily on the chair behind the desk. Every time she saw Braith he was older. More handsome to be sure, but older. In her time, he was a seriously ill old man who slept twenty-three hours a day. One day, no one knew when, but one day, he wouldn't be in her dreams anymore and she wouldn't be in his.

He handed her his shiny blue anodised cup of water and fanned her with one of the books. 'Go easy on the spine of that book,' she said. 'It's worth a mint.'

He laughed but kept fanning her. 'I'm not short of money, I'd rather not see you faint.'

'I'm fine, I just… I'll be going home soon, and I won't see you anymore.'

He leaned against the edge of the desk. 'This may be an old romantic speaking but, Thalia, muse of comedy and idyllic poetry, you will always be in my heart and as you have seen today, in my home. I see your hand in all my work. I would not be the writer I am if not for your loving guidance.'

Thalia stared up at him. She desperately wanted to jump up and down and shout, *I am not your muse,* but what if she was? What if, one wacky, drug-addled Burning Man, Zeus himself had shagged her mother? She sat back in the chair and relaxed a little. 'You've changed my life, too.' She lifted the camera and snapped another candid shot. He was looking directly at her.

'I have?' He seemed genuinely surprised by the news.

'Yes, of course. All the little helpful tips you keep adding to my work. Is it wrong that I'm getting your help? Is it cheating?'

He smiled and took her hand. 'Of course not. But if it makes you feel better you can list me as co-author.'

Thalia laughed out loud. 'Imagine what my agent would say.' She stood and put her arms around him. 'I will dedicate one of my poems to you.'

223

He nodded and appeared to be thinking. 'Your writing is fine. It is rushed, however. To read it leaves one breathless. Slow down and everything will be better.'

'Can we go for a walk? I'd like to take some photos of the house… of you, and I'd really like to see the grounds. Oh, can we see the orangery?'

His face lit up. Braith loved the old mansion and Thalia knew how deeply he loved his wife and baby daughter… to be leaving his home, so cheerfully. She wondered what had brought him back.

She followed him through the house and photographed him in front of the swimming pool in a shot she hoped was reminiscent of a Slim Aarons. He was a willing model, happy to pose in front of anything she wanted to capture, even when she would have preferred it on its own. They left the removalists to their work and took the gravel path through the grounds. She looked back and took a shot of the façade, the sun making deep shadows on the terrace, lace curtains covering the windows in what would be her room in a few decades. He posed in front of the orangery, its woodwork and window frames already showing signs of wear and tear. Rattling the first set of French doors he soon swung them open for Thalia to enter the space. She pointed at the doors with her thumb in what she hoped was a casual manner.

'Do you think you have time to get some locks on those doors?'

'There is nothing here for people to steal. Just a big empty space. Why would I lock the doors?'

Thalia shrugged with an exaggerated double shoulder action.

'Aah, I see. I will ask Henri from the farm next door to bring some chains. He will be keeping his eye on the place in exchange for using the fields beyond the stone fences.' He pointed across the already overgrown garden. She could see huge bales of hay stacked in a far-off field. It caused an almost physical pain to think how built up the local area had… would… become.

She checked the number of shots she had taken. Seven left. Braith was already walking towards the writing nook, a leather office chair and heavy black typewriter was still in place. He sat and struck a pose. Thalia snapped a shot.

'I think I'll leave this baby right here for you.' He patted it lovingly.

'No,' she said, the word coming out more forcefully than she'd intended. 'You can't, it was in the cave. You must store it, or I won't find it, and everything will be ruined.'

He was suddenly at her side, her hand grasped in his. She was crying and he was trying to console her. He promised her he would store the typewriter in the cave and have Henri from next door put chains on the doors. She suggested he install a CCTV system but from the look on his face, it was possible such a thing hadn't been invented yet.

Champagne tulle

After Thalia shot the 36th frame on the film, she wound the film to the end and flicked the off button. They had walked around the magnificent property, Braith proudly showing her his favourite nooks in the garden. She hoped this curious and gentle man was a good husband and father. Her own father and grandfather had been less than stellar in those roles, both choosing wine, women, and song over bath, bedtime, and birthdays. He certainly said all the right things, but she had met plenty of men with families who talked the talk but couldn't walk the walk due to the stripper on their laps.

As they walked back to the house, she wondered if she might ask Pamela what her father was like, but then Mrs Grant struck her as a driven woman so maybe she had something to prove. Maybe there were some Daddy issues? Thalia had her fair share of those, not to mention a heavy dose of mummy issues.

The removalists had left their work and set up their lunch on a trestle table under a big tree. Thalia longed to join them or at least to take photos of their rustic baskets and check tablecloths. She looked up at Braith as he talked about his latest project, the novel that she knew would bring him the fame he sought. She should have been listening, but she was thinking about crusty bread and olives.

They wandered back through the house to the office and she gathered up the things to take back to 2019. She stuck Cam's phone in the pocket of her shorts and tucked the sea-glass lady under her arm. She slipped

Phillip's razor and Benito's spatula into her other pocket and walked towards the door. The razor and the spatula clattered to the floor.

'These pockets are too small,' she said carefully retrieving the dropped items.

'The shorts are very small,' he said, smiling like an indulgent father.

She poked her tongue at him and looked at the safe. 'Nobody asked you, dad. I'll take the cameras and the sculpture…and these.' She really wanted that Harry Potter book.

He stood staring into the safe as Thalia tried out different ways to carry everything. 'You live in this house, in 2019.' He turned to face her. 'Do you know this room?'

Thalia shook her head. 'I haven't even seen the swimming pool. Your room is over this way, like past the parlour…' she pointed at the wall but was referring to the rooms on the other side of it.

He stared at her. 'I am…there? Here? In your time?'

She nodded.

He tapped his hands on the desk. 'You mean to tell me, in 2019, I am still alive? I will live to be… 100 years.'

'It's your birthday tomorrow. Everyone is coming. It's a big event. The minister for culture is coming and your daughter.'

'My daughter! My little Pammy? My little Pammy will be two in May.'

Thalia smiled at the thought of calling the stupendous force that was Mrs Grant, *Pammy*. He sat on the edge of the desk, shook his head slowly and smiled at Thalia.

'Do you know my daughter? Is she a strong woman? My wife is a very strong woman, a talented businesswoman.'

'Then I would say Pamela is just like her mother.' Thalia imagined bringing Pamela here to meet her father in his prime.

'There is a big party? For me? That's marvellous.'

Thalia nodded. 'I'm really looking forward to it.' After a month of hard work, she was keen to let off a little steam. She had done more work in the previous thirty days than she had in her entire life. Braith clapped his hands, shaking her from the daydream. She had been picturing Phillip in a dinner suit, dancing with her in her white sheath dress. Too bad she didn't have her white sheath dress.

The disappointment must have showed on her face because Braith asked her what she was worried about. She explained her lack of a party dress. She had clothes in London but hadn't really packed for a party.

'In that case, I have another surprise for you. You can't celebrate my birthday in short shorts.'

He left the room and she looked down at her short shorts. She could celebrate his birthday in anything she damn well pleased, but curiosity got the better of her and she ran after him just as he called to her from the pool room, camera bobbing around her neck.

He was striding through the parlour by the time she caught up with him. He was smiling and whistling quietly. Thalia recognised the tune. Cam would remember the name, he played it all the time. He chatted about the music they should play at the party, the menu, the cocktails. He was quite the event planner. She told him he'd missed his calling. Before Thalia realised, they were standing in the upstairs hall in front of her bedroom door. She drew a sudden breath. Would the messy bedroom of her waking hours be behind the door? He opened the door and to Thalia's delight, the room was even messier than she had left it, with every space covered in tulle, satin and silk.

'A woman from Paris is here to pack my mother's gowns and take them to a museum. You can have any dress you want.'

Thalia wandered into the room and looked around at the stunning dresses. The armoires were packed with them and they were piled on the four-poster bed. She looked up at the ceiling, at the bright red rosebuds with little green stems.

'I had the room painted for my daughter, for Pammy. She loved it but she only slept here for a few weeks before we decided to return to America. The museum will take the bed and the dressing table, they also belonged to my mother.' He looked around the room, smiling as though he was remembering something lovely.

'And the armoires?'

He shook his head. 'Too heavy, and the era is all wrong. They're old but not Deco or Nouveau so no one is interested in them.'

She wanted to tell him about all the Americans, Brits, and Germans who would descend on rural France in the 90s, snapping up anything with a bit of dust on it, then taking it home to flog for exorbitant prices. Thalia lifted one gown and then another, gently cradling each glorious vintage piece and running her fingers over the fine beading and stitching. She lifted the camera strap over her head and went to put it on the dressing table, a stunning piece of art nouveau furniture. Braith cleared his throat before she could put it down on the polished walnut top and so she changed direction, putting it on the bed.

A pale blue silk ballgown lay on the top of the pile of dresses. She held it up against her body and looked at Braith. He nodded to the full-length mirror in the corner of the room and started to leave the room to give her some privacy.

'No, wait!' she shrieked, and he spun on his heel. 'Just don't shut the door. Please. This is my room, in 2019 and I don't want to go back just yet.'

'I will be just outside,' he said and left the door ajar.

Thalia took a deep breath and pulled the zip down on the gown. From the corner of her eye she spied a pile of champagne tulle. She cocked her head and walked over to it very slowly as though it were a tiny creature she might startle.

Hello my pretty…

She draped the blue ballgown, as lovely as it was, over the pile on the bed and eased the silky tulle cocktail dress from its hiding place. It was the softest, most glorious dress she had ever seen and the perfect thing for the big party. It would be a miracle if it fit her but then what was this magic all about if not miracles? She slipped her tank top over her head and found the hidden zip tucked into the seam of the gown. She drew it down slowly, accustomed to being very careful with vintage clothes. She stopped. She used to have a stand-up bit where she talked about the two things *Alia* was careful with, vintage clothes and choosing her dealer. She looked out the tall windows, the light muted by soft lace curtains for a change. What a difference it made, and what a difference a month had made for her. She went to the window and opened one of the tall panels. The breeze gusted in, lifting the lace curtains. She looked down at the driveway recalling her arrival, that first real conversation with Phillip. She simply wasn't the same person she had been those few short weeks before. She slipped the dress over her head and it fell soft as a down blanket onto her breasts and she reached around to zip it up.

There was a knock at the door and Thalia tried to call out 'come in' but she had that lump of emotion in her throat. It wasn't really about the dress, although she had to admit it looked stunning and fit perfectly (well nothing a bit of fashion tape wouldn't fix.) The emotion had surfaced when she realised how her life had changed in that short time.

Braith stuck his head through the door and asked if she was happy. She nodded. He stood back and clasped his hands, looking every bit the proud dad on his daughter's wedding day. Thalia looked down at her bare feet.

'Did your mum happen to have any blush pumps, size 8?' Thalia was surprised when he nodded and left the room. She stood in front of the ornate dressing mirror and let the soft breeze play on her skin. The dress would be perfect for the party and she hoped if she was able to meet Braith, he might recognise it.

The breeze lifted the curtains and ruffled the hem of her skirt. Her heart nearly burst from her chest as the bedroom door slammed. She stood staring at it for a moment, willing Braith to open it, hoping he was still there, that she was still in… what year did he say it was? 1968? She walked slowly to the door and put her hand on the brass knob, her heart threatening to surge through her ribs. Opening the door just a crack, she peered into the hallway. It was dark. Behind her, a bright sunny day in 1968, in front, a dark hallway in 2019.

'Braith?' She called out in a voice too loud for the middle of the night. Nothing.

She let the door sit ajar, marvelling at the meeting of light and darkness, but the light was fading, the bedroom, hers but still *little Pammy's* somehow. Her camera sat on the bed amongst piles of satin and silk and she was still wearing the champagne tulle dress. As the light faded, she lunged for the camera and fell in a heap on the bedroom floor.

'No!' she screamed.

She scrambled onto her knees and peered around the dark room. Her own messy piles of clothes had replaced the lavish gowns and the curtain-less windows seemed to loom over her without their soft lace coverings. The adored Pammy's room full of her grandmother's dresses was gone. Thalia put her head on the cool timber floor and closed her eyes.

Footsteps behind her made her sit up with a sharp intake of air.

'Okay, hen?' Camryn was standing in the doorway in her fluffy robe, a torch in her hand.

Thalia sat up and stared up at her friend. 'He was here, and this room was full of his mother's gowns. It was Pammy's room, Pamela's. He painted the rosebuds for her.' Thalia was crying and looking at her empty hands. 'And now my camera's gone again and all the things. Benny's spatula.'

Camryn flicked the torch off and laid it on the table. There was more than enough light coming in from the almost full moon. She sat on the floor next to Thalia and pulled her into a hug and rocked her like a small child.

'He was right here, Cam.'

Camryn pulled a tissue from the arm of her robe and handed it to Thalia, who dabbed at her eyes. 'I only used to cry when I was dead-tired or dead-drunk. This place has got me crazy,' Thalia said.

Cam stroked Thalia's hair. 'That's a lovely dress.'

Thalia caressed the fine silk tulle and nodded. 'It's for the party,' she sniffled.

'Okay, so let's get it onto a hanger and get you into bed.'

Thalia hauled herself up and let Camryn help her out of the dress. She crawled into bed and lay on her side, staring out into the night. She felt Camryn sit on the bed and rolled over to say thank you but couldn't get the words out. Camryn just nodded and rubbed her shoulder until she was asleep.

Safe

The sound of distant hammering woke Thalia from her deep sleep. She had learnt to cover her eyes on her morning stagger to the bathroom and she had it down to a fine art. Still exhausted, she looked at her red rimmed eyes in the bathroom mirror, but her watch told her it was after one. Her watch? She stopped mid-yawn and gaped at the timepiece on her wrist. Rushing back out into the bright bedroom, she shielded her eyes as she stood in front of the armoire, the champagne cocktail dress hanging where Cam had left it.

She showered quickly, threw on some clothes and went in search of food, Camryn, and Phillip. They had a safe to crack but she couldn't do it on an empty stomach.

Food proved harder to find than she thought. Benito was commanding his small army of chefs and helpers and shooed her from the kitchen, rambling on about foraging as he shoved an apple and some pastries in her hands. As though it was an afterthought, he stuck his head back through the door and urged her to be quiet. A little baffled considering the noisy hammering that had woken her, she tried the studio, but it was deserted. Back in the château, there were people everywhere, cleaning walls, putting finishing touches on paintwork, and hanging artwork.

Stomach still rumbling after the two tiny pastries, Thalia found Camryn supervising the installation of the new parlour doors. The glass panels in the doors shone like diamonds. They were perfect. Thalia looked across the room that had once been the master's den, his favourite room filled with books, glowing lamps, and an ever-evolving bar in the

233

corner. Braith, the senior version of him, no doubt lay sleeping behind the closed doors on the other side of the room beyond, hence the need for quiet.

The contractor used a hand drill to screw in the hinges. How many times had Thalia walked through those doors to enjoy a drink and a laugh or a challenging conversation with one of the most fascinating men she would ever meet? Camryn smiled when she spotted her but put a finger to her lips.

'Cam the doors are divine,' Thalia whispered, leaning her cheek against her friend's. Watermelon stood silently beside his mistress and Thalia reached down to scratch the dog's ears.

Cam nodded solemnly but a Mona Lisa smile played on her lips. She whispered to Thalia, 'You okay…rough night?'

Thalia nodded and munched on the apple Benito had thrust at her. Camryn took her elbow and steered her gently along the corridor, towards where the spiral stairs had once stood, and perhaps one day may again.

'Where did you get the dress?' Cam still whispered.

'From him. He was right there. He went to get me some shoes.'

Camryn stood staring at her, obviously confused.

'To match the dress. He had his late-mother's wardrobe. Long story short, have you seen a safe in this place?'

Cam shook her head, her eyebrows high in surprise. 'Phil might know.'

'I was counting on it.'

After asking numerous workers, they eventually found Phillip at the top of a ladder changing lightbulbs. She turned around twice and looked back at the parlour doors on the far side. 'Was this the swimming pool? Cam, this was the swimming pool!'

She couldn't believe the transformation. Phillip looked down at them. 'How did you know this had been a swimming pool?' He spoke quietly as always.

The two women exchanged a glance and shrugged. 'Lucky guess?' they said in unison and laughed.

Phillip screwed a new bulb into place.

'Hey Cam,' Thalia called as Cam walked around the large space. Phillip shushed her. 'Sorry,' she whispered. 'Cam… how many hotties does it take to change a light bulb?' Thalia grinned up at him and Camryn walked back to her side.

'One,' he whispered, not missing a beat.

Thalia clapped her hands and gave out a whoop setting off Watermelon. Phillip shushed them both and Cam picked the dog up, her hand on his snout.

'Things are pretty tense in the old château. The guest list has swelled with a lot of last-minute acceptances and Benny is stressed out trying to cater for the crowd.' Thalia held the ladder as he climbed down.

'And Mr Evans-Lewis woke up last night. He spoke. Apparently, a door slammed somewhere in the house and he reached out for the nurse. She nearly died of fright.'

Thalia wanted to let out another whoop but clamped her hand over her mouth.

'What did he say? To the nurse?' Camryn asked.

'He was a little distressed and wanted to go upstairs. She couldn't really understand much. He was saying something about Pammy, Pamela, his daughter. And something about his muse. Pamela arrived an hour ago. She's in with him.'

Thalia and Camryn looked at each other and bumped fists. Phillip regarded them both with one eyebrow raised.

'I'd love to see…ah, meet him, but I don't want to intrude.'

Phillip folded the ladder up and gestured for them to follow him, heading towards the very room Thalia was sure held the safe. He pushed a sliding panel with his foot revealing a utility room lined with shelves of spare lightbulbs and AV equipment.

'This is the room, Cam. This is where the safe is.'

Phillip leaned the ladder against the wall. 'How did you know about the safe?'

'I dreamt it,' she said.

She let the words hang in the air for a few moments. 'Your razor is in there. Well, it was…in 1968 and my sea-glass lady, and Benny's spatula and Cam's phone. Cam, he had your phone. It was so funny.'

Camryn was silent, her eyes wide. Phillip was staring at both of them, his head watching a tennis match as his gaze bounced from one to the other. Cam spoke up. 'Phil, there's been all kinds of shenanigans going on and my suggestion is we find this safe.'

'I know where…' Phillip started, interrupted by a stifled squeal from Thalia. Her hands went to her mouth to cover the sound, but Watermelon's ears still pricked up. 'The mural, oh my goddess, the mural. We have to take another look at the mural. Cam,' she turned and took her friend's hands. 'Cam, it's me. He painted it for me. It's not old, but it was done by an Italian.'

Watermelon zoomed around the room and Phillip slid the door shut before he could bark and disturb anyone.

'What are you raving about?' Phillip was losing patience.

Cam picked the dog up again, gently talking to him, he relaxed in her arms. 'Phillip was going to tell us about the safe. Thalia, you can talk about the mural in a moment. Phil, you were saying?'

Phillip was still eyeing Thalia who had re-clamped her hand over her mouth. 'The safe is right here, but no one knows the code.'

'I do,' Thalia said, too loud, raising her hand like a schoolchild. 'It's his birthday.'

Phillip shook his head. 'No, they've tried that.'

'But I saw him do it…7-1-5-1-9-1-9.'

'In your dream? You saw him do it in your dream? His birthday is today, the 14th.'

Thalia shook his head. 'No, it's not, it's tomorrow, the 15th.'

Phillip rolled his eyes. 'No, it's not, I've seen his papers, it's all there in my thesis. You've read it, or at least you said you had.'

'I don't care what his papers say, he told me his birthday was the 15th.'

Phillip stared at her again.

'Cam, tell him.'

Camryn cleared her throat. 'To be honest, I can't explain any of it, but one night, before we went to Paris, Thalia took me with her. We met Braith, ah, Mr Evans-Lewis and we had a smoke and a chat.'

Thalia directed a look of triumph at Phillip who directed a look of exasperation at both of them. 'It's not real. You had a dream.'

'Okay, we both had a dream. The same dream.' Thalia said, crossing her arms. 'Let's just try the code and if it doesn't work then we can forget about it.' She looked around the room and walked over to the only blank wall. The desk with the hidden mechanism was gone but she could see a faint line in the plasterboard. 'I believe if I just push here…' She pushed the wall panel and it popped open.

Phillip, who had also crossed his arms across his chest let out a small grunt. 'I don't know how you knew the safe was there, but I suppose it's obviously the only panel that doesn't have shelves or anything stacked against it.'

'Yep, you got me Phil. I used my famous skills of deduction to find it.' She pulled open the panel to reveal the old black safe. 'You can do the honours.'

'I can't touch that. What if it's full of gold or something.'

'Give me your phone and I'll film you. No one is going to accuse good-old perfect Phil of trying to steal anything.' She smiled at him and held out her hand.

'You do it,' he said, lifting his phone, ready to film.

Thalia nodded and turned to face the dial. 'He did the month first, American style.' She turned the dial right to seven, then left to one, then right to five. 'He might have told people his birthday was on Bastille Day to be more exotic or something but it's definitely the 15th.' She clicked it left to the number one and right to the nine, then repeated the action. Left to one, right to nine. The door popped open.

'I forgot to press go on the video,' Phillip groaned. He pressed it and walked over to the safe, commentating on what he was doing for the imagined audience. Thalia ducked in front of the camera, fingers raised in a V for Victory sign and opened the safe door wide.

The dark space inside was piled high with objects and Thalia took them out one by one, showing the camera. Camryn was almost reverent when she took her phone and peered around Phil's broad bicep as he videoed the rest of the haul. Benito would be happy to see his spatula and a stainless-steel fitting for a mixer. There was a small hoard of books and magazines dating from 2016 onwards that had somehow found their way back in time.

'When did Braith move back in here?' she said, flicking through the magazines.

'Ah, Mr Evans-Lewis came here in…'

'2016,' they said simultaneously.

Phillip nodded. Thalia held Phillip's father's razor up to him and he gasped. 'How on earth…?'

Thalia laughed when she pulled a black bundle from the safe and unwrapped it to find her tank top wrapped around her old Canon. She popped open the film housing, but it was empty. Leaving the camera on the table, she handed a bundle of letters and papers to Phillip. He gave up on filming and sat on the floor to sort through them.

An object wrapped in canvas lay on top of a shoebox. Thalia unwrapped it and let out an 'ooh' sound and held up her sea-glass lady to Camryn. She put the sculpture on the table as Thalia pulled the lid from the box. Wrapped in layers of white tissue were a pair of size 8 blush pumps. She felt like Cinderella as she slid them onto her feet. Phillip held out a letter and handed it to her. 'It's for you. I don't bloody know how, but it is,' he said, his father's razor still in his hand.

Thalia opened the envelope and read the letter, tears streaming down her face by the end. She handed it to Camryn and leaned on the wall looking down at the shoes. Camryn read the first few lines then spoke in a reverent tone.

'It's on printed stationery. It says *from the desk of Robert Evans.* He's handwritten Braith next to it and the date 6/11/78.' She smiled up at them both. Thalia was beaming through her tears. Poor Phillip just looked confused.

'It says:

"My dearest Thalia,

My muse, my inspiration, my deepest wish. It has been ten years since you 'graced' my presence, but I still hope. Ten long years of happiness, success, and peace. Writing has been my passion and my tormentor, my paycheck and my burden. As a wise woman once said to me, writing is harder than you think.

Heartache has visited. We lost our boy, our bundle of joy, but Pammy grows each day in height, yes, but also in strength, talent and humour. My marriage has survived throughout the darkest moments due to one thing: the strength of my wife.

Cuba opened my eyes. I found, unlike my idol, my desire to write dampened with each drink. Finally, my agent has a sober writer on his hands, and we are all the better for it.

I have returned to France for a vacation. The house is much the same. The old girl still stands despite your fears for her safety.

I know in my heart I will see you again.

Forever your Braith

p.s. your photographs were a success – yet another marvellous talent.'

Camryn was breathless when she finished reading.

Phillip was staring up at her, but she just shook her head. She couldn't explain it in a way he would understand. The pile of envelopes held a treasure of letters, documents and a manilla dossier full of 8x10 photos of the writer posing around the house. Thalia's photos. She held up the image of the bird flying in front of the moon. 'These are good, if I can say that about my own work. There's one missing,' she said, gently paging through the photos, hands quivering. 'The one of him sitting at the typewriter. In the orangery.'

Phillip bundled up the envelopes and stood. 'Mrs Grant has that photo in her office. I hope it will be the cover of my book, but we could never find the photographer to gain permission. She said her father always said his…'

Thalia and Cam looked at him as a slight smile crept over his face. 'His?' Camryn said.

'Muse. He told her his *muse* took the photo.' He laughed out loud for the first time in Thalia's company. 'It's… not…' He shook his head. 'Possible.'

They stood silently for a few moments before Phillip cleared his throat. 'Thalia, would you like to meet Mr Evans-Lewis?' She nodded and Camryn burst into tears.

Himself

The new parlour doors were closed but there were numerous people in uniforms and one with the stethoscope around her neck, in the room. Phillip knocked gently on the door and waited for someone to notice. A nurse, smiling broadly, opened the door but put a finger to her lips in the universal symbol of *quiet please*.

'How is he?' Phillip said.

'He's awake and seems quite coherent but we're keeping things calm so as not to exhaust him for tonight. He's excited about the party.' The nurse was still grinning.

'The ladies would like to meet him if that's okay. Just for a few moments.'

The doctor walked over, her eyes not leaving the chart in her hands. 'One at a time.'

Camryn put her hand on Thalia's arm. 'You go in, Thalia. I'll see him tonight. He won't even remember me.'

The doctor looked up. 'Who is Thalia?'

She put her hand up slowly.

'He's asking for you.' Phillip gaped at the doctor then turned to Thalia, shrugged and stepped back, allowing her to go in. Cam reached out and squeezed her arm gently then the doctor led her across the bland but comfortable room. It was hard to believe that space had once been Braith's favourite room, filled with books, his beloved lamps, gramophone, and an ever-evolving bar in the far corner. The doctor opened the door to a large plain room that appeared to have been plucked out of a hospital and transplanted into the château. White walls and floor, machines beeping, the whole works, except that one wall of glass panels, giving out to the terrace with a view of the gardens. The gardens were not what they had been in the 50s, but they were better than staring at a wall.

Mrs Grant sat on a high stool beside the bed, holding her father's hand, chatting quietly. The doctor went to the patient's side and checked his vitals. 'Mr Evans-Lewis, there is someone here to see you,' she said nodding at Thalia.

Mrs Grant turned and smiled at her. 'Alia, or should I say *Thalia*? My father… Robert, or should I say Braith.' She motioned for Thalia to join her at the bedside.

Alia swallowed and reminded herself to breathe. She found her voice, but only a whisper. 'This room isn't you at all. You need a couple of lamps in here, maybe a bar in the corner.' Mrs Grant placed her father's hand in Thalia's and stood back.

'My Thalia,' he said.

Thalia made a noise that was half sob and half hiccough and sat on the stool Pamela had just vacated. 'I'm here and…and I'm wearing the shoes.' She lifted one leg at a right angle and showed him the elegant pumps on her feet. The doctor gasped and her eyes bulged but Braith laughed in a raspy chuckle.

'You found the safe.'

She nodded. 'Phillip helped me.'

'Aah, good old Phillip… a good man. Did you know he is writing a book about me? Pammy told me.' Thalia nodded at him and turned to smile at Pamela. 'He should mention my muse.'

'I'm not sure Phillip believes in all that stuff,' Pamela said.

Braith snickered softly. 'What's to believe? She's standing right here in front of me.'

Star

A woman in white Dior stood on the terrace looking down at her phone, dark hair falling across her face. Thalia looked at the shoes. Louboutin. Patent leather. White. A tiny array of tattooed stars splashed across the top of the left foot. She took another step down and crouched on the stairs. Star. She wasn't sure she wanted to speak to her agent. Not now. Not at the party, not ever.

Star wouldn't understand. She wouldn't know how much she'd changed. She would think she was the same old Alia. The Louboutin clad feet took a few steps and suddenly Star was standing at the foot of the stairs looking up at her. 'Oh, hey…you…' was all Thalia could manage.

There was a ping. Star looked down at her phone and up again, holding up one finger, signalling Thalia to wait. The phone went to her ear and Star retraced her footsteps to the terrace, talking at the top of her voice with one finger stuffed in her ear. Thalia stood, adjusted her dress, and continued down the stairs. The dress had pinched just a little across her boobs, but Cam had done something tricky and it fit perfectly. A light breeze played with the crystal leaves in the chandelier and the scent of the huge floral decorations in the foyer wafted up the stairs. She was eager to avoid Star but knew it was best to get it over and done with, like leg waxing. Star was wandering around on the drive, angrily poking her finger at the air as she spoke. Alia hadn't had much luck with Star in 'angry' mode. She decided to see if Benito could use her help in the kitchen.

The dining room chairs had been moved and a huge floral display dominated the table. The secret door stood open. New light fittings in black wrought iron dotted the ceiling of the passageway leading to the cave and a red velvet rope hung across the opening. She knocked on the kitchen door and pushed it open only to be shooed from the room. The door shut in front of her with a familiar whoosh and click of the lock.

'I guess they don't need any help,' said a voice behind her.

Thalia turned to see Star on the other side of the table. 'No, well their loss, really. I know my way around a kitchen. How are you?'

Star walked over and peered over the velvet rope and along the passageway. 'This place is incredible. No wonder you look so good. I think I need a month here.'

Thalia nodded her head towards her agent. 'Thanks, it has agreed with me far more than jail would have, I suspect.'

'No doubt,' Star said. The two stood awkward as new kids on the first day at school. 'Nice dress. Vintage?'

'Thanks for that, the jail thing, I mean, and yeah, the dress. It's vintage. A gift.' She smoothed the soft tulle beneath her fingers, marvelling at the colour. 'How's your dad?'

Star looked at her, a slight frown on her face. 'Why?'

Thalia didn't react. She knew there were all kinds of thoughts whirring around in Star's head and she had to give her time. Star needed to see the new Alia or should that be Thalia. She wondered if her old alter-ego still existed somewhere.

A couple of lines and a bottle of tequila might answer that question.

'Your dad was poorly, you said… last time we spoke.'

'He's much better. Thank you.' She sounded confused, as though she couldn't remember why she was saying thank you.

'Great. Star, I really meant it. Thank you, that is, for the jail thing, for everything. What I did was ridiculous, and you saved my ass, literally, and I can't even tell you how much I've learned from all this and I have written so much, and I am going by Thalia now.' She was rambling.

Star held her hand up. 'I know. I mean, that's great, but you can't. You have to be Alia for the book tour but in private, I know it will be relief to everyone if you can be Thalia for the rest of the time.' She kept her hand up and closed her eyes to stop Thalia interrupting. '…and Phil says you're doing well and from the pages he sent… Well, everyone is impressed.'

Thalia was about to launch into an explanation of why she could not possibly be Alia ever again but realised she could try if it meant she could go on a book tour. 'So, they are not going to use the ghost writer?'

She wondered if she'd ever be able to explain how she'd come to find her very own ghostly writer there in the château.

Star shook her head. 'They're giving you a chance, the work you've sent is great. It's good to see you've grown up a little, but you better keep writing. Don't go home, get back on the party-train and lose focus.'

Thalia squealed and jumped up and down. There was a click and the kitchen door opened behind her. 'Did you tell her eyeliner was on special?' Phillip said, entering the room carrying an electrical cable. Startled, Thalia turned, mid squeal and mid-jump to see the source of the voice and landed heavily on her left heel, ending up in a mass of tulle on the floor.

'Oh, my goddess!' Thalia howled, grabbing her ankle, her eyes scrunched in pain. 'Oh… balls.'

When she opened them, Star, Phillip, and Mrs Grant were crouching around her with an audience of onlookers. 'No, Phillip, I was congratulating her on her new-found maturity,' Star said.

Benito opened the kitchen door, a scowl on his face. He looked down at the gathering on the floor around Thalia. 'The official party will be here in fifteen minutes so can you all get off the floor.' He rolled his eyes and pulled the door shut.

'Can you walk?' Mrs Grant asked.

Thalia crawled onto her hands and knees and put weight on the damaged ankle that was already bruising. 'You should probably take the shoes off.' Phillip offered.

'I don't want to, they're so pretty.' She smiled at Mrs Grant.

'I still haven't gotten to the bottom of all this shoe business, but I do know you've helped my father. Phil, can you help her up? We can't have the Minister arriving with one of the guests in a nest of tulle on the floor.'

He handed the cable to Star and bent to help Thalia but stopped a slight smile playing on his lips. 'May I?'

'Of course, Phillip would ask for consent to help a woman up,' Mrs Grant said.

Thalia looked up at Phil. 'That would be great thanks.' He bent and put his arm around her waist, and she waited for him to pull her to her feet.

'Go on…' he said.

'Really?' she squeaked out. He nodded.

She looped her arms around his neck, and he scooped her up, a huge grin on her face that no-one could see because she tucked it into his neck, Bodyguard-style.

The Party

Phillip had found her a comfortable resting place while he guided the rest of the guests on a tour of the lower completed floor of the château. Earlier, he, Camryn, and Thalia had stood peering at the faces of the muses in the fresco and snapping photos until they found Thalia, Goddess of Poetry, who looked remarkably like Thalia, Socialite, and Instagram-poet.

The party venue was the enormous space, once home to the indoor pool. The glass conservatory roof glowed in the evening light. Although she had promised to dance on tables, Thalia spent the evening on one side of Braith's fancy wheelchair, one leg propped on a chair with an icepack on it, Pamela on the other side introducing a never-ending stream of well-wishers to her father. Braith was wide awake, carried on conversations and made jokes, the life of the party, although he did complain at times about the music. Star finally made her way to the head of the queue and seemed a little star-struck meeting the famous writer, her eyebrow almost arching off the top of her head when he introduced Thalia to her as his muse.

'We've met,' she said, eyeing her famous client.

After moving on from the guest of honour, Star sat beside Thalia and handed her a small gift box.

'For me?' Alia said.

Star shrugged, picked up her phone and began dialling. A moment later, the gift box buzzed. The two women laughed, Star leaning across and nudging Thalia's shoulder.

'Good to have it back?' Star asked, as Thalia turned the box over, rattling it, as though trying to work out what it was.

'Good to have *you* back,' Thalia said, smiling at her agent.

Camryn had been helping Benito but had made her way to Braith's wheelchair where they were speaking Welsh, her hand in his. Her cheeks were flushed when she joined Thalia, introducing herself to Star.

'Do artists need an agent, Star? Because if they do, you should give your card to Cam. She's a Rockstar.'

'Oh, stop it. No don't, keep talking,' Camryn giggled.

'Where's Watermelon?' Alia asked.

Cam put her hands on her heart. 'He's being very well taken care of. Benny made a little bed for him in the passageway behind the kitchen so he can supervise but keep out of the way. He's wearing a little black bow tie, which is darling, but there are too many people in here for him. There are almost too many people in here for me. You know, he hasn't barked at an empty room since before Paris. Ooh, I see you have your phone back.'

Camryn took a deep breath. 'Sorry, I'm rambling. I videoed Phil's tour of the house. It was really good. He has such a way with people, but then I don't need to tell you that. I'll send you the video. Number?' She punched the number into her phone and a little whooshing sound told them it was winging its way to Thalia's phone.

Camryn flicked through her photos and turned the screen to show a good-looking man's face, filling the screen, wearing the startled expression of someone who discovers the camera is on selfie-mode. It was Braith, circa 1959. She jumped up to show the photo to Pamela and her father.

Star looked puzzled. 'You ladies are very tight with the birthday boy.'

'It's a long story,' Thalia said, smiling over at Camryn.

Star eyed her again. 'You can tell me all about it, on the drive back to London.'

Thalia felt her heart contract at the idea of leaving the château. Leaving Camryn, Benito, Phillip, and Braith.

Braith.

Would she see him again? She picked up her phone, but it wasn't a social media account she was looking for. Star and Regina had done an amazing job with that and could continue as far as she cared. She handed the phone to Star. 'Can you ask the DJ to play this?'

A few moments later, the voice of Billie Holiday filled the room and Braith's face lit up. He took his daughter's hand and waved it back and forth as guests made their way to the dance floor. A beaming Benito led Camryn out among the dancers and Pamela smiled over at Thalia. Phillip stopped to speak to his idol again. They had spent the afternoon together. Phillip's book would have the scoop that B.R.E.L and Robert Evans were one and the same. Braith, as Thalia had discovered over the weeks, loved nothing more than to talk about himself, but at one hundred, his childlike enthusiasm for the subject was endearing.

'Would you like to dance?' Phillip stood in front of them. Thalia looked at Star. 'No, ah, you, Thalia. No offense, Star.'

'None taken, I have to work the room a bit more anyway,' she said and wandered into the crowd.

Thalia motioned to her foot. He shrugged. 'I got you,' he said, and leaned in. 'May I?'

Her whole body tingled. 'Oh goddess, yes. Please, just take me,' she said and held her arms up to him.

Epilogue

The photographer seemed terribly pleased with the light in the newly renamed Rosebud Room. It hadn't been great for writing but apparently it was perfect for the promotional shots for a soon-to-be published author. Thalia assumed one or two photos would be sufficient, but after an hour, the photographer was still enjoying herself. As they made their way around the château, Thalia ensured each pose featured Camryn's creations.

Even after just a few months it was strange being back at the old house. Benito had met them at the door, wrapping them both in a huge hug, but the place felt empty without its master. After the birthday celebrations, Braith had only rallied for a few weeks before leaving the world completely.

He was gone, but he lived on through his magnificent former home, his own works, and Thalia's new books. Whitehall had engaged Phillip to adapt his thesis to publish Braith's biography and of course, there was L'Ecrivain, the restaurant and hotel in Paris. Thalia intended to volunteer at the retreats for artists and writers, and she was working with Phillip to create Summer programmes for high school students. Cam was planning a series of workshops in the new year, after her triumphant return from Venice, and she and Benito were planning their own summer wedding at the château.

Phillip appeared at the cave entrance. He had arrived in a suit but had obviously found work clothes somewhere. He was covered in dust.

'Ready for lunch, sweetheart? Benny's thrown together one of his famous picnics.'

'Absolutely, *Doctor* Hobbs' Thalia said.

Her heart leapt when he called her sweetheart. She skipped over to him and he was laughing by the time she joined him on the stairs. It had always been her goal in life to entertain, and it was indeed a pleasure to see him relax and laugh. He reached for her hand as she approached and pulled her to him. She giggled as he kissed her neck. She could have stayed like that forever, but the photographer had work to do. Reluctantly, she pulled away and cocked her eyebrow at his appearance. Brushing dust from his face, she shook her head at him. 'Can't leave you alone for five minutes.'

He looked down at his clothes. 'I've been in the attic. Benny needed something.' He grinned.

'Of course, he did,' she said. She ran her fingers through his hair, freeing some dust bunnies. Thalia turned to the photographer. 'Will you stay for lunch? You can take Phil's author photos after he's cleaned up a bit?'

The photographer didn't respond. She was lying on the flagstone floor, her camera pointed up at the ceiling. She took a few shots and checked the digital display. 'Hey Alia...' she called. 'One of these goddesses looks just like you.'

'Really?' Thalia said. 'What a strange coincidence.'

About the Author

Hi! I'm Christine. I am an Australian writer, but I left my heart in Paris years ago. You can catch me on Facebook and Instagram by searching @ParisTimeTravel. I love to network with other writers and have a growing community of authors who love France as much as I do, sometimes more! If you're a writer with works set in France, email me at christine@writerpainter.com if you'd like to join us.

Most days I can be found at the beach. Like everyone, I am a work in progress. I write about art, creativity and personal development over at www.writerpainter.com

If you enjoyed Alia Henry and the Ghost Writer, I'd really appreciate a 5-star review on the platform you purchased from or on Goodreads. This helps others find my work and makes me do a happy dance. If there was something you think I could improve or if you just want to say hello, you can email me at christine@writerpainter.com

Some notes about the story

Alia Henry and the Ghost Writer was my Nanowrimo project for November 2019. Dubbed #nanoslowmo by some other writers on Twitter, I too struggled to make time to write but still had around 30K words by the first of December. I had been working on a couple of other projects (The Circle of Ashes and Mimi gets Away with Murder, my husband's least favourite book title…) but Alia took up residence in the front of my brain until I told her story.

Where did I get the idea for this story? Perhaps from the muse…?

I like the idea that we fill our consciousness over the years with all kinds of ideas and the act of writing, especially long hand, allows those ideas to bubble to the surface. The basic concept was inspired by my favourite childhood novel, Tom's Midnight Garden by Philippa Pearce. Phillip, our hunky, sweet, brooding love interest, is named for her. I adore Tom's Midnight Garden. I also loved Grease and Xanadu as a teenager. Although I couldn't really identify with either of the characters Olivia Newton-John played, I love the idea of transformation, stepping into who we truly are or maybe who we would like to be for a day. Did Sandy feel empowered wearing the spray-on pants, or did she peel them off when she got home in favour of a pair of stylish Capri pants? Even if it's only a matter of wearing a costume for a day, surely something of the motivation for wearing the costume remains.

I am fascinated by people who can write a book this length in a month. My ideas seem to bubble out over the weeks of playing with the words. I can't rush it. I write as though I am making a pinch-pot out of words; starting with a small amount of clay (words) and slowly adding more and more clay (words…obviously…) until I have a large and hopefully beautiful pot. Although this is a romance, the story is very much Alia's. She falls in love with everyone she meets, but in this story, she has fallen in love with herself more than anyone else.

Hotel Déjà Vu

Christine Betts

Arrivals

Gare du Nord, Paris. June 2016

Arriving in Paris should only happen by train, and on a Sunday, Rachel often told anyone who asked, and even many who didn't. Many years of arriving in Paris on weekdays, surrounded by commuters and confused tourists had convinced Rachel of this fact. She stood a little apart from the group to phone the drivers to let them know they could pull the cars around. Catching sight of herself in the plate glass windows she smoothed her pencil skirt and adjusted her sunglasses. Perfect scarf, black boots shiny, and not a hair out of place, umbrella hooked over her arm. Her friend Steph said she was rocking a sexy Mary Poppins vibe, and she was happy enough with that. At forty-two, she would take sexy-anything, even Mary Poppins.

Taking a deep breath, she walked back to the group, tucking her phone into its pocket on her tote. The women gathered in a group on the pavement, shielding their eyes from the early morning sun, beside piles of luggage. Rachel was relieved she had opted for two cars for the arrival, knowing that everyone over-packs. The tour details package sent to each participant always urged them to bring as little as possible. Shopping opportunities would be many and varied, and evening wear available to borrow.

The suggestion that they travel light had clearly been taken as a guide only by everyone except Betty, who had a Kelly bag over one arm and pulled a matching carry-on. A seasoned traveller she knew how to travel light, but Rachel knew Betty had the means to simply purchase anything she may need on the fly. Betty's friend Janet stood behind her facing away from the group.

The women began to introduce themselves, sharing names and small details of their lives. Scanning the cluster of eager, smiling faces, Rachel listened to the excited chatter. She pondered, as she did each time a new group arrived, where the week would take them. There would be plenty of tears and laughter, that was always a given. Occasionally other emotions reared their ugly heads, but Rachel knew she had the experience and the training to deal with anything her charges could throw at her. She had been there too and knew the twists and turns life could take. Paris was a great place to confront your demons and practice some self-care. The City of Light was an amazing place to discover your own light all over again.

As she stood exchanging pleasantries with the group, she wondered, as she always did, who would decide to stay and make a life for themselves in Paris. And of course, who might decide to opt for a total life makeover, so to speak.

One previous client had taken the direction to heart, arriving in Paris with little more than the clothes on her back, so determined was she to create a new life for herself and leave the old one behind. Rachel often wondered about the Stayers as she liked to call them. It wasn't for the faint of heart, and she only offered that extra service to those truly in need. They had to be ready to make a go of it. Occasionally, even in a city the size of Paris, she would run into one of her Stayers. As expected, most didn't remember her although she knew firsthand that overwhelming sense of déjà vu it brought with it. She knew it would make sense to them as time passed. Time heals all wounds they say. Rachel knew this to be true.

One of the clients who had flown into London the previous afternoon from Australia, stood away from the group and seem distressed that her phone wasn't working. Rachel moved towards her to offer some help with the phone when it sprang to life and a torrent of text messages came pouring in. Her chosen ringtone, a little like a clown would choose for the horn on his car, rang out through the early morning air to the stares and eye-rolls of passers-by. She seemed unfazed by the attention, visibly relieved to finally receive her messages again. She smiled and began scrolling through the phone, her manicured nails tick-ticking against the phone screen. She began muttering under her breath while the rest of the group stood silently, embarrassed, as the barrage of text messages continued, ringing out loudly over the noise of the train station.

'Oh, it's my son,' she said, as she looked up and saw the nine other women looking at her. 'He misses his mummy, you know.'

A tall woman in jeans, her messy bun piled on her head cleared her throat. 'How old is your son?' Her voice was calm.

This is Carole, Rachel thought. Carole was travelling with her sister and had left her own small children at home with their father.

'Seventeen,' Paula replied. 'He and his partner are looking after the house.'

Text messages continued to pour in. Rachel noticed side-eye glances and disapproving frowns directed at Paula.

'Nonsense. Seventeen-year-olds don't have a partner. At seventeen it's a girlfriend or boyfriend. Turn that phone off, would you?' Betty looked directly at Paula. She looked bored rather than annoyed.

The rest of the group looked aghast at the outburst but then each woman seemed completely fascinated by the contents of their hand luggage. Rachel took a deep breath, as deep as her tight skirt would allow, and prepared herself to mediate a slanging match in the middle of the Gare du Nord but it was clearly water off-a-Dior-raincoat to Paula. She was already busying herself replying to her son's latest missive.

'So cute,' she gushed, 'He wants to know where the toaster is kept.'

'Seriously, can you please put that on silent or something?' Betty said. Janet was rubbing her temples. The rest of the group stood awkwardly by, but Paula seemed to be made of Teflon.

'Seriously,' she mimicked Betty's tone, 'can you mind your own business?' Paula didn't look up from the phone.

Betty took Janet by the hand and steered her away from the group. The group turned to look at Rachel as two sleek stretch limousines pulled up to the curb. Previous groups had made their own way into Paris and met at the hotel, but Rachel's friends in the tourism industry had suggested the stretch limos. It had seemed like a great idea after a glass of wine or three.

Hire a driver, they said. All together in a limo will be fun, they said.

As the group stood in awkward silence, Rachel mentally cursed her friends and their wine-fuelled 'excellent' idea, quickly calculating how she would get Betty and Paula in separate cars. To be fair, the shiny cars were lovely, and they were certainly attracting attention. The passengers snapped a few photos, standing politely back to allow the lucky passengers access to their vehicles. The lead driver rounded the back of the car and opened the rear door with a flourish.

Rachel took her cue and stepped forward. 'Your chariots await,' she said.

Smiles spread across the face of even the weariest traveller as it dawned on them that the elegant stretch limos were for them. Tick that one off the bucket list, ladies, Rachel thought. Perhaps it hadn't been such a bad idea after all.

The caring driver ushered Betty and Janet in first. Rachel waved Ingrid, Sam and Paula toward the car purring behind, handsome driver waiting by the open door, but it was too late. Ingrid and Sam had jumped into the lead car, laughing like children. Paula followed her friends. There was no more room, so Rachel joined sisters Carole and Wendy, and mother-daughter duo Georgia and Judy in the rear limo. Perhaps Betty and Paula will be best of friends by the time they reach Saint Germaine, she thought. Luggage was stowed, champagne poured, and doors shut, and the cars eased their way into the almost non-existent Sunday morning traffic.

Rachel began to point out various sights as they drove, but the passengers seemed more interested in chatting about a Paris wish-list that seemed quite handbag-centric. She sat back and let the conversation wash over her. Although she had travelled over from London with the group, Rachel had had little time to speak to them before the Eurostar. They all appeared quite relaxed on the train, so Rachel left them to their own thoughts, although she was able to take a little time to chat with each lady, put a face to each name from the applications. Rachel used the information in written submissions to match her client groups. It was essential to have like-minded people in a group where rest and relaxation, and often personal transformation, was the motivation for the vacation. She had toyed with the idea of calling her tours 'retreats' but her friends and colleagues who, like her, had worked with tourists for years, felt the clubbing, shopping, and eating aspect of the tours was the main attraction for many of her clients. They feared calling it a retreat would conjure images of waking at dawn for yoga and drinking green smoothies for a week. Not that there was anything wrong with that, it just wasn't what Rachel offered. Unless that was what the group wanted.

Rachel smiled and nodded at an enthusiastic Georgia who was regaling the others with stories of her few months in Paris as part of a study abroad programme.

This is going to be a great week, Rachel thought, but then realised she had her fingers crossed. She uncrossed them and rubbed the tiny dents where her fingernails had marked her skin. Her tour company tended to attract a diverse group of potential clients who had one thing in common; they all viewed Paris as a restorative place to visit. Some groups wanted to look at museums, others were passionate about cooking, and often the wine that went with the cooking, and some wanted to party for a week, but this group seemed…special. Their booking requests all arrived within a week, the group forming organically each time she checked her emails. Each applicant seemed to have come to a turning point in her life. Some were at the lowest point. An illness, disintegration of a marriage, a bereavement, had literally sent them packing, and there were all looking for a way up, or out.

As she had at the station, Paula had stood out in the application process. In her own words, she already had an incredible life and wanted to use this time in Paris to take it to the next level. She wasn't broken-hearted, divorcing, or sick, she wrote, she simply wanted to return to Paris to have fun and let her hair down and come into her own power as a woman. Rachel wasn't at all sure she could help anyone come into their own power, but as her friends were on the tour, she couldn't really refuse her.

Rachel found Paula intriguing. It was refreshing to encounter such a confident and successful woman. Although she normally only took eight guests, Judy's daughter Georgia was not officially attending the tour, so Rachel felt Paula would be easy to accommodate. She obviously did not intend relocating to Paris or appear to need any special help apart from a few days shopping, time at the day spa, and some nights on the town.

After reading their applications, Rachel was excited about the group. She sent acceptance packages and deposits began to roll in. Then Paula's extensive wish list arrived via separate email.

Bienvenue à l'hôtel De la Roche

Rachel smiled at the eager faces around her, congratulating herself and finally deciding that the stretch limousines had been a good idea. Carole, Wendy, Judy and Georgia were relaxed and chatting quietly discovering that they had much in common. Wendy and Judy even knew some of the same people from their teen years surfing around Sydney's northern beaches.

Rachel wondered how things were going in the other car. Betty and Paula were both what Human Resources departments would call strong personalities. Rachel hated the term. They say opposites attract, but these two successful women were so similar they seemed to repel each other like poles on a battery. Rachel had heard many times over the years that you really get to know someone when you travel with them. Betty was obviously used to pulling no punches, and Paula was noticeably adept at ignoring others' opinion of her.

Lost in her own thoughts, Rachel hadn't realised that all four of the other women in the vehicle were looking at her expectantly, remarking how successful the application process was and how well matched they seemed.

'I'm not sure the ladies in the other car will have the same opinion,' Wendy said, almost under her breath.

Georgia and Judy chuckled, and Carole scolded her sister for being rude.

'My sister would be nice to a carjacker,' Wendy said with a loving smile in her sister's direction.

'Here you go Mr. Carjacker, would you like my purse, too?' Wendy laughed, patting her sister on the leg. 'Sorry, sissy. I'm bitter and old, I know.'

Wendy leaned back and closed her eyes. They were sisters but as Wendy was eleven years older than Carole, according to their applications, they were very different people with very different lives. Carole had filled out her application in a hurry, moments when her children were in bed or playing happily, which, with four children under five, a home-based business and a hard-working FIFO husband, were few and far between. She had simply written 'I'm not unhappy, I'm boring! I want a Sabrina Experience!' scrawled in red pen with three exclamation points. Sabrina was one of Rachel's favourite old movies and she had a great week planned for Carole. A session with a personal shopper to whisk her around the famous shopping districts and department stores, a couple of hours at the spa and lots of time to enjoy Paris with her sister. At the end of the week, some of the other women would join in for a photo shoot with a photographer who specialises in vacation shoots around Paris.

Carole was most definitely not a candidate for moving to Paris. She had a happy marriage and small children, and, like Paula, she wanted to let her hair down and enjoy her week in Paris.

Wendy, on the other hand, was more than ready for a new life. This was probably because her old one had completely disintegrated. Her application had brought Rachel to tears. Her marriage break-up and unfulfilled desire to start a family was a little close to home. To add insult to injury, technically, Wendy was homeless, having left the marital home to her husband and his new girlfriend. A real contender for making a permanent home in Paris, either now or at some point in the future…or past, Rachel thought with a smile. A successful partner in an international law firm, she would have no problem finding her way in Paris and would certainly not be homeless, technically or otherwise.

Wendy's application said she had researched the Louvre and wanted to spend a lot of time there. Under the heading 'secret desire' she wrote of her desire to have a 'rustic picnic on the Champs de Mars with a gorgeous Paris fireman then go out dancing and see where the night took them.' With a handful of exclamation points at the end. Secret desire indeed. Rachel often marvelled at how many people's Parisian fantasies involved the legendary Pompiers of Paris.

Rachel looked up to see that the limos were about to cross the bridge to the Left Bank. The car stopped, the driver smiled at Rachel in the rear-view mirror and gestured at the lead car.

'Tourists,' he said, rolling his eyes theatrically.

Rachel pressed the button, the tinted window sliding silently down into the door. The lead limo was waiting at a pedestrian crossing as a large tour group traipsed after their guide who was holding aloft a bright yellow umbrella covered in sunflowers. Rachel smiled, reaching down to touch the Burberry umbrella that was now a permanent fixture in her daily life.

Georgia took advantage of the pause and, opening the sunroof, stood up with her head out of the vehicle. She took a few quick photos then urged the other passengers to do the same. Each woman stood head and shoulders out of the limo, taking their first photos of Paris for this visit. The inclusion of the young Georgia may help everyone relax a little, Rachel thought.

The women were staring at her again.

'Your turn,' Georgia said.

She could hardly say no, so Rachel stood and popped her head through the open sunroof. She watched another tour group cross the road, led by the same bright yellow umbrella. A drone whizzed over her head. Confused, she looked up and down the street, spying the real reason for the hold up. A common sight in Paris, a movie set had taken over the bridge and surrounding streets. A voice on a loudspeaker bellowed 'Cut' and people running left and right.

Would she be in a movie poking her head through a limo sunroof? Rachel hoped not. Filming seemed to be centred on the bridge with their limousines and the small snake of traffic behind out of shot. A young man with a bright orange vest that said 'C R E W' was talking to her.

'It will be a few more minutes, ma'am, is that okay?' the New York accent asked.

'Sure, of course,' she said, flipping her own camera over to video to get some footage for the website. The lead limo gleamed in the sun. She pressed the little red button to start filming when the sunroof on the other car opened. Perfect timing, Rachel thought. Then a bright pink, bejewelled mobile phone flew from the car, disappearing over the railing of the bridge. Rachel almost dropped her own phone and would not have believed it if she hadn't caught it on camera. Sinking back down into the car she fought the sinking feeling in her stomach.

'Oh geez,' Rachel gulped.

'What's wrong, Rachel?' Judy asked.

Georgia jumped up again and stuck her head through the sunroof. Paula's head could be seen protruding from the top of the lead limousine. She appeared to be talking to the others in the car.

'I can see Paula, she's pointing at the film crew I think, and telling the others in the limo what's going on.'

'Well, mmmm…I think Paula has thrown her cell phone through the sunroof, and it went into the river,' Rachel said hoping that was what happened. Something told her that perhaps that wasn't what had happened at all. What she knew for certain was that someone had thrown Paula's phone from the sunroof. Her heart sunk as she showed the women the video she had taken. Sure enough, the bright pink projectile disappeared over the side of the bridge leaving little doubt to its final resting place. Unless it had landed on a barge it would now be making its way to the bottom of the Seine, to rest among the thousands of rusting keys, shopping carts and bicycles. The group had been together a little over three hours, but everyone knew exactly whose phone it was.

As much as she encouraged responsible tourism, Rachel hoped that Paula had simply decided she needed a fresh start, which included a new phone, in Paris. She tried to ignore the butterflies in her stomach.

Georgia was standing up with her head through the sunroof again. Rachel opened her window, craning her neck to see if anything else would be ejected from the limo, and hoping it wouldn't be one of the other passengers. She found herself regretting the limos again. I'm on a rollercoaster, she thought, not an elegant journey into Paris. She was often surprised she got anything done considering how often she over-thought every decision. The limos were lovely but as luxurious as they were, encouraging the client to arrive at the hotel under their own steam often gave them either a sense of ownership over their fate, or left them reeling at the enormity of the city. Dragging a rolling bag up dozens of Metro stairs and across cobblestones was a great workout plus it taught clients a little resilience. It could also bring out some much-needed vulnerability.

Closing her eyes, Rachel leaned back against the leather seat and contemplated the wisdom of making decisions concerning her business while on a wine tour with colleagues, all of whom ran various unique tour companies in and around Paris. She berated herself for a long list of stupid ideas, starting with the limousines.

Stop it. Stop this minute…Rachel told herself. Clearly someone had to take control of the voices in her head. They were being mean! She could hardly blame herself for a phone being thrown into the river, could she? Who knew what had been said in that car during the ride from Gare du Nord?

'Ooh, I hope the director caught it on film! Like Andie in Devil Wears Prada,' Georgia said.

'She's making a new start,' Judy said, 'Good on her. I should do it too!'

'Or maybe,' Wendy said slowly, 'one of the other women couldn't take it any longer and threw it for her.' Clearly Rachel wasn't the only one who had come to that conclusion.

'Oh, do you think someone would do that?' Carole asked, looking anxious.

'I would have,' Wendy replied.

Carole had taken her sister's hand, Rachel noted. She was getting nervous. Her application, despite its rushed nature, revealed high hopes for her time in Paris. She clearly didn't want anything to jeopardise it.

'Wendy warned me that being on a tour with other people can be…interesting…' Carole said, looking at her sister.

'I don't want you to get too attached to the outcome. Just take a chill-pill,' Wendy said, rubbing the skin between her eyes.

'I told you I won't take any drugs,' Carole whispered to her sister. She smiled apologetically at Rachel.

Wendy laughed.

'What's so funny, sissy?' Carole said, an edge in her voice.

Judy leaned across and patted Carole's hand.

'Georgie explained that to me one day. There's no pill, it's something people say, like whatever floats your boat.'

Georgia was laughing too, and Wendy had hunched over in her seat, her back heaving with laughter. Rachel watched Carole for any sign she was getting upset. She did not want to come across as a crotchety teacher supervising the bus to camp.

'You can be such a 'B' sometimes, you know.' Carole turned to face her sister.

'Oh, stop it, I'm going to wet myself,' Wendy said, wiping her eyes with a tissue. 'Okay, everyone, take a deep breath,' she said. She inhaled deeply, held it for a second and let it out slowly. The other women followed her lead.

'Wow, that is an amazing trick,' Georgia said.

'Very handy in court, let me tell you…and when your husband is trying to mansplain why he cheated.'

'If I'd known how to stop myself from laughing, I would have avoided so many detentions at school.' Her mother raised her eyebrow at this news, so Georgia jumped up, her head and shoulders through the sunroof again. 'Paris is so beautiful, even if you're just sitting in one spot watching the same people walk across a street over and over.' She called out to the other car.

'Georgia, please don't shout in Paris,' Judy said.

The young woman sat down again.

'The other girls are taking turns popping their heads through the sunroof, too. Sam asked if there was room for her in here. But then she laughed, so….'

Rachel was about to open the car door to see when they could get moving, but she could see the crew dismantling the barricade.

'My guess is that Betty hurled that damn phone out the window as an alternative to shoving it where the sun don't shine,' Georgia said. Judy looked at her daughter over her sunglasses and Wendy grinned at her sister who was looking anxious again. Rachel took a deep breath, mimicking the technique Wendy had taught them.

This will just be another straight-forward week with a lovely group of ladies, she affirmed under her breath. Her mind, as well as her heart, was racing so she took another deep breath. It had been a strange morning and she really didn't need any drama right now. She'd woken early from an odd dream, drenched in sweat. She had seen her own face, floating in front of her. There was a tiger…no, a cat… She couldn't quite get a handle on all the images, but the old familiar feeling of déjà vu was settling over her.

Just as she had calmed herself enough to leave the house, she had found the embossed invitation under her door. The opening of an art show at a gallery that didn't exist, with a painting of her that she couldn't explain.

She opened her eyes to see Wendy studying her. A strand of hair had escaped her ponytail. Tucking it behind her ear, she felt as though she was falling apart. She smiled at Judy. Dreams mean nothing, and one strand of hair does not constitute a bad hair day, she told herself silently as the cars finally began to move.

They crossed the river. 'On your right, you will see Notre Dame,' Rachel said.

'Yes, ladies, Paris awaits,' Wendy said, a little too sarcastically for Rachel's liking.

I am equal to this task, Rachel told herself, hoping the affirmations would start working soon. Despite Wendy's cynicism, the passengers all swivelled in their seats, oohed and aahed at the ancient cathedral forgetting momentarily about the potential drama unfolding in the other limo. The towers of Notre Dame are the cathedral's most photographed features, but the eastern view of the structure with its flying buttresses and formal gardens, were Rachel's favourite view in Paris. Even after years living and working in the city, she still thrilled at the sights as though seeing them for the first time.

The limo stopped at a red light, tourists stopping halfway across the road to photograph the cars with the cathedral in the background. Judy quickly took the opportunity to play tourist, poking her head through the sunroof. She couldn't believe it herself, that she was standing with her head out of a sunroof, in a limo, driving through Paris. If her husband could see her now, she thought.

Ex-husband, she corrected herself.

Judy rested her arms on the warm roof of the car and took it all in, not wanting to break the spell of the city by trying to capture it on her phone. She could see the lead car easily, but no-one was using the sunroof. She wondered what might be going on in there, grateful she wasn't involved. She had had enough drama for one lifetime. She carefully eased herself back down into the car. Had she made a mistake taking a tour? Should she and Georgia have simply rented an apartment where she didn't have to deal with other people?

'I've been here a few times in my life, but I was always working, I never saw the sights, but I feel like I'm home finally. That's strange isn't it?' Judy said.

'No, I feel the same. It sounds nuts, because I've spent so little time here as an adult,' Carole admitted.

'Yes, well you will see the sights this time and I hope you love it even more when it's time to go home, or make it your home, whatever the case may be!' Rachel said. 'You'll be a virtual local by the time I'm finished with you!'

'Oh yes please,' Georgia pleaded, 'I'm definitely moving here. I love Paris so much. I'm going to write and take photos, and paint and live in a gorgeous apartment. A small one, of course, but nice. With a view. Dad said he'd help me,' she finished, not looking at her mother.

'Perhaps I will become a local, too,' Judy mused quietly.

'Mum, yes! We can be room-mates,' Georgia laughed.

The limousine slowed to a crawl as it made its way down a narrow alley. Finally, they stopped again, and the chauffeur opened the door for the passengers. Smiling as he welcomed each passenger to Paris, reaching his hand out to help each lady exit the vehicle with style, their smiles lighting up as he did so. When the clients were standing in the laneway, Rachel took another deep breath and, taking Myles' hand, stepped out into the bright sunlight.

The women were already tumbling from the other limo, not waiting for the driver to help them from the vehicle. Betty and Janet, were first, followed by Sam. All three were clenching their lips, as though trying to keep a straight face. Paula emerged, red faced, and tear stained. Rachel raced to her side, placing a protective arm around the woman's shoulders. Ingrid scrambled from the car, immediately going to her friend's side, making soothing sounds, like she was trying to pacify a toddler.

'Stupid old bitch,' Paula hissed at Betty as Janet held her friends' shoulders. Rachel wasn't sure if she was holding her back, or upright.

Sara, their host, stood in the shadows of the carriage entrance, unseen by everyone but Rachel. Having worked in her mother's private hotel for years she was used to highly strung clients arriving for their 'retreat', but Rachel suspected today's events had taken things to a whole new level. Ingrid moved forward and took her crying friend's hand. The rest of the group held back to give Paula some space.

'Oh, screw it,' Betty said, scanning the faces that were desperately trying to avoid eye-contact with her. 'Aren't we all here to enjoy ourselves, to leave our old lives behind for a bit. Maybe even to start again?'

'Betty, please…stop,' Rachel interrupted.

'No, I won't stop. That damn phone beeped and shrilled the whole way here. I asked you to silence it. Everyone did.'

Paula's tear-stained face blushed red, while Ingrid and Sam stared at the cobblestones.

'We're all here to have a good time and we owe ourselves a little bit of self-love, ladies. You can't move forward if you're looking backwards, well you can, but you'll probably fall flat on your arse. Your son will be fine, Paula,' she said, placing herself in front of Paula. 'Give him the opportunity to miss you, or at least to have to find the toaster or make do with bread. Woman let it go,' she said, now standing in front of Paula, looking directly into her eyes.

'Let it go,' she said again. She took Paula's hand and held it.

Paula stood staring at her own hand, gently resting on Betty's own tiny hand. Paula appeared to be traveling through a full spectrum of emotions, no doubt wondering how to extricate her hand from this crazy woman in front of her. Rachel towered over both, her boots making her at least twenty centimetres taller than them. Two petite women would be easy to pull apart if there was a catfight in the street.

'Leave me alone. I don't need you to tell me how to behave. I am a surgeon!' Paula hissed.

Betty put her hands up in surrender. The sounds of Paris seemed to drop away as the group stood in the lane, unsure what to do next. Rachel looked over Paula's shoulder and gave Sara a look that said, "Get your butt out here lady, and help me." At least she hoped that's what the look was saying.

Sara pretended to step back into the foyer and close the door, silently laughing the whole time. Rachel shot her another look that hopefully said, "don't you dare."

Sara took a deep breath.

'Welcome to Paris, Mesdames, Bievenue à l'hôtel De la Roche,'' said a voice from the shadows as their stylish host stepped out of the old carriage entrance and into the bright sunshine.

Lunch at the Hotel Déjà Vu

The scene in the laneway was a first for the hotel, somehow managing to operate for ten years without guests screaming obscenities at each other in the quiet street. Sara was glad her parents were not present to witness the scene. Quickly regaining her composure and politely waving at the neighbours, she stood welcoming each lady in turn as they walked through the enormous doorway and into the cool dark foyer.

Young and effortlessly stylish, but with a wisdom beyond her years, Sara often sat listening to a crying client well into the early hours of the morning and had seen her fair share of bad behaviour from drunken guests. She had a nonchalance about her that came with youth, but she cared deeply for her clients, and showed it in very practical ways. Singling out the distressed Paula, she put her arm through hers and led her to the elevator that whisked them to the top floor kitchen. Leaving the rest of the clients to mill around in the foyer while she paid special attention to Paula could have seemed antagonistic, but no-one begrudged Paula a little special treatment.

In truth, they were relieved, glad to be spared any more drama, making themselves comfortable in the spacious foyer, sinking into chairs and sofas, grabbing magazines from the huge coffee table. Rachel waited for the luggage to be unloaded, the drivers leaving it neatly stacked in the carriage entry. She thanked them and confirmed with Myles the collection time for the next morning. He would be their driver for the next week. Ten in the morning and not a minute before, she reminded him, experience telling her that no-one would be ready to leave the hotel before mid-morning.

Rachel had only two important tasks on this introduction day before she could have a well-earned dinner with Sara and Marie. The first thoroughly enjoyable task was the tour of the magnificent private hotel they would call home for the next week. As they walked through the stunning building, each guest gushed appreciatively at the luxurious bedrooms, the comfortable living rooms complete with library, music room and inviting over-stuffed couches piled with feather-filled cushions. The group, one-short while Paula was being fussed over by Sara, made their way down the carved stone steps to the basement. They were gobsmacked by the sparkling swimming pool in the cavernous area; dipping their toes and splashing each other. Not one woman glanced in the direction of the gym equipment which made Rachel laugh.

'Paula and I will probably go running each morning. Like we do at home. If anyone wants to join us…' Ingrid asked, looking at Sam, who screwed her nose up at the idea.

'There is a great gym-club just off Boulevard Saint Germaine. It has an indoor running track,' Rachel explained. 'I suggest people use this as a safer alternative to running on the street. A previous guest had a nasty fall on a slippery cobble-stone, so if you're running, please make sure you take care, and take a companion with you, and of course there is the gym equipment here.'

Two-by-two they made their way up the stairs to emerge at the fourth-floor landing. Tall glasses of sparkling water waited for them on the terrace with views towards the towers of Notre Dame and each lady took turns posing for photos in the beautiful space. They turned at last to enter the heart of the home, even though it was on the top floor, the incredible farm-house style kitchen and dining room where they would meet each morning for brunch.

'Brunch at nine,' Rachel reminded them. Shoulders relaxed and deep breaths were taken. She winked at Sara.

'We believe that nothing worth talking about ever happened before nine in the morning,' Sara said.

Paula looked up from her steaming cup of tea and seemed restored to her previous poise. Ingrid went to her and hugged her shoulders.

'So, Mesdames, welcome to my home, and yours for the next week. This house has been in my family for more than one hundred years. My great-great grand-Père was born in this house in 1889, the year that the Eiffel Tower was built. My ancestor was a prominent physician, his wife who I have been told I resemble, an artist. Many of the paintings you see on the walls here are her work, including the self-portrait on the landing that many believe is moi,' Sara said. She walked over and stood under the ornately framed painting. She struck a pose to mimic the artwork, to murmurs of surprise and amusement. Well-rehearsed at her spiel she could have done it in her sleep. She loved her home and loved to share it and its history with her guests.

'You are welcome everywhere in the hotel, except of course for the maintenance rooms near the pool and the third floor, which is my family residence. My mother and father, and my brothers live here also. Ben is a chef and Sebastien, or Bas for short, is in IT. They help with the hotel sometimes, but they work in day jobs too, so you probably won't see them at all. Bas is home today so he can help with your phones or laptops if you have any problems with the Wi-Fi. You can simply ask Rachel and she will organise it. We have Claudine who helps us with the housekeeping. I think you will find everything you need in your rooms, in the living room and here in the kitchen, but if you need anything at all, please let us know, or once again, ask Rachel.'

She looked over and smiled at Rachel who took her cue.

'Thank you, Sara. And thank you for hosting us over this week in your unique and beautiful home. I welcome you all officially and express my deepest gratitude that you chose to spend this week with me, to re-discover what makes you smile, what is truly important to you and what turns your light on!'

A polite round of applause followed, and Rachel waited, a small smile on her face. She never really knew what to do while people applauded as they always seemed to do at this point, so she stood awkwardly, looking at Sara. She made a mental note to change her introduction speech to something less likely to inspire spontaneous applause.

277

'Thank you. It's going to be a lot of fun. Sam and Ingrid, could you please show Paula your room and give her the quick tour after lunch? Here are your keys.'

Rachel handed antique iron door keys each with a different jewel-coloured ribbon attached. She stressed the importance that the keys stay here in the hotel as they were almost impossible to replace.

Sam, Ingrid and Paula were sharing the only triple room; a large space with its own kitchen, which they all vowed to avoid using for anything more taxing than making a cup of tea. Carole and Wendy, Judy and Georgia took the three rooms on the second floor overlooking the walled garden, mother and daughter sharing a room. Wendy, having paid for her sister's trip, had splurged on separate rooms for them knowing she would welcome the space and her sister would welcome the novelty of a King size bed all to herself. Janet and Betty had spectacular adjoining rooms in the original attic of the home with private lift access. It had once been servant's quarters, but now housed a luxurious suite with a private bathroom and views across the roofs of the arrondissement to the Pantheon.

'In your tour documents you have been given a time slot this afternoon. This is your special opportunity to sit with me and discuss the week, how you are feeling, and if there is anything you have forgotten that you would like to do here in Paris. I will give you the phone numbers you need, including the contact number for Myles, our driver for the week.'

There were smiles all round. The limos had been a huge success after all, and Myles was such a sweet young man.

'I will answer any questions you have, in person or via text, during the week, you can also make suggestions and we will endeavour to make your dreams a reality. A point of housekeeping, none of the antique clocks here in the house are functioning. Sara and her family keep them for sentimental and decorative reasons. There is a digital clock here in the kitchen, one in the lift and one by the pool. It can make for some confusing times, but please don't try to adjust the clocks. You don't know what might happen in a magical old house like this. You might end up in the 19th Century!' She winked theatrically at Sara to laughter all round.

'Let's get washed up for lunch and then, when we are all finished, around 4.30pm, we will synchronise our watches and phones, and you are free to go crazy and take in the sights of Paris. Tomorrow morning is our first day-spa session, and the car will collect us here at 10am.'

The buzzing group moved away to their respective rooms to freshen up before lunch. They hadn't eaten since breakfast in London, hours before. Paula chattered noisily about how much she loved the unique space the three women would share over the coming week. She threw herself on the fluffy duvet on her bed and rolled around. She seemed happy to shake off the frustrations of the morning. Splashing water on their faces and running fingers through their hair, they all but raced back up the stairs, meeting the rest of the group on the landing. It seems they had all decided to make their way back to the dining room quickly. The traffic jam on the stairs forced them to admire the paintings and the smooth stone steps.

'Imagine the stories in a house like this,' Carole said to hums of agreement all round.

'Lunch is served,' Sara announced.

The group made their way from the landing through the cosy sitting room and found their places at the enormous table, exclaiming all at once about the food and the setting. The view through large plate windows was dominated by the ancient building opposite. Sara explained a little of the history of the street but only Carole seemed interested. She sat giving Sara her undivided attention while the others were focussed on the delicious meal.

After lunch, amid offers to help with the dishes that were declined by Sara and Claudine, the guests headed to their rooms to settle in. Rachel sighed, grateful for the opportunity to stop smiling for a few minutes. Sara left Claudine to clean the kitchen, coming to the table to hug her friend.

'How are you? How's your mother?' she asked Rachel.

'Got the all-clear, apparently. She's feeling much better but I hope she wasn't saying that so I would be back in Paris in time for this tour, but she insisted.'

'And the doctors? How are they coping?' Sara asked, a cheeky grin on her face.

'You know my mother! She wasn't impressed with the diagnosis and told the doctors she would recover fully within the year, and well, she did. Even cancer can't keep that woman down. I thought I was going home to bring her back here for some much-needed Paris-time, but she's fine. Miraculous really,' Rachel explained.

'Are you okay?' Sara asked.

'Yes, I'm fine. I hated leaving her. I can relax around mum. Being in Australia was so weird though. I was overdressed everywhere I went. Mum thought it was hilarious when I took her for physiotherapy in vintage Dior. She laughed so hard the doctor thought she would hurt herself. She's always cheering me up and she's the one with cancer!'

'She is a touch cookie,' Sara said.

'Tough,' Rachel corrected, laughing. 'She's a tough cookie. Yes, she is!' She hugged her young, but somehow old, friend tightly and they both laughed.

'I will never understand those silly sayings. All our sayings in French make sense.'

'Oh, like Aller se faire cuire un œuf?'

'Oui! This makes total sense. You are annoying me, so go and cook yourself an egg, instead of annoying me!'

'Bon, tu a un pet de travers,' Rachel replied, triumphant to Sara's look of surprise. 'Telling someone they are farting crooked. Now, that makes no sense!'

Sara laughed until she couldn't breathe. Rachel had lived and worked in Paris for years and still struggled with the more complex aspects of the language at times, but she had worked out every idiom, curse word and insult known to the average French dock worker.

'I will go so you can do your work with your lovely ladies, so then we can go for a drink, you Aussie Legend.' Sara loved using Australian,

English and American idioms as much as Rachel loved the silly French sayings whose origins were now lost to time. 'Do we have any free nights this week, chérie? Can you find time to have a nice meal?

'Of course. There's Thursday night while the ladies are going to the clubs with Stephanie…but first I'm going to…an art show. I think. It's across the lane here. There was an invitation slipped under my door today. Will you come with me? And then we can go to dinner...' She was rambling and her heart was racing.

Rachel placed on the table a creamy white folded card with the words Mère du temps in matt black lettering and what appeared to be splashes of watercolour paint across it. She pushed it towards Sara. Sara looked up at her friend's face.

'Déjà vu?' Sara said, eyes sparkling, her hand lifted for a high five.

'Déjà vu!' Rachel confirmed, laughing, slapping her friend's hand.

Sara looked down at the gallery invitation. 'Oh, it's you! With your hair all loose, like you used to wear it,' Sara exclaimed, delighted to see a portrait of Rachel that was simple in its style but rendered such an instantly recognisable likeness.

'That's beautiful work. A friend of yours? Oh, this is going to be across the street. In the old shoemakers. That's a bit - weird.'

'No, it's very weird. Very, very…I always… saw a gallery there…remember? I don't know the artist, but they obviously know me,' Rachel said.

She lay her hands flat on the table as though examining them.

'At first, I was creeped out, I thought I had a stalker. But I did a little online stalking myself. Mère du temps, is the nom de plume she uses. Do you call it a nom de plume when it's a painter? Her pseudonym, I guess...' She trailed off unsure whether to continue with Claudine, the Housekeeper, in the room.

'Mother Time…' Sara said. They both sat staring at the card.

'Sara, I think it's Karen. You know…the artist that had the…the drug problem…? She went… back…?' she whispered, raising her eyebrows at Sara and motioning towards the stairwell.

'Ah, mon dieu! I have that memory too. Do you think it is her? Have you never met her? I mean, again?'

'No, but she knows me on some level. She put this under my door, at least someone did,' she said, pointing at the gallery card portrait. 'You know how strong the feeling of déjà vu is? We live it every day…I told her to write it all down. As Marie told me. Just like you do every time you go…back,' Rachel whispered.

Her eyes were glued on Claudine at the sink for any sign that she might be listening, although the headphones firmly planted in her ears and the tuneless humming suggested Bruno Mars was the only thing on her mind. Sara put her finger up to her lips and tilted her head signalling a move to the cosy sitting room off the kitchen. They shut the door behind them.

Rachel felt as though she had been holding her breath again. 'It's been years though. She wanted to go back to…was it Christmas, 1992? That's 25 years ago! Look at the photo on the back. She's absolutely covered in tattoos. It's strange, I recall so much of that night, the first time she and I met, on the stairs…in, was it 1999? Who knows what's changed? Oh, it's hard to remember. Anyway, I remember showing her my little 'A' tattoo. She was horrified at the idea of the needle, of getting a tattoo, even though she was all scarred from the drugs. I think her husband is a chef, not that those things are related, but he's just taken up as Chef de cuisine at Entre Amis…' She laughed awkwardly staring again at the invitation to the exhibition that stared back at her with her own eyes. 'I'm rambling again…'

'Yes, you are…so he's at Entre Amis, where maman worked all those years! That's a funny coincidence, isn't it?'

'I know, right? It's all too weird. But I know it's her now. Speaking to you like this, I can feel it. If only she had put her name on the invitation and not just the pseudonym. It's puzzling why she waited this long to contact me,' Rachel said.

'Maybe she found her notebooks again. You lost yours for years and forgot all about it…remember?' Sara crossed her eyes and laughed. The grammar of time travel was, is, always tricky.

'What do I do? I can't just waltz into the gallery and say 'hey, this portrait looks exactly like me. Is this a neighbourly thing or were you a drug addict in an alternate time-loop and I sent you back through a time portal and well, you seem to have made a better go of it second time around!'

They both laughed.

'No, this isn't something that happens every day,' Sara said.

'Are you worried she might…tell people…' Rachel made circular hand gestures.

Sara copied them. 'I don't know what this is.' She waved her hands around in circles, 'But no, I'm not worried. Who on earth would believe in time travel?'

www.ingramcontent.com/pod-product-compliance
Lightning Source LLC
Chambersburg PA
CBHW050035120726
47903CB00006B/2043